P9-CQL-543

Donovan blurted, "I want you to marry me."

"Marry you?" Bobbie echoed, incredulous. "Why would I do that?"

"I love Rose a great deal," he said quietly. "I don't want to lose her."

Bobbie had no doubt of that. If only some of the devotion he felt for his daughter would spill over onto her, she'd accept that leftover love in a New York minute.

"We can make it work," he urged. "Bobbie? What are you thinking?"

She was thinking she must be crazy to consider his offer for even a moment. What chance did she have of holding the interest of a man like Big D, even if she lived with him and wore his ring? She'd seen the kind of women he was used to. The competition was formidable.

More to the point, how—exactly—would he expect her to compete?

Dear Reader,

Welcome to Silhouette **Special Edition**...welcome to romance. March has six wonderful books in store for you that are guaranteed to become some of your all-time favorites!

Our THAT SPECIAL WOMAN! title for March is *Sisters* by Penny Richards. A dramatic and emotional love story, this book about family and the special relationship between a mother and daughter is one you won't want to miss!

Also in March, it's time to meet another of the irresistible Adams men in the new series by Sherryl Woods, AND BABY MAKES THREE, which continues with *The Rancher and His Unexpected Daughter*. And continuing this month is Pamela Toth's newest miniseries, BUCKLES AND BRONCOS. In *Buchanan's Baby*, a cowboy is hearing wedding bells and the call of fatherhood. Rounding out the month are *For Love of Her Child*, a touching and emotional story from Tracy Sinclair, Diana Whitney's *The Reformer*, the next tale in her THE BLACKTHORN BROTHERHOOD series, and *Playing Daddy* by Lorraine Carroll.

These books are sure to make the month of March an exciting and unforgettable one! I hope you enjoy these books, and all the stories to come!

Sincerely,

Tara Gavin
Senior Editor

Please address questions and book requests to:
Silhouette Reader Service
U.S.: 3010 Walden Ave., P.O. Box 1325, Buffalo, NY 14269
Canadian: P.O. Box 609, Fort Erie, Ont. L2A 5X3

PAMELA TOTH
BUCHANAN'S BABY

Published by Silhouette Books
America's Publisher of Contemporary Romance

If you purchased this book without a cover you should be aware
that this book is stolen property. It was reported as "unsold and
destroyed" to the publisher, and neither the author nor the
publisher has received any payment for this "stripped book."

To Ginny Sloan, whose friendship and support have
always made the good times better and the bad times easier.

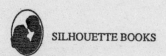 SILHOUETTE BOOKS

ISBN 0-373-24017-1

BUCHANAN'S BABY

Copyright © 1996 by Pamela Toth

All rights reserved. Except for use in any review, the reproduction
or utilization of this work in whole or in part in any form by any
electronic, mechanical or other means, now known or hereafter
invented, including xerography, photocopying and recording, or in
any information storage or retrieval system, is forbidden without
the written permission of the editorial office, Silhouette Books,
300 East 42nd Street, New York, NY 10017 U.S.A.

All characters in this book have no existence outside the imagination of
the author and have no relation whatsoever to anyone bearing the same
name or names. They are not even distantly inspired by any individual
known or unknown to the author, and all incidents are pure invention.

This edition published by arrangement with Harlequin Books S.A.

® and TM are trademarks of Harlequin Books S.A., used under
license. Trademarks indicated with ® are registered in the United States
Patent and Trademark Office, the Canadian Trade Marks Office and in
other countries.

Printed in U.S.A.

Books by Pamela Toth

Silhouette Special Edition

Thunderstruck #411
Dark Angel #515
Old Enough To Know Better #624
Two Sets of Footprints #729
A Warming Trend #760
Walk Away, Joe #850
The Wedding Knot #905
Rocky Mountain Rancher #951
*Buchanan's Bride #1012
*Buchanan's Baby #1017

*Buckles and Broncos

Silhouette Romance

Kissing Games #500
The Ladybug Lady #595

PAMELA TOTH

was born in Wisconsin, but grew up in Seattle, where she attended the University of Washington and majored in art. She still lives in western Washington, and she enjoys reading, traveling and quilting when she isn't spending time with her two daughters and her Siamese cats. Three of her books, *Two Sets of Footprints*, *Walk Away, Joe* and *The Wedding Knot*, have won the *Romantic Times* WISH Award, and she has been nominated for two *Romantic Times* Reviewer's Choice awards.

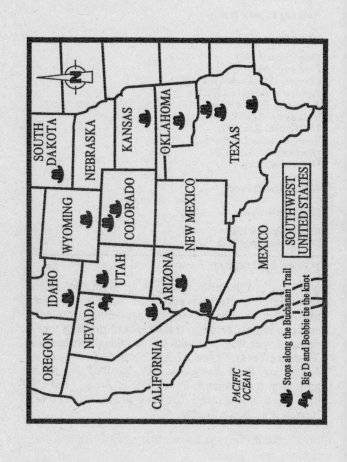

Prologue

Bobbie McBride stood by the hospital bed and gazed down at her daughter. Four-year-old Rose was asleep, her face almost as pale as the pillowcase beneath her head.

Pulling a chair up to the bed, Bobbie perched on the edge of the seat and wiped the tears from her eyes. Gently, she took her daughter's hand, mindful of the IV taped in place. Rose didn't stir. The long lashes that framed her brown eyes lay still against her cheeks.

"That's right, sweetie, get some sleep," Bobbie crooned softly. She, too, was exhausted from the ordeal they had been through together. At first Rose had come down with a virus, but then her blood count plummeted. Just this morning the doctor had broken the news to Bobbie—it was serious . . . very serious.

Suddenly there was talk of a bone-marrow transplant, and Bobbie had immediately volunteered to be Rose's donor. A few moments ago Dr. Richards had come to tell her that her test results were back. She was borderline compatible with Rose, but not an ideal match.

"What about her father?" the doctor had asked. "Chances are he'd be a better match for Rose. If that's the case, a transplant from him could increase her chances substantially."

Rose's father. The rodeo cowboy she had known for two weeks and slept with just once before he rode into the sunset and left her to cope with an unplanned pregnancy and raise her daughter alone. Now Bobbie didn't even know where he was.

"I'm not sure I can locate him," she had told Dr. Richards.

"It might be very important that you do," he'd replied with a grave expression. "For your daughter's sake, you had better try. Aplastic anemia can be very unpredictable."

Now Bobbie gave Rose's hand a gentle squeeze and then laid it carefully back against the covers. Restlessly Bobbie got to her feet and leaned over her baby to brush the tangled golden hair off her face. Golden hair she'd inherited from her father, along with the faint cleft in her rounded chin.

"I love you, honey," Bobbie whispered. "I'll be back as soon as I can."

Just like Sleeping Beauty, Rose didn't awaken. This time, though, the only man who could save her was definitely no Prince Charming.

Bobbie knew what she had to do. Pressing a kiss to her daughter's forehead, she put aside her own pride. She had written Rose's father when she first discovered she was pregnant and again after she had given birth, but he'd ignored both letters. At the time, the pain of his silent rejection when she needed him so desperately had been almost more than she could take.

Now, thanks to a terrifying twist of fate, she needed him again. Only to save her daughter was Bobbie willing to track down and face the man who had stolen her heart, the man she had no desire ever to see again.

This time when she confronted him, she wasn't taking no for an answer.

Chapter One

Donovan Buchanan shifted in his seat in the grandstand and glanced at his watch. Down in the rodeo arena a mounted drill team was going through its paces. Outside, the Arizona sun baked everything in the unrelenting summer heat. It was nearly time for Donovan to go down to the dressing room and prepare for the last event of the afternoon, bull riding.

Tomorrow he would be in Texas. Next week he would hit three more rodeos on his way to defending his title at the National Finals Rodeo in December, where the top fifteen contenders in each event would compete for the national championship. Donovan had won the NFR bull-riding title four out of the last five years and he planned to win again. Nothing was going to get in his way. Meanwhile, there was a bull waiting for him in the chutes here in Flagstaff.

Donovan was walking down the aisle toward the cowboys' dressing room when he noticed a slim brunette standing outside the door. Her head was bent and her long brown hair fell forward, partially hiding her profile, but something about her looked familiar.

Curious, Donovan propped one shoulder against the wall and studied her more closely. She was dressed like a hundred other women, in jeans, a flowered blouse and sandals, but there was something about her that tugged at his memory, something he couldn't quite place.

He wished she would lift her head so he could get a glimpse of her face. Then he caught himself. He had probably seen her at any one of a hundred or more rodeos. There must be a lot of women with hair that particular shade of dark brown.

Before he could straighten away from the wall and go around her, she turned her head and stared directly at him. Stunned, Donovan froze as someone bumped into him and mumbled an apology. He couldn't take his eyes off the woman who was walking toward him. Could it be her, after all this time? Common sense told him it wasn't possible, but the sudden hard thud of his heart said otherwise.

He stared, barely breathing, as she stopped a couple feet away from where he remained rooted in the crowded aisle. He was only vaguely aware of people pushing past him. Unless his gaze was playing tricks on him, the woman gazing up at him with the prettiest brown eyes he had ever seen was indeed Bobbie McBride.

"My God," he muttered, blinking, "I don't believe it."

Except for the length of her brown hair, her appearance hadn't changed all that much since the night, years ago, that they had spent in each other's arms.

"Bobbie! It *is* you!" he exclaimed, starting to grin as shock was replaced by a burst of exhilaration so pure it left him dizzy. He reached out, intent on wrapping her in his arms. Part of him had refused to believe he would never see her again, and now she was standing before him.

To his surprise, she didn't return his smile and she resisted his embrace. "Hello, Donovan," she replied breathlessly, holding him off with hands splayed against his chest. "We need to talk."

Her words hit him like a trough full of cold water. Disconcerted, he straightened, dropping his arms, and studied her face. Now that she was closer, he could see lines of tension around her mouth and shadows beneath her dark eyes. She was still pretty, but the girlish freshness he remembered so clearly had been replaced by a softer, more mature beauty. Right now it was underlined with strain.

"Of course we'll talk," he replied, confused by her words, as well as her attitude. She didn't appear to share his surprise. "What are you doing here? How long are you staying?" The last time he had seen her was in Las Vegas and he had never imagined he'd run into her again at a rodeo in Arizona.

He glanced behind her. "Are you with anyone?" A chill was quelling his excitement. Something was obviously wrong, but he couldn't think what it might be or why she had suddenly popped up like an image from the past. He wanted to touch her, to make sure she was real and not a product of his fevered imagination.

"I'm here alone," she said.

Did she remember those ten days in Las Vegas as clearly as he did? After all this time, it wasn't likely. Still, she must remember something or she wouldn't be standing in front of him now.

"I've been looking for you, but I don't have a lot of time." Her words were a mystery. "Is there somewhere more private we can go?"

"You were looking for me?" he echoed. "I don't understand." As much as he would like to believe that she hadn't been able to forget him, something about her expression told him this was no lover's reunion. But why else would she want to find him?

He would have liked to suggest she go back to his hotel with him, so he could find out where she had disappeared to and what she'd been doing since they had been together—not to mention why she had suddenly sought him out and what she meant about having to talk. He wanted to tell her, too, how much he had missed her.

Another cowboy jostled him with a bony elbow, reminding Donovan where he was and why.

"I've got a bull to ride," he told Bobbie, half-afraid she would disappear again if he let her out of his sight. "If you'd wait until I'm done, we could go back to my hotel and have some dinner. Get caught up." She had never seen him ride and he found that he wanted to show off for her, like a teenage boy flexing his muscles. He couldn't keep from smiling and now he did reach out to touch her cheek.

To his surprise, she flinched. Had someone hurt her? Was that why she looked so serious, even worried? Was she in trouble? It was hard to stop himself from pulling her into his arms and telling her that everything was going to be all right.

Bobbie stared up at the golden-haired cowboy with the mustache and sideburns who had shoved his way into her thoughts so many times over the years. Indeed, she had followed his bull-riding career on its meteoric rise. The four-time national champion was still lean and broad shouldered. A few more lines fanned out from his narrowed green eyes and bracketed his smile, but they only added to his attraction. How she had loved him once!

Now she took a deep breath as he turned away to reply to a shouted greeting. His blue-striped Western shirt bore the name of one of his sponsors down the sleeve. Snug faded jeans hugged his lean hips and long legs. The intervening years, spent in one of the world's most dangerous professions, had been remarkably kind to him.

Much kinder than they had been to Bobbie. When Donovan turned his attention back to her, she hardened her resolve against his potent though shallow appeal. She had been taken in by it once, but never again.

"This isn't something I want to chat about over dinner," she replied tensely. "It's a matter of life and death."

His brows went up and she realized how melodramatic she must sound. Frustrated, she stepped closer as if to form a pocket of privacy within the crowd swirling around them. "It's about your daughter."

Her words hit Donovan like a surprise left hook. His impulse was to reply that he didn't have a daughter. He had never been married; nor had he ever been careless enough to father a child accidentally. Now, as the meaning behind her words sank in, bitter disappointment replaced the joyous disbelief he had felt when he first saw her. Thank God he hadn't revealed that initial reaction and blurted out something he'd regret now that he knew why she was here.

The term *gold digger* leaped into his mind, but he could hardly accept it. Not Bobbie, not the one woman he had never been able to put completely out of his mind, no matter how much time went by.

His business manager had often cautioned him about bogus paternity suits, but Donovan had barely listened. "I'm not some rock star who makes a gazillion dollars a year and beds groupies by the gross," he had remarked at the time.

No, he was only a fairly successful, extremely lucky rodeo cowboy with a healthy income from prize money and endorsement contracts. Now anger replaced his first surge of disappointment. Boy, was he a lousy judge of character. He had actually believed she cared more for him than the gold buckle that held up his pants. The only thing he couldn't understand was why she had waited so long to try to collect.

He let his mouth curve into a cynical smile. "We both know that's impossible," he finally drawled. "I wore protection when I slept with you. I always do."

She gasped, but then her chin went up and her eyes blazed. No doubt she had hoped he'd whip out his checkbook the moment she mentioned a child.

"Protection fails," she replied. "And we have a daughter to prove it."

"What's the matter?" he demanded, too bitter and disappointed to worry about the people dodging around them. "Is the kid's real father so broke he's not worth going after, or is he in on this little scam with you?"

She blanched, and for a heartbeat his certainty that she was lying faltered. Then his anger surged again and he grabbed her arm. "Your little game won't work. I'm not quite as trusting as I used to be."

"Neither am I!" She struggled to pull loose as his fingers tightened below the sleeve of her flowered blouse. Her scent wafted around him, invoking memories he wanted only to forget. The woman he remembered obviously no longer existed, replaced by someone he was starting to wish he had never met.

"Let me go!" she cried, drawing curious glances from a couple of cowboys who hesitated until they recognized Donovan. Then, obviously puzzled by what looked like a well-respected colleague manhandling a woman, they kept going.

The announcer's voice boomed out with the news that the bull riding was about to start. Damn. If Donovan missed his turn in the chutes he'd be awarded a goose egg for his trouble.

A goose egg he couldn't afford, not with only a few dollars in winnings separating him from the bull rider bearing down on him from second place in the standings.

"I have to go," he told the woman trying to free herself from his iron grip. "I suggest you leave by whatever door you came in." It hurt him to say the words; he'd hoped for so long that they would meet again, but not like this.

"No!" She lowered her voice. "I won't go. You owe me. I'm telling the truth, no matter what you think." She dug a hand into her purse. "There isn't time to go through channels. If this doesn't convince you that I'm right, I'll take my story to the newspapers." She pulled out a photograph. "If you can't see the family resemblance, maybe some reporter will."

With that, she shoved the photo under Donovan's nose. He looked at it and his eyes widened.

"Where did you get this?" he demanded. It was a picture of his little sister, Kirby, but it was one he didn't remember ever seeing before.

"I told you," Bobbie insisted as he studied the photo hungrily. "This is your daughter. Her name is Rose and she's four years old. Now do I have your attention?"

Stunned, he tore his gaze from the picture and looked at Bobbie, whose expression oddly bore no triumph. Only weariness.

"We need to talk," he said, barely aware that his words echoed hers from when she had first approached him. He raised his head and glanced around, still reeling.

Now that she had his attention, she was apparently no longer in such a burning hurry. "Go take your ride," she said in a mocking tone. "You wouldn't want to disappoint your fans. We'll discuss this little matter when you're done."

He swallowed dryly, feeling as if he'd just been kicked in the head. He didn't want to let her out of his sight until he could sort this through, but he had no choice.

"We can't talk here. I'll wait for you in the lobby at your hotel," she said. "Where are you staying?"

Common sense took over. He realized that she wasn't going to disappear, not now. He gave her the name of his hotel and brief directions. Then he asked the question that burned his gut like raw acid.

"Why?" he demanded, struggling to keep the betrayal from seeping into his voice. "If this is true, why didn't you ever tell me about her?"

To his astonishment, pure hatred narrowed Bobbie's eyes. Her lips parted, but she didn't speak. Then she pressed them together again and swallowed, as if she were forcefully holding something back. "Good luck on your ride," she said instead, and her tone made it clear she wished him anything but luck.

Before he could stop her, she ducked around a group of giggling teenage girls and disappeared into the crowd.

An hour later, as she waited for Donovan Buchanan in the lobby of the fancy hotel, Bobbie was still trembling from their confrontation. She'd never realized that seeing him again would be so gut-wrenching or that she would still find him so attractive on some primal level where good sense had no say.

A glass of iced tea sat untouched at her elbow. After the shocking price she had paid for the beverage, she'd better drink it, she thought distractedly. Instead, she dragged in a breath and twisted her fingers nervously around the strap of the worn leather purse in her lap as she remembered the first time she had seen him.

It had been a slow night, as usual, at the diner where Bobbie worked, and her tip money reflected the lack of customers. Her boss had remarked just that evening when she came on duty that he didn't know how much longer they could hang on unless business picked up considerably.

When a man walked in the front door wearing a cowboy hat and Western clothing, Bobbie smiled a welcome. He made her think of the waiters at the Wild West Casino, except that his jeans and shirt weren't covered with sequins and braid.

"Evening," she said. "We're pretty full, but I think I can find you a single at the counter."

She watched his startled glance take in the empty booths and stools. Then he broke into a grin that deepened the creases in his cheeks on either side of his full gold mustache.

"How long's the wait?" he drawled.

Bobbie grabbed a menu and moved toward him, delighted at his response to her outrageous statement. "I think I see an empty seat opening up," she replied, putting the menu on the counter near where he stood. "This okay?"

He set down his hat and swept a hand through his blond hair as his green eyes crinkled at the corners. "I feel lucky to get it." He straddled the stool and put aside the menu without opening it. "All I want's coffee," he said, glancing up and down the length of the empty counter. "I hope it's okay for me to take up a seat for just that."

She set a thick white cup and saucer in front of him and filled it from the steaming pot. "If someone better comes along, you may have to move." She made sure he had a spoon and that the sugar container was full. "Cream?" she asked.

"No, thanks. Black's fine."

She was dying to ask where the fair-haired stranger was from and how long he was going to be in town. Usually she had no trouble quizzing her customers, especially when business was slow. For some reason, though, this cowboy with the intriguing sideburns and dashing mustache intimidated the heck out of her. All the usual questions dried up on her tongue.

"Do you live around here?" she finally blurted as he sipped his coffee.

He shook his head. "I'm in town for the rodeo."

Vaguely, she had heard some big rodeo was here this week. No wonder he was dressed like the bronco busters she had seen on TV, right down to his fancy boots.

"Are you competing?" she asked.

"I'm a bull rider," he volunteered as he set down his half-empty cup.

She wasn't sure just what that meant, but it sounded dangerous. She was about to ask him about it when he put on his hat and stood, towering over her. "How much do I owe you?"

Hating to see him leave, she totaled his ticket and handed it to him. As he dug the money from his wallet, she eyed his wide shoulders appreciatively.

"Keep the change." He handed her some bills and then he touched two fingers politely to the wide brim of his hat.

Utterly charmed by the gesture, she glanced down at the money in her hand. He had overpaid her by five dollars. "Are you sure?"

His grin widened. "I'm sure," he drawled. "I appreciate your squeezing me in without a reservation."

As soon as she caught his meaning, Bobbie laughed. For a second his eyes narrowed, screened by thick lashes several shades darker than his hair.

After she had thanked him, he turned away. He was almost to the door when she thought to ask, "When do you ride?"

"Day after tomorrow," he replied, glancing back over his shoulder.

"Good luck, then," she said.

"Thanks." With a last wave of his hand, he was gone.

She wished she knew his name, in case she saw something about the rodeo in the newspaper. Oh, well, she would probably never see him again, anyway, so it didn't really matter....

A burst of laughter from a nearby table brought Bobbie sharply back to the present. She blinked, recalling with painful clarity why she was sitting in this fancy hotel lobby.

How dare Donovan pretend not to believe Rose was his! Bobbie had tried phoning and had written him twice—once when she found out she was pregnant, a second time after she had Rose, just in case her first letter had gone astray. Neither time had he so much as bothered to reply, let alone taken the slightest interest in his own child.

Bobbie blinked back tears of remembrance. Even if he'd had doubts about the baby's paternity, there were tests that could prove she was his. After the ten days they had spent talking and getting to know each other, culminated by that one magical night after the NFR banquet, it had never occurred to Bobbie that he might not believe her, let alone ignore the news completely.

Lord, had he fooled her or what? Being so wrong about him hurt almost as much as his callous abandonment. But neither was as painful as the fear of losing the precious little angel Bobbie had raised alone. Rose's illness was a far bigger heartache than her own lack of insight or Donovan's cruel indifference.

Rose could die. Nothing less than sheer desperation would have ever made Bobbie seek out her baby's father now, but there was nothing she wouldn't do for Rose. That was the reason Bobbie was here—the only reason.

She saw Donovan coming toward her across the opulent lobby, followed by another man in a dark suit. Bracing herself for the fight of her life, she gripped the strap of her purse tighter and got to her feet.

Donovan's expression was grim, no doubt because he finally had to face the mess he'd hoped to avoid. His head was bare, but he was still dressed in the same jeans and shirt he'd been wearing back at the rodeo grounds. His icy green eyes locked with hers for a moment and then they slid away.

"This is Bill Crouch, my business manager. I'd like to discuss this in my suite, and I thought you might be more comfortable with a third party present." He turned to his companion.

"This is the woman I told you about."

Bobbie flushed at the impersonal description as the other man nodded, smiling slightly but not offering his hand. He was barely taller than her own medium height, with thinning brown hair and a ruddy complexion. It was clear from his cautious manner that for whatever reason, he considered Bobbie the enemy. How many times had the man handled this kind of situation for his client?

A tiny part of her ached with regret for the final betrayal of the fantasy she had refused to let die for so long, despite Donovan's silence over the years. The fantasy that he would show up to sweep her into his arms and tell her he had never stopped loving her, that all he wanted was to be a family with her and the daughter they had conceived together.

Well, she reminded herself with a deep, steadying breath, at least she had managed to track Donovan down and get him to talk. That was the first step in enlisting his help. Help only he could give.

"If we're going to your suite, let's do it," she said, striving for assertiveness. She liked to think that over the years she had gotten tougher and more capable of standing up for herself. She had to win this battle; her daughter's life might very well depend on it.

Donovan's mouth flattened into a grim line and he nodded. "Right." Without another word he turned and headed for the elevator, leaving Bobbie and his business manager to follow. Bill looked at her inquiringly.

"After you," he said.

Forcing down the butterflies flapping wildly in her stomach, Bobbie hurried across the lobby. Damn Donovan's arrogance, she thought. It would serve him right if she walked out, leaving him to turn and wonder what had happened to her.

She caught up with him at the elevator, but he didn't even glance at her. Only the way he jabbed the Up button a second time revealed his impatience.

In moments they were seated comfortably in a room decorated in soft tans and blues, with a huge pot of dried weeds in one corner and a glassed-in display of Hopi kachina dolls on the wall. The room was cool and quiet, the nubby curtains open to the gathering darkness beyond the hotel complex.

A shiver went through Bobbie, making her tremble.

"Are you cold?" Donovan asked.

How could she admit she was scared he would still refuse to help her? "No, I'm fine."

Bill cleared his throat. "Donovan has already filled me in on the history you two share," he said quietly. "Why don't you tell us just what it is you want from him?"

She almost flinched at the impersonal way he worded something that had changed her entire life. History. It sounded just as dry as the list of facts she had memorized in school.

Her chin went up as irritation flowed through her. "Our shared history produced a child," she said coolly.

"A child I knew nothing about," Donovan replied.

"A child you chose to ignore," she contradicted.

He leaned forward on the love seat, clasped hands hanging between his knees. "That's not true. If I had known—"

"Let's not waste time arguing," Bill cut in. He met Bobbie's gaze. "Tell us about the child."

She took a deep breath. "She's four and her name is Rose." Part of Bobbie hated sharing anything about her little girl with this man who just happened to be her biological father.

"Paternity can be determined by a blood test," Bill said, looking at his client. "You don't have to—"

"Let me see that picture again." Donovan's direct gaze pinned Bobbie like a spear as he extended his hand.

She fumbled in her purse and brought out the most recent snapshot she had of Rose, taken in the park in Yuma near their tiny apartment. Bobbie glanced at it fondly, eyes misting, and then she relinquished it.

She watched Donovan's face while he studied the photo intently. "She looks just like my sister Kirby did at that age," he muttered.

"She looks like you." Bobbie hated admitting it, but the resemblance was plain to see. Rose had pale blond hair surrounding a face that was a softly blurred copy of his, right down to the faint duplicate of the cleft in his chin. The only feature the child had inherited from Bobbie was her brown eyes, startlingly attractive with her light hair. Even those were topped by Donovan's straighter brows.

"Kirby's eyes were green," he muttered.

"Let me see." Bill extended his hand. After a moment Donovan gave him the picture. "Well, I do see some resemblance," he said, "but it's certainly not conclusive."

"Why did you come after all this time?" Donovan demanded, ignoring his companion.

Now that the moment was here, Bobbie found herself blinking back tears as she struggled to maintain her composure. "Rose is sick," she said through lips that trembled despite her best efforts to steady them. "She has aplastic anemia."

"And you want someone to pay her medical bills?" the business manager guessed.

She glared at him.

Donovan hunched forward, his gaze riveted on hers. "What exactly does that mean—aplastic anemia?"

She swallowed, remembering the way Rose looked, huddled in the hospital bed. "Her blood count is dangerously low. She may need a bone-marrow transplant. I'm compatible, but apparently there's a range and I'm not an ideal match. The doctors told me her natural father's bone marrow might have a much greater chance of helping her."

"How serious is this?" Donovan asked.

She had been staring at her hands, but now she looked up at him. For the first time since she had mentioned Rose, his expression had softened, showing Bobbie a glimpse of the gentle man she remembered.

"It's very serious. Without the transplant, she could die." Bobbie's throat closed and she swallowed. Honesty compelled her to give him the total picture. "On the other hand, she could recover spontaneously, without any do-nated marrow.'' She shrugged, tension making the move-ment jerky. "At this point they just don't know what to expect.''

"How could it be that it's life threatening, but she could recover on her own?'' Bill interjected.

Bobbie shrugged. "It happens, I guess, but we can't count on it.''

"Where is she?'' Donovan asked, rising.

Bobbie's heart climbed into her throat. Was he done talking to her? What if he refused to help?

"She's at the hospital down in Yuma, where we live. I need to get back to her as soon as I can.''

He looked at Bill. "I'll call the airport and file a flight plan. We can leave in an hour.''

"Wait a minute,'' Bill exclaimed. "You don't even know—''

Donovan held up the photo he hadn't yet returned to Bobbie. "Look at this,'' he said. "If it's really a picture of Rose, it's all the proof I need.''

Bill rolled his eyes. A flush of anger burned Bobbie's cheeks.

"What do you mean, if this is her? Do you honestly think I'd try to pull some kind of trick on you?'' She struggled to keep from slapping Donovan's face. "What good would your bone marrow do if she *wasn't* your daughter?'' she asked. "Have you thought of that?''

He glanced down at his feet, clad in hand-tooled boots. "I don't know.'' For the first time he sounded unsure. "Maybe you'd hit me up for money, once we were at the hospital.''

"Have I ever asked for money?'' Her temper flared.

He shook his head.

"Do you think I'd even be here if I didn't have to be?"
she continued, incensed. "She's *my* daughter, understand? When you ignored my letters, I raised her alone. It
wasn't easy, but I've been the only parent she's known."

"Just a damn minute!" His expression hardened. "What
letters?" Color raced across his cheeks, darkening his natural tan even further.

"Don't play innocent with me," she shot back. "You
may be able to fool your business manager with this caring
father act, but you can't fool me. I tried calling. And then
I wrote you twice."

"The hell you did."

"That's right, I did." Her hands were on her hips and she
had stepped forward so they were almost nose to nose, despite the disparity in height.

Now he stepped back, blinking. "Where did you send
them?"

She ticked off on her fingers. "I sent one to your brother's ranch in Colorado when I found out I was pregnant."
Embarrassed, she glanced at the other man, who was
watching them closely. "I sent the other in care of the rodeo association after I had her." She sniffed angrily. "I
thought you had a right to know."

"Damned straight I did," Donovan replied. "Only I
never got any letters. And the chance of two letters going
astray is pretty preposterous."

"All I know is that I wrote you," she insisted. "What
was I supposed to do, show up at one of your rodeos, baby
in arms?"

"Yeah," he replied. "That would have been the next
logical step."

How could she ever explain how she had felt, watching
the mailbox for a reply to her letter, so sure he would get in

touch? Praying he would want more than a long-distance relationship with his little girl.

"I was alone and pregnant," she said instead. "I lost my job when the diner closed and I didn't have the money to run all over the country chasing you. You didn't exactly stay in touch after we parted company, you know."

His frown deepened. "How did you manage alone? Was there anyone to help you? Any family?"

Tears threatened to overflow, but she jerked her chin up a notch. "All that doesn't matter now. I need to get back to the hospital. Are you really coming, or not?" She half expected him to weasel out. After all, he hadn't exactly proved himself to be reliable in a pinch.

"Of course I'm coming. We'll fly, like I said. We can be there in no time."

"How do you know there's a flight?" she countered.

He had been reaching for the phone. Now he turned back toward her. "I have a small plane at a strip near here," he said. "I fly it between shows and it seats four. We'll take it to Yuma."

Bobbie had only flown once and that had been on a huge commercial jet. She hadn't much cared for the idea of being thousands of feet above land. A small plane was even worse. Didn't they crash all the time?

"I took the bus up here," she said. "We could rent a car and drive back to Yuma."

Donovan's gaze narrowed. "I thought you were in a hurry."

"I am. It's just—"

"Afraid to fly?" he jeered.

Her jaw tightened. "Of course not."

His smile was humorless. "Good."

* * *

Donovan's feelings were in a jumble as he turned the car he had rented at the airstrip into the hospital parking lot and eased it into an empty space. As he glanced at Bobbie in the rearview mirror, he couldn't help but remember the first time he had ever seen her.

He had been bored with the endless parties and negotiations going on before the actual start of the NFR, so he'd ignored Bill's protests and walked out on the latest lavish reception.

When he got outside, he'd spotted the pink-and-green neon sign across the street flashing Mo 's H me Co king. A cup of coffee before he walked back to the hotel sounded like a good idea.

Bobbie had been wearing a pink nylon uniform with a short skirt that drew attention to her great legs and a white apron that tied at her tiny waist. Her brown hair was cut short then, baring her neck and feathering across her brow in an uneven fringe that emphasized her high cheekbones and pointed chin. He remembered thinking at the time that the name on her little plastic name tag suited her, as did the tiny mole at the corner of her full mouth. She still had the mole, but the name tag was long gone, as was the warmth in her eyes when she smiled.

Now he slid out of the car and pocketed the keys. Before they left Donovan's hotel in Flagstaff, Bobbie had called the hospital, but all she told him was that there had been no change. Rose's blood count was still dangerously low, but so far she was resting comfortably.

On the short flight to Yuma, Bill had sat next to Donovan in the cockpit while Bobbie sat alone behind them. If she was frightened of flying, she managed to keep her fear to herself. Donovan would have preferred that she sit up front and fill him in on the four years of his daughter's life that she had deprived him of. Still, he could see that she was worried, and even as angry as he was, he had enough compassion not to push her when she was so exhausted. Too bad she hadn't grabbed a catnap during the short flight.

Now as Donovan held open Bobbie's car door, Bill came around the car and put a detaining hand on Donovan's arm.

"I still want you to have that blood test before you go committing yourself to anything," he said in a low voice.

Donovan knew Bobbie could hear every word. He shook off Bill's hand. "I just want to see Rose," he said stubbornly. He hadn't ruled out the test. Perhaps he would see that there really wasn't much resemblance in person. Deep in his gut, though, he felt that she was his. He didn't bother to examine the feeling as he followed Bobbie into the hospital. Some things couldn't be picked apart and analyzed—they just were.

Like the way he had felt about Bobbie after only ten days spent mostly talking at the little diner. If that was as well as his gut instinct worked, perhaps he needed to examine it closer, after all.

"She's up in pediatrics on the third floor," Bobbie said quietly as they paused in front of the elevator. "I'll go in first and explain to her that you're here."

"Does she know about me?" Donovan demanded.

Bobbie shook her head. "Not exactly. She's never asked about her father, so I haven't said anything."

"And who are you going to tell her that I am?" Donovan asked, still furious inside at her deception and lies. If Rose proved to be his child, he still wouldn't have known about her if she hadn't gotten sick. The realization sliced through him viciously. He had lost his parents and his sister, so the idea of never knowing his own child was an especially painful one.

Why had Bobbie lied about writing him?

Her face paled at his tone and she glanced away. "I'll tell her the truth," she said.

"And what's that?" he pressed.

Now she turned to look full into his face. God, but she was still beautiful, he thought, distracted.

"I'll tell Rose that you're her father," she said firmly. "Because, no matter how much you'd like to pretend otherwise, that's the truth."

He started to argue about her last words, but the elevator door opened and three people got out. Two nurses stayed on, so he had no opportunity to refute Bobbie's statement during the brief ride. Once they were following her down the third floor hallway, Donovan realized that arguing was futile. Besides, he was too full of conflicting feelings about the prospect of meeting Rose to bother.

When they got to the nurses' station, Bobbie turned to him and Bill. "Wait here," she commanded.

Donovan would have liked to tell her she had kept him from Rose long enough and he wasn't going to wait another minute. He remained silent only for the child's sake. Bobbie had admitted earlier that she hadn't yet said a word to Rose about where she was going in case she couldn't find him or he refused to help her. When she had told him she didn't want her child disappointed, pain slashed through him.

The possibility that such a young child might not survive this illness made him want to lash out at the injustice of it, whether or not she was really his. Hell, meeting her was a formality; in his heart he had already decided that she was. All based on that photo.

Briefly he wondered if he would have preferred never knowing about her at all rather than facing the risk of losing her to this illness right after he found her. He had lost so many people he loved—his parents, Kirby, even Bobbie, although that was in a different way.

He tried to remind himself this whole thing might be a ruse, with Bobbie hoping he would decide to claim the child, just as he had. Deep down, he couldn't make himself believe it. Where was his good old common horse sense when he needed it?

Probably lying in the dust along with his pride after that last bull ride back in Flagstaff, he thought wryly. Distracted by Bobbie's sudden appearance and her startling news, Donovan hadn't stood a chance against Copenhagen Devil's Spawn. He'd gone flying on the second buck like a greenhorn and was probably lucky to have escaped without being gored for his trouble.

When Bobbie came back out of Rose's room a few moments later, Donovan stopped the pacing he had begun when the waiting got to him. With her was a short man in a white coat with a stethoscope sticking out of his pocket.

"This is Dr. Richards," she said. "Donovan Buchanan, Rose's father, and Bill Crouch, his . . ." Her gaze flickered between Bill and Donovan, and then her lips tightened. "His advisor," she finished. "Donovan isn't convinced that Rose is his child."

A protest surged to Donovan's lips, but the doctor seemed unfazed by her words. Instead, he began explaining Rose's medical condition.

"Naturally we want the best odds we can get with the transplant," he said in conclusion. "So we'd like to start with a blood test." He glanced at Bobbie almost apologetically.

Donovan felt a surprising surge of jealousy.

"Her mother is only borderline compatible," the doctor continued before Donovan could even begin to analyze that shocking burst of possessiveness. "If you're a better match and she needs the transplant, we would want to go with you.''

Donovan nodded impatiently. All he wanted was to see his daughter. ''Of course. That won't be a problem.''

''You'll be here if we need you?'' the doctor pressed.

''Yeah. I'll be here.'' Donovan glanced toward Rose's room. ''May I see her now?''

He had asked the question of Dr. Richards, but Donovan glanced at Bobbie. ''Is it okay with you?''

His automatic gesture made him realize that, for now at least, she called the shots. If he wanted any rights where Rose was concerned, he was probably going to have to fight Bobbie for them.

He had no sooner come to that conclusion than her brown eyes searched his. She looked worried. Donovan's certainty wavered. Was she trying to deceive him, after all, or merely concerned that his sudden appearance would upset the child she insisted belonged to both of them? Her face revealed no clues.

''I'll introduce you,'' she said quietly. ''Come on.''

As he followed her the short distance down the hallway, Donovan was surprised to realize that he was trembling and his mouth had gone dry. He was a man who faced danger every time he settled himself on the back of a bucking bull. How could one four-year-old girl make his knees go weak and cause his heart to pound like a ceremonial drum?

Following Bobbie into the hospital room, Donovan stopped at the side of the bed. Taking a deep breath, he looked down at the small blond child who lay there gazing up at him with her mother's big brown eyes, and he fell head over heels in love.

Chapter Two

Rose's gaze shifted from Donovan to her mother, standing on the other side of the bed. "Who's the man?" she asked as his fingers tightened on the brim of the hat he was holding.

Her voice reminded him of Kirby's. He could remember it as clearly as if he had last heard his sister speak only days before. Pain and exultation shot through him. He could sense Bobbie's hesitation. This must be difficult for her.

"This is—"

Before she could tell Rose some half-truth, he cut her off. "I'm your daddy, honey," he said quietly as he squatted down beside the bed.

Rose's eyes widened and she studied him with a thoroughness that was disconcerting. Her skin was so fine it appeared poreless, and it was pale except for faint shadows beneath her dark eyes. Her hair, lighter than his own by several shades, hung in limp waves past her thin shoulders. The sight of her tiny hospital gown reminded him how sick she was. A lump rose in his throat and stuck there.

"You're really my daddy?" she asked gravely.

"Really," he echoed, feeling more cowardly than he ever had facing down a bull. What if she wanted nothing to do with him? Oh, God, what if she didn't recover?

A cautious smile crossed her small face, wiping away the telltale signs of her exhaustion. "What's your name?"

He glanced up at Bobbie, who was watching him with a mother's protectiveness. "My name's Donovan Buchanan," he replied.

Rose frowned thoughtfully and a chill slid over him. "Then why is my name McBride? Joey's name is the same as his daddy's."

Donovan looked again at Bobbie. He had no idea how she wanted this handled.

"Joey's a neighbor she plays with." She was studying the tiny figure under the covers, tenderness softening her expression. "Your daddy and I aren't married, so we have different last names."

Donovan braced himself for more difficult questions. Instead of pursuing the subject, Rose eyed the hat he had been turning around and around in his hands. The dented brim bore signs of his nervousness.

"Are you a cowboy?" Her voice held a note of awe he found deeply gratifying, considering that she might have been rejecting him instead.

"Your daddy is a rodeo cowboy," Bobbie said.

If he hadn't known better, Donovan might have thought the pride in her voice was real. For a moment, part of him wished it were.

"That's right," he added, clearing his throat when his voice faltered. "I ride bucking bulls."

The frown was back, pleating Rose's forehead. "Are you on TV?"

He couldn't help but smile, wondering just what her impression of a cowboy really was. "Not very often," he admitted. "Is that okay?"

"I'm glad you're here instead," she said. "Can I wear your hat?"

"I don't think—" Bobbie began.

"Sure." He set it gently on Rose's head. It slid forward, covering her face and causing her to giggle.

If he hadn't already fallen for her, the childish sound would have done it. Her laughter was the sweetest music he had ever heard. As Rose lifted the hat so she could see, he caught an expression in Bobbie's eyes that made his heart stutter. For just a second they had glowed with approval. That fractional softening reminded him of how she had hung on his every word, back in Las Vegas so many years before. The memory both warmed him and made him unutterably sad.

He had never realized how precious what he and Bobbie had shared was, until after he had tossed it so thoughtlessly aside. Until blind panic, fear of involvement and the subsequent hurt it could bring sent him scrambling for the hills—as cowardly as any coyote with its tail between its legs. By the time he had come to his senses and tried to undo his mistake, it had been too late, the trail too cold to follow.

It was too late now as well—too late to recapture that feeling, but not to forge a relationship with Rose. At least he had a chance for that.

"You need to rest," Bobbie was telling her daughter, leaning forward to smooth the blond hair off her face. "We don't want to wear you out."

"I'm not tired," Rose protested, but it was easy to see she was near the end of her strength. Surely that couldn't be good for her.

"Your mama's right, sweetheart," Donovan told her. Automatically his gaze flicked to Bobbie's. If it was more approval he sought, he wasn't going to find it now. Instead, her eyes were cold. She might very well have been trying to tell him that his help was the last thing she needed.

Except she did need him, he reminded himself. She might hate the idea, but she needed him a lot.

"Will you come back and see me again?" Rose asked, distracting him.

"Of course I will. I'll be right here until you're all better," he promised rashly.

Bobbie made an involuntary sound. She leaned over Rose protectively. "Daddy may not be able to stay," she said, glaring across the bed. "His work—"

"His work will keep," Donovan interrupted. Alarm filled Rose's face. He took a deep breath and modified his voice. "I'm not going anywhere for a little while," he told her. "I'll be back to visit you first thing in the morning, as long as Dr. Richards approves."

Rose's expression relaxed again. "Thank you," she said.

For some reason the simple words cracked his composure as nothing else had. He turned his head away, swallowing the prickling at the back of his throat as he straightened.

"Daddy!" Rose exclaimed as he was about to beat a hasty retreat from her room. "Aren't you going to kiss me good-night?"

His vision blurred as he bent down and touched his mouth to her cheek. The scent of her—warmth and innocence and sunshine—filled his head. Her skin was feather soft against his lips. For a moment her arms fastened around his neck. Long before he was ready, she released him.

"Your mustache tickles."

"I'll see you in the morning," he whispered hoarsely. Without looking at either Rose or Bobbie again, he made his escape.

Outside in the hallway he leaned against the wall and struggled for composure.

"Are you okay?" Bill demanded.

Donovan had forgotten that the other man was even there. "Yeah, why?" he asked, firmly back in control.

Bill was watching him closely. "How's she doing?"

Donovan pinched the bridge of his nose between two fingers. "She's my daughter," he muttered. "And she's sick."

"Now wait a minute," Bill protested. "We need to arrange for a blood test—"

Donovan looked at him hard. "The only blood test I need is the one to make sure we're a good match."

"I know how you feel," Bill said, regrouping. "But it's essential we establish paternity beyond a shadow of a doubt."

"I don't have any doubts," Donovan argued, realizing in some dim corner of his brain that Bill was only doing his job and that he was right.

"Thank you for that." Bobbie's voice was soft as she came out of Rose's room.

"I'm sorry I didn't believe you right away." Without warning, cold anger swept over Donovan as the realization of what this woman had cost him sank in. He had lost four years of Rose's life that he could never regain.

Bobbie must have seen something of what he was feeling in his face, because her faint smile faded. What had happened to the warmth he remembered? Now she looked almost hard.

"Are you married?" he asked her suddenly. He knew nothing about her recent life, but it was unlikely that she had been alone all these years.

His question stunned Bobbie, who could only stare. For a moment she had hoped they might become...if not friends, at least amicable. Especially when he seemed to accept his responsibility for Rose. Fresh resentment surged through her.

"What business is that of yours?" she demanded, moving deliberately away from the door to her daughter's room.

"I think I have a right to know. Are you?" Donovan's eyes had narrowed. Even so, his thick dark lashes only made him more attractive. Somehow she had to find a way to stay immune to his potentially lethal charm.

"No. Are you?" It had never occurred to her that he might have a wife, or a serious girlfriend, but of course it was possible. Not that it made any difference to *her*.

"Hell, no." His face bore distaste. Someone had hurt him badly, she thought. Then she wondered if he had ever found his family. During one of their long conversations back at Mom's Diner, he had told her how his parents had disappeared suddenly, leaving him and his brother to the mercy of the foster-care system while their little sister had been adopted. Maybe Bobbie would have the chance to ask him about it, but not now. He would probably tell her in no uncertain terms to mind her own business.

"How many boyfriends have you had?" he asked.

Bobbie had been walking along with him as he headed down the hall. Now she stopped abruptly, itching to slap the smug expression off his handsome face. Instead, she made do with glaring up at him. Damn him for being so tall, anyway. Somewhere she had read that bull riders were short, wiry men. Not this one, though.

"Where do you get off asking me something like that?" she demanded. "How many lady friends have *you* had in the last five years? Or can't you count that high?"

Bill made a choking sound. When she glanced at him, he had put a hand over his mouth and turned away.

"Not that many," Donovan replied coolly. "But then, I haven't been raising an impressionable child."

Unexpected fury roared through Bobbie and she took an aggressive step toward him. "Don't you even presume to lecture me," she told him, her body rigid with tension and the desire to do physical violence. "I was alone and pregnant. I worked and I managed and I raised *my daughter* without any help from you or from any 'uncles.'" Her voice dripped loathing. "It wasn't easy and it wasn't always fun. Sometimes I was scared and sometimes—" Sudden tears blocked her throat as memories crowded her mind. Memories of crummy apartments, bare cupboards and her own crushing doubts that keeping Rose was fair to the child.

Abruptly Bobbie whirled away, refusing to give in to tears.

"This isn't getting us anywhere," Bill interjected. "We all need food and rest. Uh, Bobbie, can we drop you off at your place or anywhere else?"

She didn't want Donovan to see the modest apartment she and Rose called home. No doubt he would find out where they lived sooner or later if he didn't get cold feet and leave, but it didn't have to be tonight.

"No, thanks." She dragged up a weak smile for the business manager. Even if he had been the one to insist on the paternity test, he was only doing his job. "I'm going to stay here for a while."

"You need rest," Donovan told her. "You look ready to collapse."

"Gee, thanks." She indulged herself in sarcasm. Without trying, he brought out the worst in her.

Impatience set his features. "You know I'm right."

She'd phone a neighbor, she thought. Her car was still parked at the bus station, but Darlene would come if Bobbie called her. "I'll be fine."

"Do you live near here?" Donovan asked. A nurse walked by them, eyeing him with interest. He didn't appear to notice.

"No, I don't live near here." Bobbie stared him down, until he shrugged and looked away.

"Suit yourself." Donovan glanced at Bill. "Let's find a hotel and a meal."

Dismissed, she reminded herself that she wanted them to go.

"I'll be back first thing in the morning," Donovan said over his shoulder. "I'll leave a number with the nurses' station as soon as we check in somewhere."

Suddenly Bobbie was so exhausted she could hardly stand. As the two men walked away, she went back in the other direction. After she checked on Rose one last time, she would make that call to Darlene.

Three days later Donovan sat with Bobbie in the pediatric lounge, waiting impatiently for Rose's doctor to bring in the results of her latest blood count. Bill had flown out by commercial jet early this morning, after he reminded Donovan about the big rodeo in Amarillo this weekend. Missing it would seriously jeopardize Donovan's standings, but all he could think about was Rose. He had to be here if she needed him.

Across the room, Bobbie flipped through the pages of a magazine while Donovan stared sightlessly at the television screen, long legs sprawled in front of him. He was used to action; all this endless waiting was driving him up the wall.

He had called his brother in Colorado the first night he was in Yuma. After getting over the shock of being an uncle, Taylor had offered to fly out, but Donovan discouraged him. Rose needed time to get used to her daddy first.

Donovan had never dreamed a four-year-old could be so fascinating. She had asked endless questions about the rodeo until he finally sent Bill to the local mall in search of picture books about the subject. He had returned with two that Rose and Donovan had read together. At least they had gotten to know each other a little better over the last couple of days.

Now he sneaked another look at Bobbie, wondering what she was thinking. Knowing he owed her a debt of gratitude for not turning Rose against him, he wanted to say something, but the time never seemed right.

The results of his blood work had come back. He was a good match for Rose and a better candidate for a bone-marrow transplant than Bobbie was. He wondered how that made her feel. Relieved? A little resentful? Her reaction had given him no clue.

Surprisingly, Rose's last blood count had also shown a slight rise, so the doctor decided to wait a day or two before starting preparation for the transplant.

If this new count showed even more improvement, it might indicate that she was getting over the anemia on her own. The doctor had explained to Donovan and Bobbie that a spontaneous recovery sometimes happened and that he didn't want to move too quickly.

"What are you reading?" Donovan asked Bobbie, to break the long silence between them. They had established a truce of sorts over the last couple of days, keeping up a friendly facade in front of Rose and polite silence the rest of the time.

Meanwhile, when he wasn't worrying about his daughter, he was aching to quiz Bobbie about the last four years. From what little she had said the other day, it must not have been easy for her. Even more puzzling was that she hadn't contacted him long ago. He still didn't buy her story about the letters.

Now she looked up and frowned at his interruption. "I'm reading about redecorating your kitchen on a shoestring," she replied, holding up the cover of the open magazine. "Something you probably haven't had to worry about much."

"How do you know I even have a kitchen to redecorate?" he asked in a lazy drawl. Perhaps sparring with Bobbie would make the time go faster.

She raised her eyebrows. "Everyone has to live somewhere. Did you buy your ranch?"

Secretly pleased that she remembered, he nodded. "I'm still fixing up the house, but I'm not there much and I haven't gotten to the kitchen yet." Although he stayed in the small two-story ranch house when he was there, he hoped to rebuild someday soon. "Maybe I should check out that article," he added lightly. "It might give me some ideas."

She didn't return his smile. Instead, she went back to her reading.

Frustrated, Donovan switched chairs, sitting in the one next to her. She glanced up and her mouth tightened, but she remained silent.

"Tell me about her," he asked in a lowered voice. "It seems like you've done a good job raising her. What's she like when she isn't sick?"

His attempt at flattery rolled off Bobbie like rain off a metal roof. "You'd know if you had bothered to answer my letters," she replied.

He leaped to his feet, temper flaring. "How many times do I have to tell you I didn't get any letters!" Before he could finish his statement, the doctor appeared. He looked from Bobbie to Donovan, obviously curious.

"What's her blood count?" Bobbie asked in a voice that trembled, setting aside the magazine as she stood up to face Dr. Richards. "Is it higher?" She didn't appear to notice when Donovan enfolded her hand in his.

The doctor was smiling. "I'm very relieved. Her count is soaring and she is definitely improving. If the numbers continue to rise, she won't need a transplant, after all."

With a whoop of elation, Donovan pulled Bobbie into a fierce hug. Shaking, she clung to him, arms wrapped around his waist.

"She's going to make it," he told her gruffly with his face buried in her hair. "Our little girl is going to make it."

He lifted Bobbie off her feet. Briefly her arms tightened. As her sweet, familiar scent drifted around him, his elation over Rose's test results altered to something else entirely. For a timeless moment, he savored the feel of the woman clamped in his arms. Memories engulfed him. He remembered their lovemaking as if it had taken place days before, not years.

"Bobbie?" He set her carefully back down, keeping his voice neutral.

Realization washed over her like an icy wave. She dropped her arms and stepped back so fast she almost stumbled over a chair. The imprint of his solid body still

tingled along her nerve endings, bringing with it images
both sweet and painful. Images of the last time he had held
her close.

Dragging in a deep, steadying breath, she glanced up at
the man standing so near she would have sworn she could
still feel his body heat.

Donovan's face had relaxed into a smile of relief and
gratitude. Happiness over the good news about Rose soared
through Bobbie, as well, bringing with it tears of joy. Then
a sudden thought stopped her cold.

She wouldn't have had to tell him about his daughter. If
she had just waited a few more days before she went charg-
ing after him, he wouldn't be here, rioting her senses and
making her remember things best left in the past. Making
her heart weep with regret over what could never be.

She stared into his handsome face, wishing she had the
power to send him back to the circuit, where he belonged.
When she had first tracked him down through the Profes-
sional Rodeo Cowboy's Association and discovered that he
was actually in Arizona and not several states away, she had
taken it as a sign that she was doing the right thing in contacting him. Apparently her ability to read signs was on a
par with picking men.

Perhaps, now that the crisis was over, Donovan would
just disappear.

He must have seen something in her expression, because
his own grin faded. "What is it?" he asked.

She resisted the urge to massage her forehead where it
had begun to throb. "Nothing. I'm just tired. It's been an
ordeal, that's all."

For a moment he looked as if he was thinking about
taking her into his arms again. Stiffening, she widened the
space between them. Then she remembered Dr. Richards.

"That's wonderful news," she said, facing the doctor.

"You bet it is." Apparently unaware of the undercurrents in the small waiting room, he beamed first at her and then at Donovan. "You can both see her if you'd like."

Out of the corner of her eye, Bobbie saw Donovan extend his hand. "Shall we?"

Ignoring it, she thanked the doctor and headed toward Rose's room.

Donovan hated to leave Yuma, but he had no choice. Now that the crisis was over, he had a living to earn. He knew that Bobbie, too, had to return to her office job. She had mentioned once that she'd used vacation time when Rose became ill.

"I'll be back real soon to visit," he told Rose, wishing he could stick around until she was ready to go home.

She clutched a rag doll he had bought for her at a local toy store the evening before on his way back to the hotel. The doll looked like a clown dressed in patchwork, and she had named it Patchy. Donovan was pleased that she kept the doll with her in the hospital bed and had carried it under one arm when they went for a long, slow walk down the corridor earlier.

"I don't want you to go, Daddy," Rose told him, tears swimming in her eyes. "You won't come back for years and years."

Donovan glanced at Bobbie, who had taken her usual place at the other side of the room. He still hadn't thanked her for not alienating Rose from him.

Ignoring one of the hospital rules, he perched carefully on the edge of the bed. "I said I'd come back and I meant it," he told Rose. "As soon as I look over my schedule, I'll call your mom and set up a time, okay?"

Rose looked doubtful. "Really?"

He made an X over his chest. "Cross my heart. You
know cowboys don't lie." It tore his guts out to see the
mistrust on her face. The two of them had made some
progress, but it had only been a few days and he had years
of neglect to overcome.

"Okay," she said, sniffing. "I'll miss you."

Leaning forward, he hugged her gently, blinking his eyes
against the emotion that threatened to well up and spill
over. Already he loved this child fiercely, and not just because she reminded him so much of his missing sister when
she had been the same age.

When he straightened, Rose gave him a brave little smile
that pierced his heart. "Good luck with those wild bulls,"
she said seriously. He had showed her a picture of a cowboy on a bucking bull in one of the books Bill had picked
up for him, but he didn't think she really understood.

"Thanks, little darlin'. One of these days we'll go to a
rodeo and you'll see them for real."

Her eyes grew wide. "Can we? Will I see you ride, too?"

"Sure." He glanced at Bobbie, who was frowning. An
idea started to form in the back of his brain, but it was too
new and he had too little time to pursue it right now. "I'll
work it out with your mom," he promised rashly instead.

After a couple more goodbyes and another hug, it was
time for him to go. "Could I talk to you for a minute?" he
asked Bobbie before he went through the open doorway.

She followed him into the hall with her hands balled into
fists. How dare he make promises to Rose without checking with her first? Just who the hell did he think he was,
anyway?

The answer came to her as she caught him sneaking a last
glance back over his shoulder as the door closed behind
them.

He was Rose's father and, as such, he had certain rights. Once again, bitterness rose inside Bobbie. She was the one who had opened this particular can of worms, and now she had to deal with it.

"I hope it's okay that I told her I'd visit," Donovan began. Then his expression changed, hardened slightly. He must have realized the absurdity of his comment. Bobbie doubted there was a court anywhere that would deny him some kind of visitation.

"Of course," she agreed crisply. She might have to concede certain things, but she didn't have to pretend to like them.

"Good." He looked relieved. Had he thought she would fight him? "I'll call you and set up something as soon as I can," he said. "I don't want her to forget me."

Bobbie gazed up at him, so dashing with his golden hair and full mustache, so striking in his Western shirt and snug jeans, even without the Stetson he always removed inside the hospital. The nurses made fools of themselves over him, Bobbie recalled scornfully. A woman doctor had stared unprofessionally, almost falling over a patient in a wheelchair.

They wouldn't feel that way if they got to know him, Bobbie started to tell herself. Then she stopped, remembering how much support he had given her since they flew back to Yuma.

He had insisted that she go to the cafeteria and choke down meals he paid for. He had brought her endless cups of coffee and nagged her about getting enough rest. Last night he had put her into a cab he also paid for, after she refused—and not too politely—his offer to drive her home.

Donovan had been terrific with Rose, spending hours reading and talking to her, patiently answering her questions. He had been a solid presence for Bobbie, offering his silent support even though he seemed to sense she would refuse any comfort he tried to give.

Confused, she glanced up at him, recalling his last comment. "Rose won't forget you," she told him. "Don't *you* forget *her*."

His gaze darkened abruptly. "I'm not going to go away, no matter how much you wish I would."

His perception brought hot color to her cheeks. "I didn't say that."

His mouth tightened, but he didn't argue. "I have your phone numbers, at home and at work," he said instead.

She had given them to him when he asked. What was the point in refusing?

"I'll call and let you know when I'll be back."

She nodded, unwilling to mouth some platitude about how welcome he would be. Despite the way he had acted in the hospital, she hadn't forgotten the last four years of silence.

He dug into his pocket and gave her a handwritten list. "These are the numbers for my brother, Taylor, and for Bill's office," he said. "I wish I could tell you where I'll be, but my location changes too quick to be much help." He watched while she tucked the list into her purse. "Bill will always know where I am," he added. "If there's any problem with Rose, I can be here in a matter of hours."

She remembered his plane and wondered how long he had been flying. There were so many things they hadn't discussed, despite the hours they had spent together in this building. She sighed. Well, it was too late now.

"Thank you for staying," she said, knowing she owed him a lot. "And for everything else." He had been good to Rose. That in itself was enough to earn him Bobbie's appreciation, not to mention his quick acceptance of his daughter and his apparent willingness to donate bone marrow—a painful procedure—if it had been necessary.

"You don't have to thank me for wanting to help my own daughter," he replied. "I would have given her anything she needed."

The thought occurred to Bobbie that his attitude since she had confronted him in Flagstaff was very much at odds with his refusal to acknowledge her letters.

Dismayed by the thought, she shoved it aside.

"Have a safe flight," she told him instead.

"Thanks." He shifted uncomfortably, surprising her. She always thought of him as totally self-assured, with no doubts to hinder him. Now he rubbed at one sideburn with his finger as his eyes searched hers.

Bracing herself, she thrust out her chin. "Was there something else?"

"Yeah." He glanced at a spot somewhere over her shoulder, and then he dragged his gaze back to hers. "I just wanted to thank you for not turning Rose against me," he said, stunning Bobbie as much with the humility in his voice as the actual words. "For not turning her against the idea of her dad, I guess. From the sound of things, you didn't always have an easy time. It must have been tempting to blame someone. As near as I can tell, you didn't, and I wanted to thank you, that's all."

Bobbie opened her mouth to reply, but the words didn't come. Instead, she shook her head and made a vague gesture with her hand. "I did it for her, not you," she said finally.

"I know that." He shifted his hat from one hand to the other and glanced at his watch. "Well, I want to see about the bill before I leave, so I'd better get going. I'll call you."

"The bill?" she echoed, confused. "What about it?" She hadn't let herself think about how much it was or where she was going to find the money. Her insurance would cover a percentage, but her deductible was huge. Even that was going to be a struggle. The hospital would have to take installments. Small ones.

Donovan's eyes narrowed and his jaw flexed, as if he sensed a fight. "I'm taking care of Rose's medical bills," he said firmly.

Bobbie shook her head. His involvement with her daughter was closing around her like barrel staves, leaving her feeling trapped and obligated. "That's not necessary," she argued, slightly horrified when she heard the words leave her mouth.

"Don't be stupid," he snapped. "Do you have any idea what hospitals charge? Where would you get the money?"

Pride stiffened Bobbie's spine and lifted her chin. "I'll manage."

As if he could see the desperation on her face, his expression softened. "Look," he said, glancing around the empty hallway, "think of it as part of the back child support I no doubt owe you. Would you deprive Rose of other things so you can pay a bill I'm perfectly willing to cover?"

She hated admitting he was right. She had struggled to keep her independence and now he was trying to sweep it away with his signature on a check.

For a long moment she studied him. If she had seen one tiny hint of smug arrogance in his expression, of pleasure over grinding her pride into the dust, she would have thrown the offer back in his face. No matter what the consequences. Instead, all she saw there was compassion. It almost broke her—as the crisis with her daughter's health hadn't quite managed to do.

She allowed one jerky nod of her head. "Thank you." Her teeth were clenched, her lips pressed together to keep them from trembling. "I'll talk to you later." Without waiting for a reply, she ducked her head and hurried back into Rose's room as if she were running away from the devil himself.

Chapter Three

"Make copies of this and send them out to everyone who's paid off a loan in the last six months, would you?" The office manager dropped a piece of paper onto Bobbie's desk on his way to the door. "Oh, and could you take them by the post office on your way home? I have to see a client."

One of the other employees looked up and then quickly ducked his head.

"But I was in the middle of a tax report." Bobbie frowned at the flier lying on the keyboard of her computer. After her absence while Rose was sick, Bobbie had a lot of work to catch up on and she resented Paul's constant interruptions. It was only four o'clock and she suspected he sometimes used visiting a client as an excuse to duck out early.

Besides, she was eager to leave on time herself. If she

stayed to mail out his letters, she would be late picking up Rose.

"Thanks, hon. I appreciate it."

Bobbie heard the outside door close behind him. With a weary sigh, she put a roll of address labels in the printer, punched a few buttons on her computer and went over to the copy machine. As soon as it began spitting out fliers, she called Marty, the woman who watched Rose while Bobbie was at work, and explained that she would be a little late.

"Rose ate a good lunch and had a nap," Marty said. "Right now she and Angie are playing dolls. Do you want to talk to her?"

"No, don't interrupt them. I'll see her when I get there. Thanks, Marty." Bobbie hung up the phone and checked on the copy machine. Working at the local branch of a large finance company beat waitressing, but the job still had its drawbacks.

Paul Baylor was one of them. He was always foisting his work off on Bobbie and leaving early to visit clients. Too often he treated her more like his personal gofer than an accounting clerk.

At least Rose was feeling better. In the week and a half since Bobbie had brought her home from the hospital, she'd recovered completely from her bout with the aplastic anemia. Her blood count had returned to normal and her color and energy were restored. To Bobbie, her recovery seemed like nothing short of a miracle.

Before she had checked Rose out of the hospital, Bobbie had asked the amount of her bill. The dollar figure had left her gasping and more than a little thankful that Donovan insisted on paying it. She was going to have a difficult enough time dealing with her short paycheck.

Only the first week of the two she had taken off was covered by vacation, but she was lucky to have gotten the extra time, even without pay. Now she was the one who had to get caught up before the end of the month. Although she was grateful to Paul for letting her miss work, he wasn't helping her get caught up by dumping extra chores on her. He was probably taking advantage because he figured she owed him.

At closing time the other two employees turned off their computers, told Bobbie good-night and left. Rubbing the back of her neck where it ached dully, she finished her regular work and retrieved the stack of fliers from the copy machine. The mindless task of folding them, stuffing them into envelopes and sticking on stamps and address labels gave her mind time to wander.

She knew she was still recuperating from the emotional toll Rose's illness and Donovan's reappearance had taken on her. In spite of Dr. Richards's reassurances that Rose was completely out of danger, Bobbie still got up at least once each night to check on her daughter while she slept.

Every time the phone rang, at home or at work, tension trickled through Bobbie like ice water as she tried to prepare for the sound of Donovan's voice. He called almost every day to ask about Rose and to speak to her. He had intended to come back to Arizona right away for a visit, but his schedule made that impossible.

He had been zigzagging all over Texas, Colorado and Oklahoma for the last two weeks. Frustration edged his voice each time he told her why he wasn't yet able to return, but part of her couldn't help wondering if he was only making excuses. Surely he could spare a day or two if he really wanted to see his daughter.

The last time he called he had explained the importance of staying in first place in the bull riding standings, something about contract bonuses with the products he endorsed. To Bobbie it sounded as if he was choosing his precious rodeo over the child they shared. Each time she had to tell Rose he wasn't coming, Bobbie got more impatient with his excuses.

She was almost finished stuffing and stamping Paul's notices when the phone on her desk rang. Technically the office was closed, but the insistent summons was almost impossible to ignore.

"I tried you at home first and then I thought you might still be at work," Donovan said when she answered.

"I've got a lot of catching up to do." She kept her tone brisk and tried not to respond to his honeyed drawl. "What is it you want?" It surprised her that he hadn't waited to call her at home when he could talk to Rose, as well.

"I'll be in Yuma tomorrow afternoon," he said. "I'd like to pick Rose up at her day care, if you'd arrange it for me."

Bobbie had told him that while she worked Rose stayed with a neighbor who took care of several other children, as well. Now she hesitated, nibbling on her lower lip thoughtfully. She had assumed that he would come to the apartment, where she could keep an eye on him, and it bothered her to think of him taking Rose off somewhere without her.

Donovan knew nothing about being a parent. What if something came up that he couldn't handle? What if Rose needed the rest room or she skinned her knee?

"Bobbie?" his voice came through the telephone receiver. "Are you still there?"

With a start, she realized he was waiting for some sort of response. "I thought you'd visit her at home first," she said. "So you could get used to each other again."

It was his turn to fall silent. "Don't you trust me with her?" he asked finally.

"It has nothing to do with trust," Bobbie exclaimed.
"She's only four and she doesn't know you that well." She
took a steadying breath. "I need to adjust to this, too," she
admitted. She hadn't meant to tell him that, but it was true.
Ever since Rose's birth, there had been just the two of
them. Sharing her was a daunting proposition.

"I understand." Donovan surprised her. "It's just that
I have so little time to spend with Rose that I hate to waste
any of it waiting around for you to get off work. Is there a
chance you could leave early?"

A humorless laugh was her reply. "Not after the two
weeks I just missed, but I guess it would be okay for you to
pick her up at Marty's," she finally relented. "I'll explain
things to Rose in the morning and I'll tell Marty to expect
you. What time will you be there?"

As soon as they had finalized the arrangements, Bobbie
hung up and finished stamping Paul's envelopes. Switch-
ing off her computer, she picked up her purse and the pile
of fliers, turned out the lights and locked the door behind
her.

Donovan took one glance at the dark, evil-looking clouds
overhead and swore under his breath before ducking into
the hangar to use the pay phone. Because of the thunder-
storm, his plane was grounded. Frustrated, he picked up the
receiver and began punching in numbers.

It was as if the Fates were conspiring to prevent him from
seeing his little girl. First a nearly impossible schedule had
him racing from show to show like a headless chicken, and
now a summer storm was keeping him pinned down in
Amarillo.

As the phone at Bobbie's office started to ring, he
thought about renting a car. Then he discarded the idea.

Not only would he be hours late in picking up Rose, but he wouldn't get to Mesquite in time for his next event, either.

As soon as he heard Bobbie's voice, he started to explain.

"But Rose is counting on you." Bobbie gripped the receiver hard as she tried to contain her frustration. A child didn't understand about weather reports and FAA regulations. This was exactly the kind of thing she'd been worried about—getting her daughter's hopes up and then disappointing her.

Through the receiver Bobbie heard Donovan's sigh, but she was too annoyed to consider his feelings.

"It's not safe to fly." He sounded frustrated. "If I could drive, I would, but it would take hours and I have to be in Mesquite first thing tomorrow."

Bobbie bit back an impatient reply. Grudgingly she admitted to herself, at least, that the situation was out of his hands.

"Why don't you give me the number where Rose is," Donovan suggested, breaking the oppressive silence. "I'll call and explain everything myself."

Bobbie's reluctance to give him Marty's number caught her by surprise. It just seemed as if he was infiltrating every part of their lives. "I'll call her," she replied. "I need to let Marty know that Rose will be staying until the regular time, after all."

She expected him to argue. Instead, he sighed again and she realized that he must be disappointed, too.

"Okay," he said, "if that's the way you want to handle it. Just tell Rose I'm sorry, okay? Make sure she understands that none of this was my fault."

What was he trying to gain by being so agreeable? Bobbie wondered. Did he think he could win her over by pretending to go along with whatever she wanted? She had thought she wanted him to disappear again, but she had reconsidered and now she wasn't so sure. Rose had a right to know her daddy; Bobbie had lost her father when her parents divorced and she couldn't do that to her own child.

"I'll see that she understands," Bobbie said. After Donovan had repeated his intention to visit Rose as soon as possible, they broke the connection.

Bobbie checked her watch. Might as well call Marty before she got involved in her work and forgot the time.

Rose was going to be disappointed. She had been looking forward to this visit. Maybe Bobbie could take her out for hamburgers after work without straining their already-stretched budget to the breaking point. It might help take Rose's mind off her disappointment.

Though Bobbie knew it wouldn't be fair to blame Donovan for the weather, his last-minute cancellation was still frustrating. Her feelings toward him had undergone so many changes: love, disappointment, bitterness. And, since he came back into her life, confusion.

Part of her was relieved that she didn't have to face him again just yet, but she ached for her daughter. Bobbie had survived his rejection; Rose might not. If he lost interest in her now, it was bound to be more painful than never having met him at all.

When Donovan had left Yuma the first time, he would never have believed that a month would go by before he had the chance to return. To make matters worse, he was running late.

Bobbie had every right to be as irritated as she sounded when he called to tell her a problem at the arena had set him back by well over two hours. As a result, he was picking Rose up at home rather than at her day care, and he wasn't sure he was ready to face Bobbie again.

Recognizing the apartment complex from her description, he parked the rental car and slid from behind the wheel. The sudden pain from his bruised ribs reminded him of the spill he had taken after the buzzer that afternoon and made him suck in his breath. The corset he wore beneath his shirt did little to ease the ache, and he had refused any pain medication since he was flying his plane to Yuma.

Now he glanced around, looking for apartment numbers. The two-story building was light gray with charcoal trim and the concrete walkways were surrounded by dead grass and a few bushes. On closer inspection, Donovan could see that the building needed paint, there were bare patches in the dry grass and the sidewalk was bisected by cracks. Someone had drawn a picture with chalk on the concrete and toys were scattered around several of the apartment doorways.

Donovan spotted the door to unit 102 and drew in as deep a breath as the corset allowed. Over the last four weeks he had been thinking a lot about Rose and trying not to think about her mother. Now he wondered just what his reception from both of them would be.

Banishing the sudden case of nerves, he pressed the doorbell below the slightly rusty porch light.

As the bell sounded inside the apartment, Bobbie saw Rose duck behind a chair, exhibiting an uncharacteristic attack of shyness. One of her thin arms clutched the patchwork clown doll she'd gotten from Donovan at the hospital.

"That's probably your daddy." Bobbie forced a smile. "Would you like to answer the door?"

Rose shook her head, brown eyes wide. "You do it."

Bobbie hesitated. Despite the fact that Rose had talked less and less often about Donovan as the weeks went by, she still seemed excited when Bobbie told her he was picking her up at Marty's. Apparently she was having second thoughts.

"You remember Daddy from the hospital, don't you?" Bobbie asked. "He read to you and brought you Patchy."

Rose gave the doll a hug. Before she could reply, the doorbell rang again. Bobbie glanced over her shoulder, frowning.

"Daddy's a cowboy," Rose said.

"That's right." Bobbie crossed to the door. "Shall I let him in?" she asked, one hand on the knob. She had no idea what she would do if Rose said no.

"Okay." She looked very small and vulnerable, standing there in her red shorts and striped T-shirt. Bobbie had recombed her hair and put it into a ponytail with a red-yarn tie, but she hadn't taken the time to change clothes herself. She had on the same wrinkled khaki skirt and plaid blouse she'd worn to work. Now she wished she'd at least run a brush through her own hair and put on fresh lip gloss.

Before the bell could sound again, she dragged in a bracing breath and opened the door.

Every time she saw Donovan, she was shocked anew by how attractive he was. More so than even her memories of him. He stood outside the screen door, wearing his trademark tan Stetson, a faded blue chambray shirt, jeans and Western boots. His face appeared leaner, the lines around his eyes and mouth deeper. Bobbie's involuntary response reared up like a wild horse before she subdued it.

"Hi, Bobbie. Thanks for letting me come by." As usual, he was unfailingly polite, his gaze meeting hers before it swept the room behind her.

Returning his greeting, she stepped aside and invited him in while she tried to see the compact living room through his eyes: worn light brown carpet with a faded grape-juice stain that had been there when they moved in; a couch with a striped slipcover; scarred end table topped by a straw mat beside a lamp from a neighbor's garage sale that she had repainted to match the dark green stripe in the couch cover. At least the apartment was clean; Bobbie had seen to that the evening before.

Donovan stopped just inside the doorway. "Hi, princess," he said.

When Rose stayed rooted beside the vinyl-covered chair, he glanced at Bobbie with a question in his eyes.

"Four-year-olds have pretty short memories," she said under her breath. "Give her a few minutes."

His puzzled frown cleared and he went down on his haunches. Long, sleek muscles bunched beneath the faded denim, pulling the fabric tight. Bobbie stared, swallowing dryly. How could she let herself respond to him after all that had happened?

"I missed you," he told Rose in a quiet voice, reminding Bobbie why he was here. "Are you feeling all better now?"

Rose clung to her doll as she stared at him. "Yes, thank you," she said politely.

"Can I have a hug?" he asked.

She glanced at Bobbie, who managed an encouraging nod and a shaky smile. If only he had come back when he'd said he would, she thought. Poor Rose looked entirely too wary. It almost broke Bobbie's heart to watch her.

When she didn't respond, Donovan must have realized he was pushing too hard. He cleared his throat. Then he took off his hat. "How about you try this on and we'll forget about the hug for a while?"

A smile of relief brightened Rose's face and she reached for his hat. When she put it on and it settled down over her eyes, she giggled and took it off again.

"Your head's too big."

Donovan straightened. His gaze locked with Bobbie's. "Probably not the last time I'll hear that," he drawled in an undertone.

She couldn't help but return his infectious grin. "I was just thinking the same thing. Why don't you sit down," she suggested nervously. "How was your flight?"

He sat on the couch and she winced at how far the ancient cushions sank beneath his weight. His knees were sticking up; it couldn't have been very comfortable for him. Probably little about this visit was.

"The flight was uneventful. I have to leave again first thing in the morning."

She assumed he was staying at a local motel, but she didn't ask. Maybe, if coming here proved too inconvenient, he would eventually give up.

Was that what Bobbie wanted, for Rose to lose her daddy just as Bobbie had hers? Or was she willing to deal with him for years to come, struggling against the attraction she still felt toward him, despite the way he had treated her before? She had no answers.

Donovan turned down her offer of iced tea, making her wish she had some beer in the fridge, before she caught herself. When she suggested that Rose show him her bedroom, he got up from the couch and followed her willingly, giving Bobbie a few much-needed minutes to compose herself. She could hear their voices, Rose's preciously familiar as she chattered about her dolls and toys, Donovan's deeper, but too soft for Bobbie to understand. She tried to stay busy in the kitchen and not eavesdrop, but curiosity was eating her up.

Eventually the two of them came back, Rose's hand tucked into his. "Would you like to go get something to eat?" he asked her.

Bobbie wondered if he had any idea what kind of place would be suitable for a small child. She was about to speak up and then decided to let him find out for himself. If he wanted to be a real father, he had to learn how.

To Donovan's obvious surprise, as well as Bobbie's own, Rose pulled her hand free and ran over to where Bobbie stood at the sink. "Are you going, too?" she demanded.

Bobbie exchanged looks with Donovan, her cheeks heating. "Don't you want to spend some time alone with your daddy?" she asked. "He's come a long way to see you."

"I want you to come with us." Rose's tone was adamant.

Bobbie hadn't thought to discuss this situation with her ahead of time. There was no way she could try to explain how uncomfortable she would feel, not in front of the *reason* for that discomfort. "Maybe you should forget about going out this time," she suggested instead. "Perhaps later on you'll feel more like going somewhere together."

"But I'm hungry." Rose's expression turned mutinous. She was usually cooperative unless she was tired—or hungry. Then she could be stubborn and difficult. "I want you to go with us."

Donovan regarded his daughter with a helpless expression. Bobbie wasn't sure what to do.

"Can't Mommy come, too?" Rose asked him.

"Sure, she can," he said magnanimously. "If she wants to." He tossed the problem neatly back into Bobbie's lap. The situation was growing more awkward by the second, but she couldn't think of a single way to resolve it. The last thing she wanted was to play happy family with Donovan, even for a free dinner, but she couldn't force Rose into an uncomfortable situation, either.

"Mommy?" Her voice quavered and Bobbie was surprised to see that she was close to tears.

"Perhaps I'd better go along this time," Bobbie suggested uncomfortably, "just until she's a little more used to you." She hoped he understood that it wasn't because she didn't trust him with her daughter or because she wanted to go.

Did she trust him? She believed he wouldn't hurt their child, not deliberately, but it would be so easy for him to hurt her feelings without thinking.

"Are we ready, then?" he asked, managing a smile.

"I guess so." She'd have to give him points for a fast recovery and a gracious surrender, she thought. "Where did you plan on eating?"

He raised his brows. "Any suggestions?"

She mentioned the hamburger place that was her daughter's favorite, smothering a grin at his grimace of distaste.

"Oh, could we?" Rose clapped her hands, all traces of her earlier reluctance gone. "Mommy says we can't afford to go there much, but they have the best fries in the whole world."

Bobbie colored at Rose's innocent commentary. What other family secrets would she inadvertently reveal? Bobbie's jaw tightened. Well, it wasn't as if they were living on the street, after all. If he dared to look down his nose at their life-style, she would—

"That's quite a testimonial," he said pleasantly.

"What's a testi-mo-ni-al?" Rose asked.

He thought for a moment. "A little like a compliment. Shall we go? I could probably eat about five of their burgers just by myself."

"Five?" Rose's eyes widened. "Can you really?"

He smiled down at her and winked. "Well, at least four. How about you?"

* * *

Three weeks went by before Donovan managed another visit to Yuma. When he finally did, Rose pulled away from his hug of greeting and was unusually quiet the whole time he was there. It was painfully obvious that his infrequent trips were doing little toward building a relationship. There had to be a better way.

"Thank you for going with me," he said when he had delivered her and her mother back to their apartment after another hamburger dinner.

"Thank you for taking us," Bobbie replied politely.

Rose remained quiet, her mouth set in a stubborn line. He walked them to their door, where he bent down to tell Rose goodbye. As he held his breath, she surprised him by finally giving him a peck on the cheek. A bolt of emotion shot through him. The intensity of his feelings for her never failed to surprise him. Three months before, he hadn't known she existed, and now she was a crucial part of his life.

"I'll see you soon," he told her.

Her smile faded. "No, you won't. You hardly ever come to see me," she shouted and then she ran inside.

Stunned by her vehemence, Donovan didn't know what to say.

"Why don't you come in," Bobbie suggested. "I'll start some coffee and then I need to tuck her into bed."

Her invitation surprised him. She had said little during dinner. All in all, it hadn't been a very satisfactory visit.

"That would be nice." He was feeling wary. Was she going to hit him up for more money? She'd thanked him for paying the hospital bill and he'd set up a regular child-support payment through Bill right after that. Perhaps she'd decided it wasn't enough.

When Bobbie came back out of Rose's room, Donovan was sitting on the uncomfortable couch, hands clasped loosely between his bent knees. When he saw her, he got to his feet.

"How's Rose?"

"I got her calmed down," Bobbie replied, her own emotions in a turmoil. "She's just too young to understand all this, I'm afraid."

"Well, thanks for trying." He looked so forlorn that, for a moment, she felt sorry for him.

"I would have poured the coffee," he added, "but I didn't think you'd want me messing around in your kitchen."

The coffee! She'd forgotten all about it, but now she could smell its rich aroma coming from the other room. Lord knew she needed a cup. "I'll get it." She spent a few moments filling their mugs and stirring sugar into hers. Finally she turned and almost ran into Donovan, who had sneaked up silently behind her.

"Let me take those," he said when the mugs threatened to spill.

Wordlessly, Bobbie followed him into the living room and sat down in the vinyl chair. Donovan handed her one of the mugs and gingerly settled back onto the sagging couch. He took a sip of his coffee and set it down on the table.

She held hers with both hands, staring into the dark brew.

"I hope my visits haven't been too disruptive," he began, giving her the opening she needed.

"Actually, I wanted to talk to you about that."

Immediately his expression grew wary. Bobbie took another sip of her coffee and plunged on.

"This arrangement isn't working."

"I know it must be inconvenient," he said, "with me springing these visits on you at the last minute, and you having to go with us—"

"It's not that," she interrupted hastily. "As you saw just now, it's too upsetting for Rose. You can't drop in and out of her life like this."

"She'll adjust."

Bobbie shook her head. "Last week when you didn't show up, I found her Patchy doll in the wastebasket."

For a moment he looked shocked. They both knew that Patchy was Rose's very favorite possession. "What do you suggest we do?"

She made a helpless gesture. "I don't know, but I have to think of my daughter's welfare. She's just a little girl. She sees the clerk at the grocery store more often than she does you."

"That's not my fault," Donovan argued. "I'm doing the best I can, but you know my schedule's a killer."

"Your schedule will always be a killer," she retorted. "Maybe it's not your fault, but Rose is starting to ask questions I can't answer."

"Like what?" His voice had sharpened, as had his expression. She mustn't forget that he could be a powerful adversary if she crossed him.

"Like why you don't come to spend more time with her." Actually Rose's words had been "with us," but Bobbie had no intention of telling him that. "She's too young to understand that you have a killer schedule."

"Maybe you just don't want this to work."

His sudden attack made her angry. She and Rose had done without him for five years, now he expected her to move over and make room for him. Containing her emotions with difficulty, she leaned forward.

"My parents were divorced when I was a child," she said. "Afterward my father deserted me just as surely as he had my mother. Believe me, after growing up with one parent, I would have done almost anything to keep the same situation from happening to my own daughter."

"Except tell me of her existence," Donovan commented.

She opened her mouth to remind him that she *had* told him, and then decided not to bother. Perhaps he was starting to believe his own lies.

He got to his feet, coffee forgotten. "I'm sorry about your father," he muttered, pacing to the front window and gazing outside. "That must have been tough. Didn't he stay in touch with you?"

Bobbie ignored the feeling of rejection that talking about him still caused. "After he moved out, I got two phone calls and a birthday card. Mom told me later that he remarried and had a little boy."

"Are you ever tempted to look him up?" Donovan asked, turning to face her.

"I have no interest in him. It's been too long. But I want you and Rose to know each other. She needs a father."

"She has a father."

"And I won't interfere with that, no matter what my own feelings happen to be," Bobbie replied crisply. "But some changes need to be made."

"I agree."

His quick compliance made her nervous. She took another swallow of her coffee while she waited for him to elaborate.

"I have another idea," he finally said.

"What's that?" Instinct told her she wasn't going to care for his new idea.

Donovan hooked his thumbs into his wide leather belt and shifted his weight to one hip. The movement drew her attention to his long legs, sheathed in denim that was worn white at the points of stress. Distracted, she dragged her gaze back to his face.

He was watching her the way a hawk watched a field mouse. She kept her expression carefully blank, praying he would see no hint of how attractive she still found him. He had abandoned her when she needed him the most. Hadn't she learned her lesson?

"What's your idea?" she prompted.

"I want her to come on the road with me."

For a moment Bobbie could only stare. "Are you out of your mind?" she finally sputtered. "I'm not letting you take her with you."

Her response didn't appear to surprise him. "It's not as crazy as it sounds," he said quickly. "She could come for a month or so. I'd hire a nanny, someone well qualified. The two of them would travel with me. Wherever we stayed, they'd have their own room. Rose would be looked after every minute."

Bobbie shook her head. "I'm not letting you take her," she repeated. "Not for a month, not for a week. No."

"Why not?" he demanded. "Divorced people do it for a summer."

Bobbie was still shocked that he would suggest such a thing. "It's not the same," she argued. "She doesn't know you well enough to go to dinner alone with you, and you want to hire a perfect stranger to take care of her? She'd be scared to death. Don't you know anything about children? Rose is way too young to be dragged all over hell and gone.

I'm the only security she's ever had. We've never been separated before and she needs me.''

"Fine.'' Donovan threw up his hands. "If she's too young to go without you, then you can damn well come along with us.''

Chapter Four

"What did you say?" Bobbie couldn't have heard Donovan right. Her ears were playing tricks on her.

"I said you could come along with us." His expression was serious; he wasn't kidding.

"That's what I thought you said." Bobbie sat back down in the vinyl chair with a soft plop. "Obviously you've lost your mind."

"No, I haven't," he replied. "And I won't lose my daughter, either. You're right about these visits not working, but that doesn't mean I'm giving up. No way. I don't have a lot of options here, you know. And I don't see why taking her with me for a month is such a bad idea."

"Just a month," she echoed. "Why not six? How about a year?"

"I've got four years of visitation to make up for," he countered. "If you're worried about her, you're welcome to come along, too."

"Oh, sure, just like that," Bobbie muttered, dazed.

"That's right, just like that." Donovan's face had settled into a stubborn expression, but she barely noticed.

"That's ludicrous." She wanted to shout at him, but Rose was asleep in the next room. Hearing her parents fight would only upset her. "I have a life here in Yuma, and a job," Bobbie said instead, trying to be reasonable. "Besides, you don't have any idea of the responsibility involved in taking care of a small child twenty-four hours a day."

"I'll learn. You'd be right there to teach me."

The idea of traveling with Donovan, of seeing him day after day for a whole month, made Bobbie's mouth go dry with fear. But she was immune to him, wasn't she?

She had fallen for his rustic brand of charm once, she reminded herself, and familiarity could breed a lot more than contempt. They already had one child between them.

"What about taking her for a week?" she countered desperately. "Maybe I could manage that somehow." The last thing she wanted was to bargain with him, but a month was impossible.

He was already shaking his head. "A week won't give me nearly the time with her that I want," he replied. "You owe me. It's a month or nothing."

She resisted the impulse to tell him that nothing was her first choice. "You expect to fly Rose all over the country in that little tin can with propellers?" she demanded instead. "It's not safe."

Donovan looked as if she had insulted his manhood. "My plane's a step or two more evolved than a tin can, and I'm an experienced pilot. My safety record is unblemished. I don't take chances. If I did, I might not have had to cancel that one visit because of the weather." He leaned toward her until they were almost nose to nose. Up close, his green eyes had flakes of gold around the pupils. "And I sure as hell wouldn't take chances with my only child." He straightened, a pleading expression softening his attractive face.

"Think of the fun she'd have," he coaxed. "She'd love the animals and the clowns, and everyone would love her, too."

For an instant Bobbie felt a bubble of jealousy. It did sound like fun, and she almost envied her own daughter the chance to go.

What was she thinking? Donovan might no longer be the unassuming cowboy she had fallen in love with—perhaps he never really was—but she was still too susceptible to risk being hurt by him again.

"I won't let Rose go alone and I can't afford to go with her," she said, folding her arms across her chest. "I just took two weeks off when she was sick and I'd never get any more time away from work."

"I'll pay you to go with me," he said bluntly. "If they won't give you the time off, you can quit. It probably wouldn't be hard to find something else when you come back."

"What planet have you been living on?" Bobbie sputtered. "I'm lucky to have that job. I can't just throw it all aside—I have a daughter to support."

He shrugged. "Couldn't they get a temp to fill in for you?"

His assumption that she could be replaced so easily grated on Bobbie's pride. "Even if they could," she said, "I won't take money from you. And how would I pay my bills while I was away? I'd still have rent and other expenses, not to mention meals and incidentals on the road."

His eyes glittered as he looked down at her, and his jaw was set with stubborn determination. "I'll pay your regular salary, just like I'd have to pay a nanny," he said. "And I bet they don't come cheap. I'll talk to your boss for you and see if he can get a replacement."

She started to interrupt and he held up one finger. "Temporarily." He rubbed his jaw thoughtfully while she scrambled to think of more reasons why his idea wouldn't work.

"Don't you dare say anything to my boss," Bobbie warned.

"I'll pay your rent while we're gone," he added. "Hell, I can afford it." His stare intensified. "Rose isn't in school yet. This would be a terrific opportunity for her. And for me. Next year would be too late. Come on, what do you say? At least think about it."

Bobbie shook her head. The idea terrified her and she knew it wasn't only her daughter's safety she was thinking about. "No," she said. "The whole scheme is impossible."

"You owe me," he repeated. "I've already lost four years of her life. Four years I can't get back. While we're on the road, you can fill me in on everything I've missed."

It was a tempting offer. To get paid to take care of her own child. Not to have to leave Rose at the baby-sitter's and spend the entire day away from her, cooped up in an office with a job that was often boring.

"No," she said again. "I don't need to think about it. The answer's no."

"If that's your attitude, you leave me no choice." Donovan paced the length of the room and then turned to give her a hard stare. "I tried to reason with you." He dragged in a breath that expanded his muscular chest and strained the snaps fastening his shirt. "Damn it, she's my kid, too."

"What do you mean?" His words alarmed her. Good Lord, he wouldn't kidnap Rose, would he? She had heard of parents who took their children and disappeared. Surely he wouldn't go to those lengths. He was a public figure, with obligations and a lucrative career. Would he give that all up for one little girl?

"Tell me what you mean," Bobbie insisted, fearing the worst.

He dragged a hand through his hair. "If you won't share Rose with me voluntarily, I'll have to sue for custody."

The words dropped between the two of them like stones plunging into a bottomless pond.

"I'm her mother," Bobbie protested, struggling for control. "You don't have a chance of taking her away from me."

"Not even when the judge hears how you kept her existence a secret until you needed me for a transplant?" he asked softly. "Mothers don't automatically win custody these days, you know. The courts are paying a lot more attention to the rights of fathers, and my rights have been violated."

"You wouldn't," she cried.

"I wouldn't want to," he replied quietly. "But what choice have you left me?"

Suddenly, something snapped deep inside her. She had fought and struggled and cried many bitter tears, trying to care for her baby. She couldn't bear to stand there and listen to any more of his threats.

"Get out." She stalked to the door and wrenched it open.

"Bobbie—" His voice held a warning. As if he, too, had been pushed too far.

Without stopping to consider what he might be feeling, she shook her head and opened the door even wider. "You heard me. No more bullying. Get out or I'll call the police." She had no idea whether they would help her, but she was too upset to reconsider.

"I'll leave for now," Donovan said, "but we're going to have to talk about this again, and soon. That's a promise."

She squeezed her eyes shut, barely refraining from putting her hands over her ears. "Not now. Please just leave."

Apparently her insistence was more convincing than her anger. He picked up his hat and brushed past her as she stood by the door. As soon as he was outside, he started to say something, but before he could, she shut the door in his face.

Appalled at what she had done, she sagged against the closed door, shaking with emotion, as she waited for the pounding of his fists and his demands that she open up. Her ears strained against the silence. Then she heard the sound of a car engine starting up. When she finally peeked out the window, she saw the tail end of his rental car as he drove away.

"Mommy, I heard yelling." Rose was standing in her bedroom doorway, rubbing one eye with her fist. "Were you and Daddy fighting?"

Dismayed that she had been disturbed by their argument, Bobbie led Rose gently back to bed. "We were having a disagreement, honey. Sometimes adults do that. I'm sorry we bothered you."

"Does that mean Daddy won't come back?" Rose asked, voice rising. "Is he mad at us?"

Bobbie let her climb back into bed, then pulled the covers up while searching for the right answer.

"You know that Daddy works far away," she said as she smoothed back Rose's hair. "He'd like to spend more time with you, but he's very busy."

"Being a cowboy," Rose said.

Bobbie couldn't hold back a smile. "That's right."

"Can't he be a cowboy here? Then he could visit us all the time, like Susie's dad, and I could go to his apartment and sleep over sometimes."

"Would you like that?"

"I think so."

Rose's words gave Bobbie a heartbreaking glimpse of just what her little girl was missing. Was Bobbie right in telling Donovan he couldn't take his daughter with him? She had never been separated from Bobbie before, not even for one night. Bobbie couldn't imagine her life without Rose in it, not for a few weeks. And she sure as heck didn't want to go with him herself. No, it was the craziest idea she had ever heard.

After she had calmed Rose down, kissed her good-night and closed her door, Bobbie poured herself another cup of coffee and stood at the front window, looking out at the street beyond the parking lot.

She wondered whether Donovan had gone back to his hotel room or if he had stopped for a drink somewhere. A man like him probably wasn't used to being alone. Perhaps he had found himself a woman with a weakness for cowboys.

Before Bobbie could block it out, the image of him in the arms of someone else formed like a hologram to taunt her. She whirled away from the window so fast that the coffee sloshed over the rim of her mug.

"Damn." Grabbing a damp dishcloth from the kitchen sink, she bent to scrub at the spot on the carpet. What did she care if he picked up a hundred other women? It was Rose who concerned her, not Donovan—and certainly not his sex life.

It had never occurred to her when she first sought him out that he might sue for custody or that he would even want to. Now, as she poured the remainder of her coffee down the drain, the idea terrified her. She couldn't lose her baby.

Donovan perched on the fence surrounding the bucking chutes and watched J. D. Reese, the bull rider who trailed him in the standings by less than a hundred dollars, as he burst from the chute on the back of an NFR Brahma crossbreed that had only been ridden twice all year. Bulls like him were called eliminators, because they eliminated cowboys from competition.

As the crowd in the huge covered arena in Mesquite, Texas, roared its approval, J.D. clung to the bull like a tick on a pig. His free hand waved high; his body followed the bull's movements with unexpected grace as the animal bucked, whirled, changed direction in midair to spin the other way and buck again. The cowbell that hung from J.D.'s rigging clanged with every movement.

The bull's eyes glowed red with hatred as it tossed its wicked horns. Saliva ran from its broad nose and open mouth while it fought to dislodge the irritation on its back.

Twice Donovan thought J.D. would surely lose his grip on the rigging. That, his spurs and the fierce determination all bull riders shared—to outlast the beast and the buzzer—were all that kept him on the raging behemoth.

Reese's hat flew off, sailing across the dirt like a Frisbee, and his leather chaps flapped wildly. His wiry body stayed centered, absorbing the ground-shaking jolts with deceptive ease. Finally, after a dizzying series of spins, the buzzer sounded and he bailed off the animal's broad back. As a clown moved in to distract it, J.D. scrambled for the rail and hauled himself up next to Donovan.

"Nice ride," he drawled as Reese's score was announced. Reese had just pulled an eighty-five, but Donovan could afford to be generous with his praise. He had

earned an eighty-seven with a hell of a ride on a decep-
tively small bull named Bad Boy. Donovan's whole body
was still protesting the way the bull had spun him into his
hand and then away, almost ripping his arm from its
socket—as smooth a ride as a cement mixer with a flat tire.

J. D. Reese only glanced at Donovan, his black eyes
opaque with silent disdain, before he cleared the fence and
walked away, entry number flapping. Not for the first time,
Donovan wondered what he had done to make the other
man dislike him. Even when the competition was at its
fiercest, rodeo bums were usually a pretty friendly group.

Not Reese. He had a reputation as a loner, though he
sometimes hung out with a few of the Indians on the circuit. With his long black hair and dark skin, Reese might
be part Native American himself. He was the only one close
enough in the rankings to snatch the lead from Donovan
this season.

Donovan still might end up eating the other man's dust
all year, he thought as he tucked his rigging into his equipment bag and headed for the locker room. Reese was one
of the most talented bull riders Donovan had ever seen,
anticipating the bull's moves and sharing its force instead
of fighting it.

Passing a pay phone in the aisle, Donovan hesitated before he walked on. He wanted to call Bobbie, to hear what
she had decided about Rose.

He could still picture her stricken expression when he had
threatened to sue for custody. The image tweaked his conscience the same way his mother used to tweak his ear when
he sassed her back. Manipulating Bobbie with her love for
their child went against everything he believed in, but she
had left him no choice. Dammit, he had every right to use
whatever weapons he could in order to build a relationship
with Rose.

Bobbie had given him that right when she kept his child a secret. So why did he still feel as though he had done something terrible?

Donovan hardened his heart as he walked into the locker room and exchanged greetings with several other competitors.

"Hell of a ride," one of the steer wrestlers, a friend of his brother's, told him. Reese was changing clothes, but he didn't even glance up. Stripping off his flak jacket and then his dirty shirt, Donovan opened his locker and pulled out a clean one. Three more days, he decided, and then he would call Bobbie McBride and find out whether she was taking his deal or facing him in court.

"He can't take my baby, can he?" Bobbie demanded. She was seated across the desk from an attorney she couldn't afford, her hands clasped together so tightly that her knuckles were turning white. Deliberately, she unclenched them and willed herself to relax.

The attorney, a gray-haired man with small round spectacles, smiled ruefully. "Unfortunately, he might be able to." His words sent a shaft of apprehension through Bobbie. "These days, the courts are bending over backward in an effort to recognize fathers' rights."

A headache began tap-dancing behind her eyes. This was not the news she was paying so dearly to hear, she thought grimly. "He's never shown any interest in her before," she argued.

Mr. Kovak steepled his fingers and pursed his lips. "Didn't you say you wrote him when your child was born?"

"Twice. He ignored both letters."

"I don't suppose you got a signed receipt for either of them?" he asked. "Or any other way of proving you attempted to notify him?"

She flushed. "No, I didn't." At the time she had never considered that she might have to prove it. In her little fantasy, Donovan had come racing to her side with a teddy bear in one hand and a ring in the other, eager to claim both his daughter and herself. How naive she had been.

The attorney's smile was sympathetic. "Unfortunately, Mr. Buchanan's claim that you kept news of the child from him can't be disproven."

"But I'll swear under oath that I wrote him," Bobbie exclaimed.

He spread his hands wide. "And he'll deny it. Your word against his."

Despair flooded through her. "Then what?"

"Then the judge could rule either way. Or he could grant joint custody, but that would only be likely if he felt there was a chance you two could share it peaceably." Mr. Kovak shook his head slowly. "Of course, if you could do that, you wouldn't be here."

"So there really is a chance I could lose Rose." Bobbie had to blink back tears of panic. She had so hoped to be told Donovan's bluff was a hollow one.

The attorney moved a folder on his desk. "I'm afraid so."

Fury boiled up unexpectedly inside Bobbie. It wasn't fair! When she had needed Donovan in her life, he hadn't been there. And now, when she didn't want him disrupting everything she had built with her daughter, he was threatening to destroy it as if it were made of straw and he was the big bad wolf.

"I'll fight him," she said, rising. "I'm Rose's mother. I raised her, not him, and I'm going to keep her." She glared at Mr. Kovak, who was watching her sadly from behind his desk. Suddenly ashamed of her outburst, Bobbie sat back down. "We have a chance, don't we?" she asked meekly, her anger draining as quickly as it had risen.

"Sure, you have a chance, and no doubt a good one, but you told me the child's father is quite successful. Do you have access to the funds to withstand the kind of legal battle he can wage against you?" he asked gently.

Bobbie wanted to tell him that she would fight as long as there was a breath in her body and hang the cost. From a practical point of view, though, she knew that was impossible. Even this one visit was a strain on her resources.

"Is there no other solution to your dilemma?" the attorney asked. "No way you can prevent Mr. Buchanan from suing?"

With a sigh, Bobbie began to describe the ludicrous plan he had suggested.

When she opened her apartment door, Donovan was struck by how tired Bobbie looked. Her face was drawn and pale, as if the intense summer heat had sucked the moisture from her. Only her eyes seemed to burn with intensity. He had to keep reminding himself that she was the one who had chosen to keep his daughter from him and then to lie about it when she had finally been backed into a corner by Rose's illness. Still, guilt turned his stomach.

Thank God the child had completely recovered. He didn't think he could have stood losing her, especially not after just learning of her existence, and he hated to think what that kind of heartbreaking loss would have done to Bobbie. She loved Rose, too.

Despite all his reminders to himself, he had a hard time maintaining his resentment toward her. No matter what she had done to him, there was no doubt in his mind that she'd had a tough time as a single parent.

"Come on in," she told him in a flat voice as he stood on the step, hat in hand. The cryptic message she had left for him, that she was ready to talk, had brought him racing back to Yuma and her apartment. That and the chance to visit his daughter again.

As he brushed past Bobbie, he searched the tiny living room for Rose. He had hoped she might feel comfortable enough to go out with him alone this time. He had heard of a park not too far from the apartment and he'd driven by there to check it out when he first got to town. There were trees and a pond with ducks, as well as a play area with swings and a slide.

He hadn't let himself think about what he was going to do if Bobbie forced him to take her to court. Although he had meant every word at the time, he dreaded the idea of doing that to her.

"Where's Rose?" he asked. The quiet apartment appeared to be empty except for Bobbie and himself. Would she have sent Rose away, hiding her from him?

He took a deep breath and struggled to keep from jumping to conclusions. Bobbie had already told him she had no family. Her mother had passed away a couple of years before. Who else would she entrust with their daughter?

"Rose is at my neighbor Darlene's," Bobbie said as she waved him over to the couch he detested.

Donovan sat down carefully as the cushions sank beneath his weight and the frame creaked. One of these times it was going to collapse altogether and he'd end up on his butt on the floor.

"Can I get you anything?" Bobbie asked. "Water? Juice? It seemed too hot out for coffee, but I can make some if you want."

He shook his head, noticing again how tired and nervous she seemed. "No thanks, I'm fine. Why did you send her away?" No point in wasting time with small talk when he was reasonably sure Bobbie was as preoccupied with their daughter's fate as he was. "What have you decided to do about my suggestion?"

Bobbie's mouth twisted bitterly as she stood over him with her arms folded across her chest. "My attorney assures me you have a chance, albeit a slim one, of winning custody," she admitted. Two spots of color appeared on her pale cheeks, and her expression was mutinous.

Donovan wasn't surprised that she had gone to a lawyer, although he'd hoped she would see the sense of his suggestion once she thought it over carefully. It was the ideal solution—an opportunity for him and Rose to become better acquainted without the pressure on him to make time to run back and forth to Yuma. Apparently Bobbie still failed to recognize the benefits of his idea and had decided to fight him instead.

Faced with the obvious strain the coming battle had already placed on her, he once again felt a sharp regret that he had ever made the threat in the first place. What kind of monster tried to separate a child from her mother?

The answer came to him swiftly. One desperate not to lose anyone else he loved.

Donovan got to his feet and faced her, resigned to a fight. "So what have you decided?" he asked in a guarded voice.

Her dark eyes sparkled with unshed tears. Her lower lip trembled until, with a visible effort, she steadied it. The loathing on her face struck him like a blow, but he had no time to wonder at the strength of his dismay before she spoke. He was too busy bracing himself for the disappointing news that they were about to become legal adversaries.

"If you still want us to," she said without meeting his gaze, "Rose and I will go with you."

Chapter Five

Bobbie had been prepared to see triumph on Donovan's face at her capitulation, or even smug satisfaction that she had no real choice but to agree to take Rose and go with him. The last thing she might have expected, had she even thought of it at all, was his obvious relief. For a second his eyes closed and the harsh line of his lips relaxed.

"Thank you," he said quietly as he opened his eyes and stared into hers.

His sincerity stunned her. She'd been too busy fighting against his custody threat to give any thought to why he had made that threat in the first place. Now the idea that he really wanted to spend time with his daughter hit Bobbie with the force of a roundhouse punch. No matter what else lay between the two of them, they shared the parentage of a child. Even though she had always thought of him as Rose's father, since before her child's birth, Bobbie realized with sudden clarity that she had never considered what that must mean to him.

In a crazy way, Donovan's determination to have Rose with him, even if that involved the time and expense of a custody suit, was reassuring. It meant he wasn't likely to abandon her baby again, as Bobbie had feared.

For once she was able to look at him without resentment, allowing herself to feel for perhaps the first time the bond of parenthood they shared.

"You're welcome," she replied. Almost immediately reality took over. "You realize," she added, "that everything hinges on my being able to take time away from work without jeopardizing my job. Rose is still too young to go off with you and some strange nanny." Bobbie didn't point out that he was nearly a stranger to her, too. "And you said you'd pay my salary and my travel expenses." She hated to bring up that part, but she had no choice.

"That's right." His gaze probed hers. "Do you want me to talk to your boss? Surely, if I explain the situation—"

She shook her head. "I'll handle it. I'll talk to Paul tomorrow and let you know what he says. If he agrees, it may take a little time to find a replacement." Paul had two children of his own. Perhaps he would understand what she was facing.

Donovan let out a long breath. "As long as I know you're both coming, I don't mind waiting for a little while."

Briefly, Bobbie let herself pretend that some of his elation was for her. The moment she realized what she was doing, she frowned and cleared her throat. "I guess we can work out the details after I've talked to Paul."

"Well," he said, "I guess I'd better be going."

"Wait a minute." She spoke without thinking, curiosity getting the best of her. "There's something I've been meaning to ask you."

His expression became guarded. "What's that?"

No doubt he would tell her to mind her own business. "I've been wondering if you ever found your parents," she said, remembering how touchy he had been about the subject. They had disappeared one evening when Donovan and his brother were just children. Donovan had confided one night back at the diner that he blamed his own misbehavior for their departure, but Bobbie hoped time had proved him wrong.

The sudden pain on his face made her wish she had kept silent. A muscle in his jaw flexed and he glanced away. "No," he said harshly. "We've never heard a word."

How difficult it must be for him to carry that self-imposed burden of guilt, never knowing what really happened or even if they were still alive. "What about your sister?" Bobbie asked softly. Kirby had been just Rose's age when she was separated from her brothers. Somehow they had lost touch, but Bobbie didn't know the details.

Donovan sighed and bowed his head. "We're still looking, but after all these years the trail is pretty cold and the records of her adoption have been lost." The closed expression Bobbie expected to see on his face didn't appear. "Thanks for asking," he said instead. "You always were easy to talk to. I've missed that." Guard temporarily lowered, he gave her a crooked grin.

Dismayed at how badly she wanted to tell him she, too, had missed their closeness, Bobbie got hastily to her feet.

"Don't give up on your family," she told him. "I can't believe you won't find them someday."

"I'm not giving up. Maybe now you see why Rose is so important to me."

What Bobbie didn't understand was how he had been able to ignore her existence for so long. Reluctant to destroy the temporary peace between them, she didn't bother

be leaving her friends and her home behind, it was clear her feelings were mixed.

Well, it was done now, or almost, Bobbie reminded herself with a sigh. Donovan would be here any moment to take them to the airport and his plane. Even Texas couldn't be any hotter than Yuma in August, and the heat was one thing she didn't mind leaving behind.

All she had to do was to stay immune to Big D for a few weeks. Under the circumstances, that shouldn't be difficult.

Without thinking, Donovan pushed open the unlocked door to Bobbie and Rose's adjoining hotel room and barged in.

"What do you think of..." His voice drained away as Bobbie, clad only in jeans and a pink bra, screeched and crossed her arms protectively in front of herself.

"Get out of here!" she cried, turning away.

"Oops! I'm sorry," he muttered, any memory of what he'd been saying wiped from his brain by the sight of her curves covered only by skimpy lace. His gaze was riveted on the enticing line of her spine, bisected only by the back of her narrow bra before it finally disappeared into her snug new jeans.

They had arrived in Dallas the night before. First thing this morning, he had taken her and Rose shopping at a nearby mall under the guise of buying a few outfits for his daughter. Despite Bobbie's protests, he'd managed to pick out several items for her, as well.

"No one would expect you to have already had suitable clothes for the rodeo," he'd reasoned, grabbing jeans and Western shirts off the rack and piling them into her arms while she sputtered a protest he ignored. "I can't let you buy these things yourself when you're here only as a favor to me." He grabbed a pair of boots in what he hoped was her size. "When would you ever wear these again?" he asked, adding them to the pile.

Whether or not she actually fell for his explanation, she had insisted on paying him back later for the clothes, as well as a Stetson he told her she couldn't do without. He had piled her purchases next to Rose's new wardrobe of miniature Western wear and paid for the whole lot before Bobbie could rustle up a second thought.

Now she grabbed one of her new Western shirts, a pink one with purple stitching on the yoke and collar that looked great with her dark hair, and held it in front of her like a shield as she glared at him. Her face was flushed the same bright pink as her skimpy undergarment.

"Go on, get! Can't you see I'm not decent?"

With an effort bordering on Herculean, he kept from commenting that she looked pretty damn decent to him.

"Yes, ma'am," he replied instead as he smothered a grin and began backing from the room. "Excuse me."

Before Donovan could apologize again for his intrusion, Rose came out of the bathroom. She, too, was wearing a new outfit. The tiny jeans and matching vest she wore over a checkered shirt were trimmed with fringe.

"Don't I look like a real cowgirl?" she demanded, heedless of the tension between her parents. Holding out her hat, she spun in a circle and waited expectantly for Donovan's reaction.

He would have bought out the store if Bobbie hadn't stopped him with the reminder that little girls outgrew their clothes pretty quickly. He had still insisted on the little red boots and matching Western hat that Rose fell in love with, while Bobbie muttered dire warnings about spoiling their daughter rotten.

The idea was a tempting one.

Now he gave Bobbie a last bemused glance as she darted into the bathroom, shirttail flapping. Then he studied Rose, who was wiggling with impatience.

In her new outfit she was as cute as any rodeo princess, and he told her so. "Why don't we go wait in my room for Mommy to finish getting dressed?"

"Okay." As he swelled with parental pride, Rose put on her Western hat and went with him into the room that was a twin of theirs. He had wanted a suite, but the hotel was filled with some writers' conference and couldn't accommodate his last-minute change.

When Bobbie knocked on the adjoining door and came in, Donovan had to bite his tongue to keep from telling her how pretty she looked.

"Are you ready to go?" he asked instead. He knew his new companions' sudden appearance at his side was bound to cause speculation, but his real friends would accept whatever explanation he chose to give.

"I'm ready." Bobbie sounded as if she were going to a hanging, quite possibly her own.

Until now Donovan hadn't given much thought to how difficult all this must be for her. They weren't married; they weren't even involved. She wouldn't be here if he hadn't forced her.

Without thinking he rested an encouraging hand on her shoulder. Through the fabric of her shirt he felt her stiffen, and the look she gave him through her long lashes was unreadable.

"It'll be fun," he said, giving her shoulder a squeeze before he dropped his hand. His palm tingled where it had touched her. Funny, he had never thought of shoulders as particularly sexy before. Now he remembered how hers had looked, bare except for the straps of her lacy pink bra.

Surprise flickered in Bobbie's big brown eyes, as if she, too, felt something unexpected from the brief contact. "What are you going to tell people?" she asked, distracting him from wondering what the silky-looking skin of her shoulders would feel like against his mouth.

"How about the truth?" he suggested, shocked at the direction his thoughts had taken. She was the last woman in Dallas he should be fantasizing about—probably in the whole state of Texas. "Rose is my daughter, you're her mother and you're both traveling with me."

"We should always tell the truth." Rose watched them as if they were the newest kids' movie released on video. Donovan was just beginning to learn how difficult it could be to have an adult conversation with an inquisitive four-year-old underfoot.

"That's right, honey," Donovan replied, distracted.

"Will that be enough?" Bobbie asked skeptically.

He shrugged. "Cowboys aren't nosy. I can't promise the same about the media, but perhaps they won't notice. It's not as if I were some big movie star."

She took a deep breath. "We'll try not to embarrass you."

So that was it. Stunned, Donovan immediately caught Rose up in one arm and Bobbie in the other. His daughter merely giggled. Bobbie tried to pull away, but he ignored her halfhearted struggle.

"Nothing about either of you embarrasses me," he said sincerely. "Any man I know would be as proud to escort the two of you as a pony with twin foals. "Besides," he added, grinning, "in your new duds you both look great."

Rose gave him a smacking kiss on the cheek and then bounced out of his embrace. "Let's go," she cried impatiently. "I want to see the clowns and the horses."

Donovan tightened his other arm around Bobbie's narrow waist as her familiar scent filled his head. "My other cheek's available," he teased, leaning closer.

She pulled away and stared. "Whatever for?"

"Don't you want to kiss me, too?" he asked in a patently innocent voice.

She shot from his loose hold as if he had waved a branding iron beneath her nose. "Not for all the gold in your teeth," she exclaimed, but she failed to hide a grin and her cheeks had gone as pink as her shirt.

The sparkle in her dark eyes ignited a response in Donovan so intense that it caught him unprepared. Despite everything, he still found her attractive. Too much so. Maybe he couldn't trust her, but that didn't mean he didn't want her. The sudden realization stopped him cold.

"What's wrong?" Bobbie demanded as she watched his grin fade. His teasing was a side of his personality she hadn't seen in a long time. It brought back memories too painful to remember. Now his wary expression made her wonder if he, too, was having trouble with the past.

No, that wasn't likely. After all, he'd been the one to walk out of her arms and never look back, just as he had warned her all along that he would—despite the magical night of love they had shared and the child they created.

He might flirt with her now just because she was here and handy, but she knew he didn't really care. He had already proved that beyond a shadow of a doubt and she had best not forget it.

"Wrong?" he echoed, frowning. "Nothing's wrong." He glanced at Rose and his smile returned. "Shall we go?"

Clutching Donovan's hand as they walked down the wide aisle to their seats, Rose swiveled her head first one way and then the other. She had already asked two dozen questions he'd done his best to answer.

Behind them, Bobbie followed silently. Every time he glanced over his shoulder, he caught her staring around as if she had beamed down onto an alien planet.

"Hey, Buchanan," called a bowlegged bullfighter named Tulsa Lewis, who had a scraggly beard and a lump of chaw in one cheek. "Gonna teach Dynamite Dan who's the boss tonight?" He stopped in the middle of the aisle and grinned at Rose, who was hugging Donovan's leg.

"I'll do my best," he replied. Dynamite Dan was the bull he had drawn, a critter with a full measure of mean and then some.

"Who's the little lady?" Tulsa asked, hooking his thumbs into his lime green suspenders.

"This is my daughter." Unexpectedly, the words caught in Donovan's throat and he had to clear it before he continued. "Rose, this is Tulsa. He's a bullfighter, a rodeo clown."

She appeared disappointed. "You don't look like a real clown."

Before Donovan could explain the difference between bullfighters and circus clowns, Tulsa gave her a wink. "Wait till you see me in the arena," he promised.

Bobbie was standing beside Donovan. When he introduced her, she greeted Tulsa and stuck out her hand.

"Mighty pretty little girl," he told her as he shook it. "Easy to see where she got her looks."

Color ran up Bobbie's cheeks. Tulsa was right, Donovan thought as he watched her. Rose might resemble him, but she got her beauty from her mother. As soon as Bobbie thanked the older man, he tipped his hat and wished Donovan luck in his ride.

"I just met my first clown," Rose exclaimed after he had walked away.

"But not your last," Donovan replied. "Let's find some seats." As they went down the steps, he tried to sort through his feelings. When it came to introducing Bobbie to Tulsa, he had stumbled, unsure how to label her, and finally settled on just using her name. It was Tulsa who'd figured out she was Rose's mother.

He and Donovan had known each other for a long time; the old rodeo hand was one of the few people who knew about the Buchanans' search for their sister Kirby. He might wonder why Donovan had never mentioned a daughter, but he was too polite ever to ask. Donovan could only hope that everyone's manners were as good as Tulsa's.

As Donovan indicated three empty seats on the aisle and let Bobbie go in first, the bareback-bronc riding started in the arena below. In less time than it took the first mount to buck off his rider, Rose bombarded him with questions.

"Why does the horse buck so much?"

"Why does the rider wear his hat pulled down so low?"

"Why doesn't he hang on with both hands?"

"Does that strap around the horse's middle hurt him?"

"Is that a boy horse or a girl horse?"

Donovan answered each question the best he could, aware of Bobbie's grin as she stared straight ahead.

After a few moments Bobbie searched his face to see if his patience was beginning to flag. For a man unused to the boundless curiosity of a four-year-old, Donovan seemed to know how to answer in ways she could understand.

As Bobbie continued watching them out of the corner of her eye, she couldn't help but notice how attractive the man and child were together. Donovan's tan Stetson was tipped close to Rose's small red one, his sideburns a shade darker

than her curls as he spoke to her in the velvety drawl that
never failed to affect Bobbie's senses. He was absently
stroking his mustache and his eyes were screened by his
short, thick lashes.

Without warning, he looked up and caught Bobbie staring. Something unreadable flared in his eyes and then his
mouth curved into a knowing grin.

Heat washed over her as she turned to watch the horse
and rider in the arena. It was a moment before she could
have identified the mount's color or said whether the cowboy on its bare back was naked or fully clothed. Gritting
her teeth, Bobbie continued to stare as if the duel between
the two was the most fascinating thing she had ever seen.

When Donovan had first brought up the idea of her and
Rose coming with him, Bobbie had been too busy with
practical considerations to think about what living almost
in his pocket was going to do to her peace of mind. Now,
when it was too late, she realized her biggest problem wasn't
how he treated Rose—parenting seemed to come naturally
to the big, tough cowboy—but whether Bobbie herself
could keep from making the second biggest mistake of her
life: falling for him all over again.

She was still watching the bronc busting when he leaned
over behind Rose, making Bobbie shy away like a skittish
filly. She glared, but he just grinned without remorse.

Good Lord, the man looked like a pirate about to plun-
der an unarmed clipper ship.

"What is it?" she demanded waspishly.

His grin deepened the grooves in his tanned cheeks.
"Want a hot dog and something to drink from the conces-
sion stand?" he asked innocently. "Rose and I are hungry."

Bobbie was about to object to such an unhealthy lunch when she noticed her daughter's face. It fairly glowed with excitement.

Bobbie swallowed her objection. Ever since Rose was born, they'd had to skimp and go without. Granted, the last two years since Bobbie had gotten the office job had been easier, but this wasn't the time to deny Rose a few treats.

Or deny Donovan the pleasure in providing them.

"Thank you," Bobbie replied, trying to banish the image of him with an eye patch and a parrot on his shoulder that kept forming in her mind. "A hot dog with ketchup and a diet soda would be nice. Do you need help carrying anything?"

He shook his head as he got to his feet. "Nah. We can manage." Politely he tipped his hat and then he took his daughter's hand. Emotions Bobbie couldn't begin to sort out washed over her as she watched them head back up the steps, Rose skipping beside the tall, lean figure of her father.

"Cute kid," remarked a woman behind Bobbie before she could turn back around. "And your husband's a hunk."

Murmuring an automatic response, Bobbie sank deeper into her seat, wishing she could pull in her head like a turtle. Husband? What in heck had she gotten herself into, anyway?

By the time the two of them returned, she had regained her composure and made friends with an old man in the seat next to hers. When she reached up to relieve Donovan of two of the full cups he carried, something about his sheepish expression caught her attention.

"What is it?" she asked as Rose hopped from one foot to the other.

"She needs the little girls' room," he replied. "I guess that's your department."

Donovan was about to go down to the locker room and prepare for his event when he realized that Rose's steady stream of questions had all but dried up in the last half hour. Feeling a soft bump, he looked down to see that her cowboy hat was in her lap and her golden head was pillowed against his arm. He hadn't stopped to think how fast she would fade without her afternoon nap. After their shopping spree and lunch in the hotel coffee shop, she had been too excited to sleep back in the room.

Guilt assailed him. He had been so caught up in playing the big important rodeo star that he had failed to consider anyone else. Even Bobbie might have found the show less than fascinating.

He glanced at Bobbie's profile. She appeared to be deeply engrossed in the team roping that was just finishing. Since she had returned from taking Rose to the rest room and eaten her hot dog, she hadn't said much. At first he had tried to include her in his explanations of the events, but he eventually gave up and confined his comments to his daughter. He had no idea what was bothering Bobbie, and now, when he needed to start concentrating on the ride ahead of him, was no time to wonder.

Instead, he signaled her silently over Rose's bowed head.

Pointing, he asked quietly, "Do you want to take the rental car back to the hotel and put her to bed? I can catch a ride or take a cab when I'm done."

Before Bobbie could answer, Rose's head popped up. "I want to see you ride the bull," she exclaimed. "And I want to see Tulsa in his clown costume."

Privately, Donovan wondered if seeing a real clown in full makeup and costume didn't rank slightly above the appeal of his own performance. "I thought you were asleep," he remarked.

She sat up straighter and blinked several times. "I'm not tired. I was only resting my eyes." She glanced at her mother pleadingly, no doubt well aware of who wielded the true authority. "Please, Mommy. Can we stay?"

Bobbie glanced at her newly energized daughter and then back at Donovan. "When will you be done?" she asked.

He glanced down at the arena and calculated swiftly. Taking someone else into consideration was a new experience, but not one he found unpleasant. "A half hour, forty-five minutes at the most."

Bobbie smiled down at Rose. "We can hold out that long, can't we?"

Rose's head bobbed emphatically. "You bet."

Donovan released the breath he hadn't even been aware he was holding as he realized just how much he wanted them here while he rode. Both of them. Ever since his brother had married and retired from the circuit, he'd missed having family cheering him on.

"That's good," he said, glancing at his watch. "I'd better go now."

Rose hugged him and Bobbie wished him luck before he left. During the eight seconds he was in the arena, he always made sure he gave a hundred percent of himself. Tonight, though, there were two reasons in the stands for him to give this ride at least a hundred and ten.

Watching the bull-riding competition, Bobbie wondered with detached curiosity why anyone would want to subject his body to such brutal punishment and life-threatening danger. Seeing these men face staggering odds to pit themselves against such huge and scary beasts was mildly interesting, until Donovan's name was announced.

"There's my daddy!" Rose cried, pointing to the figure they could see sticking up above the top rails of the chute, no doubt poised over the wide back of the next fire-breathing killing machine to tear up the dirt of the arena.

Bobbie took one look at Donovan's familiar face as he pulled his hat down low and stuck one arm in the air—and the hot dog she had eaten earlier threatened to make a return appearance. Pressing a hand to her suddenly churning stomach, she clenched her teeth together and forced herself to watch the pair locked in mortal combat below.

When the buzzer sounded and Donovan leaped from the bull, her head began to spin and she realized she had forgotten to breathe during the entire eight-second ordeal. As she did, the bull whirled, curved horns cutting a deadly swath. It lowered its huge head and charged after Donovan, who stumbled in his rush for the fence. The crowd gasped and Rose screamed a warning as Bobbie watched helplessly, fear freezing her in her seat. Her mouth flew open, but no sound came out.

Tulsa and the other clown dashed between Donovan and the bull, effectively distracting it as he hit the fence running and scrambled to the top. Only when he was safely out of the arena did Bobbie unfurl the fists she had clenched and see the rows of half-moon-shaped indentations her nails had made in the skin of her palms.

"Wow," Rose exclaimed, no doubt blessedly oblivious to the danger, "that was pretty neat."

"Yeah," Bobbie squeaked, voice thin. "That was neat, all right." What had she been thinking, bringing her daughter here so she could see her own father skewered like a hunk of meat or trampled to death in front of her very eyes?

As Bobbie waited impatiently for Donovan to return, she barely noticed that his score was the highest yet. Only when it was announced that he had won the go-round and he made a victory lap around the arena on a borrowed horse, waving his hat to the crowd that clearly adored him, did she even recognize how well he had done.

Later, after Donovan had kissed Rose good-night and returned to his own room to watch a little television, he realized that he hadn't given much thought to the mechanics of life on the road with family in tow. He knew Bobbie wouldn't have objected if he dropped her and Rose off at the hotel and went out with the boys, but he wouldn't have felt right about it. Nor would he feel right about meeting up with another woman and paying her attention while they were with him. Having any of his rowdy friends up to his room for drinks and poker was probably out, too, since his daughter was trying to sleep next door.

That left a book or the TV. Since he didn't have anything to read, the small screen was his only option. He had removed his boots, opened a beer from the tiny fridge and was flipping through channels with the remote when there was a soft knock on the adjoining door.

Damn. He hadn't even thought to invite Bobbie over to watch television with him. No doubt she didn't keep the same hours as a preschooler, but she would have little option sharing a hotel room. He hoped Bill had managed to reserve suites with a sitting room for the rest of the time they'd be traveling together.

Donovan crossed the spacious room and reached for the knob. He was curious to hear what Bobbie thought of his world. She'd had little to say on the ride back to the hotel, but he'd assumed it was because Rose had fallen asleep again in the seat between them.

"Hi," he said quietly after he had pulled open the door. "Come on in. What did you think of the bull riding?"

She stepped into his room, still wearing the pink shirt and jeans. Softly, he shut the heavy door behind her and then he waited expectantly for her reply. To his surprise, her features were set in stubborn lines and her hands were clenched at her sides.

"This has all been a terrible mistake," she exclaimed before he could ask what was wrong. "First thing tomorrow morning, Rose and I are going home and we aren't coming back."

Chapter Six

As soon as Bobbie made the announcement that she was taking Rose and going home, she braced herself for the blast of Donovan's anger. Instead of shouting at her or threatening, as she expected him to do, he sank down onto the corner of his king-size bed and stared. The soft glow of the brass lamp turned his hair to gold and caressed the planes of his deeply tanned face.

"Where's this coming from?" he asked quietly. "You've only been here for a little over twenty-four hours. What's happened to change your mind? Rose seemed to enjoy herself. Did she say something to you?"

Reluctantly, Bobbie shook her head. "Rose did enjoy herself, but I never realized before just how dangerous what you do really is." She folded her arms across her chest. "I refuse to let our daughter see her father laid open by a bull's horn or watch the stuffing being stomped out of him before her eyes." The idea made Bobbie's stomach churn, but she told herself she would feel that way about anyone, even a complete stranger.

To her surprise, Donovan got to his feet. He reached out to grip her elbows gently as he peered into her face. There was a blur of whiskers along his jaw. They surrounded the cleft in his chin. She remembered kissing that cleft after they made love. The memory distracted her, as did the warm touch of his hands.

"Bobbie, honey," he said, making her wonder if the endearment was a slip of his tongue or a blatant attempt to soften her up, "I've been riding bulls for a long time and I don't plan on getting either gored or stomped, believe me."

"What about the other riders?" she asked. "You can't possibly vouch for their safety."

He tipped back his head and closed his eyes, but he didn't release her. "No, I can't, but Rose is liable to see more violence on television than she ever would in the arena."

"But the violence on television isn't real," Bobbie argued, keenly aware of his touch. "The people getting hurt aren't her family."

His hands slid up and down her arms in a rough attempt at comfort. "Is it Rose's reaction you're really concerned about, or your own?" he asked, voice suddenly husky. "Are you worried about me?"

"Don't be ridiculous." Bobbie tried to step back and free herself, but his fingers tightened. "My concerns are always for my daughter."

"A minute ago she was our daughter." Donovan loomed closer.

Bobbie stared up at him, mesmerized by the way his eyes had darkened, more black than green. He was standing so near that she could see each individual eyelash, tipped with gold. Heat washed through her, replacing sense with sensation. Without conscious thought, she raised her chin and her lips parted.

Donovan dragged in a sharp breath.

Reality hit her like a blast of arctic air. Yanking her arms free to scrub frantically at the burning spots where his hands had touched her skin, she retreated until her back was pressed against the door separating their two rooms.

She was shaking and her heart raced. What on earth had she been thinking?

That was the problem—she hadn't been thinking at all. Horrified, she watched a tiny muscle in his cheek jump as his hands dropped to his sides.

"I grew up on a ranch." His voice was harsh and his abrupt change of subject confused her. "Injuries, even death, are part of life," he continued. "Believe me, Rose isn't going to be traumatized by a little roughness in the rodeo ring. If she sees anyone get hurt, we'll talk to her about it."

"I still think I made a big mistake in agreeing to this," Bobbie argued, deeply shaken by what had almost happened between them. She didn't want to be drawn back into his net. He had hurt her once; she'd be a fool to let him hurt her again.

Donovan walked over to a compact fridge that was tucked into an entertainment center next to the television. "Want a beer?"

She shook her head. "No, thanks."

"How about a soda?"

When she turned that down, too, he shrugged and took a long swallow of his own beer. "Give this a little more time," he suggested. "You're tired and it's all new to you. We're flying out tomorrow afternoon as soon as I'm done riding. I'm going to the arena first thing in the morning for some publicity shots, but you can sleep late if you like. I'll come back for you and Rose. We can grab some lunch before the show."

"I guess you've never tried to sleep in when a four-year-old wants breakfast." She was relieved that her heartbeat had finally slowed to normal. Had he actually been going to kiss her or had she jumped to conclusions?

Donovan raked a hand through his hair, leaving it in silken disarray. With the first three snaps on his shirt undone and the start of whiskers on his cheeks, he looked untamed and slightly dangerous.

"Why don't I take Rose with me in the morning, then?"

The suggestion surprised Bobbie. She had assumed he would expect her to look after Rose while he went about his business, as usual.

"The two of us can have breakfast downstairs and then I'll take her to the photo shoot. After lunch she'll have time for a quick nap before the show starts."

His offer was tempting; Bobbie was emotionally and physically drained. "You'd have to keep an eye on her every minute," she cautioned. "You have no idea—"

"So let me find out," he interrupted gently. "I promise I'll watch her like a hawk. She won't be in the way. We'll have fun."

Rose was still a novelty and he wanted to show her off. Bobbie's resolve wavered, until she remembered she had originally come to his room to tell him she was taking Rose back to Yuma.

"I don't know." She wasn't sure what to do. If Rose was too much trouble, perhaps he'd let them leave.

No, Rose wasn't a pawn. "Maybe we should just go home."

While Bobbie gazed up at him, his expression hardened until his eyes glittered like green ice. "Don't forget my terms," he said softly. "I haven't changed my mind about having her with me, and I'll do whatever I have to."

Before Bobbie could react to the threat, the harsh lines of his face relaxed. "Give me a chance," he coaxed. "This experience could be a positive one for Rose, if you'd just let it." He set the beer bottle back down on the table and spread his hands in supplication. "I promise I won't let anything hurt her, or you. Believe me, that's the last thing I'd want."

The apparent sincerity of his words weakened Bobbie's determination. She wanted to do what was fair for all of them, but the bottom line was that she had no more choice than before and she didn't dare risk a court battle.

"Okay, we'll stay," she said, resigned.

His shoulders slumped with obvious relief and his expression softened. She did her best to ignore the way her own resolve began melting in response. He might seem placated now, but what she needed to remember was how ruthless he could be when there was something he wanted.

She should be darned glad he didn't want her.

"You won't regret this," he said. "I'll make sure of it."

She wished she could be as certain as he sounded. When she didn't reply, he added that he would pick Rose up at nine in the morning.

Bobbie didn't bother to tell him sleeping in wasn't what she needed. What she did need, and desperately, was some time away from him.

Slowly she was learning that he could be trusted with Rose. Perhaps Bobbie would go shopping or sightseeing in the morning, anything to put some space between them.

She reached for the knob behind her and opened the door. "I'll have her ready by nine."

"Good night," Donovan said quietly as she slipped through the door.

Without bothering to reply, she closed it gently behind her.

As he watched it shut, he wondered who had really won their little skirmish just now. Sure, he'd dissuaded her from taking Rose and leaving, but to do so he'd had to bring out his big gun, the threat of a custody suit.

The more he saw Bobbie with Rose, the more he realized how much she loved the child they had created together—and he felt like a bastard for using that love to manipulate Bobbie. Even before she had come to his room tonight, he'd been wondering what she would do if he were to admit it was a threat he'd never be able to carry out.

Now he knew what Bobbie would do. She'd take Rose and leave.

He couldn't give up the only leverage he had. Not yet. For the time being at least, he needed Bobbie to believe he was ruthless enough to haul her into court if she didn't keep up her part of their bargain.

As much as it sickened him, there was no way he could abandon the charade. And as long as he kept it up, he and Bobbie would never be friends—or anything else.

That meant kissing her was probably out of the question. But when had not being able to kiss her started to be a problem?

For just a moment when she had been standing so close to him and his head filled with her scent, wild and sweet, he'd needed to kiss her almost as much as he needed his next breath.

Now the memory of that moment of devastating hunger turned his sigh ragged. Stripping off his clothes, he headed for the shower and turned the faucet to cold.

Bobbie had known they'd be on the move, but she'd had no idea just how hectic Donovan's schedule really was. For the next couple of weeks they flew in, rented a car at the airstrip or hitched a ride with some friend of his and raced to the arena—all so that he could sit a bull for eight seconds. Then they tore back to the plane and flew to the next town and the next show, hitting several each week. Bobbie felt sorry for the cowboys who had to drive between rodeos.

Between bull rides they ate and slept and—when Donovan wasn't on the phone with his business manager or some rodeo secretary, calling in future entries or finding out what bull he'd drawn—he made personal appearances. If there was a cowboy in a local hospital, Donovan found time to visit. Dressed in a costume that often included an oversize buckle and leather chaps, he'd swing by the children's ward before he left.

He did radio interviews, posed for print ads and dragged Bobbie and Rose to more than one charity event where he dispensed autographs and charm in equal measure. Seeing the way other women looked at him shook Bobbie's determined indifference to its foundations.

Most important, he rode bucking bulls better than anyone else on the circuit. After two weeks following him around, Bobbie was amazed he'd found any time at all to visit Rose in Yuma. The fact that he had, and more than once, was a clear indication of his commitment to his daughter.

"Bill Crouch sure earns whatever you pay him," she told Donovan over breakfast one morning after she glanced at the next week's itinerary he'd just handed her. He had already explained that it was Bill's job to draw up the schedule and coordinate everything from hotel reservations to interviews.

When Bobbie asked Donovan why he didn't slow down a little and compete at fewer rodeos, he pointed to a man with long black hair sitting alone at another table.

"That's J. D. Reese. He's heading out to Tulsa," Donovan told her as the waitress poured their coffee. "He'll be in Colorado after that."

"Colorado's where we're going next," Rose piped up. Donovan had made a habit of pointing out to her on a map where they were going each week. Bobbie hadn't thought she really understood, but it was clear from her comment that she did.

"Very good," he told Rose as he leaned close and smiled. Then he fixed his attention back on Bobbie. "If J.D. wins in Tulsa and beats me in Boulder, he'll pull ahead of me in the rankings. And he's only one man. Who knows how many shows the rest of the boys in the top fifteen are hitting this week while we do four." He took a sip of his coffee. "Now do you understand why I stay so busy?"

His explanation made her think of wolves nipping at his heels. "But what about the interviews and personal appearances?" She spread jam on Rose's toast. "Surely they aren't all necessary."

Donovan bit into a strip of bacon and chewed thoughtfully. "Maybe they aren't," he said, "but I'm not going to ride bulls forever. Endorsements are a part of my earnings. The bigger my name, the more value my sponsors put on it."

As the waitress refilled their cups, Bobbie sat back and mulled over what he had said. Someday he would retire and live a more settled life on his ranch. He would have a home that Rose could visit.

Bobbie pictured their daughter spending summers with him in Colorado while she sweltered alone in Yuma. Tears blocked her throat. Swallowing, she wondered if it was only Rose's company she would miss.

When Bobbie glanced up, Donovan was cutting Rose's waffle as she watched him adoringly. He'd been right about one thing—spending time together on the road was cementing the bond between his daughter and himself.

Bobbie was about to ask him more about his retirement when a young woman approached their table. She was holding a cassette tape and a pen.

"Would you mind signing this?" she asked Donovan. "I don't mean to bother you while you're eating, but I wanted to thank you for recording this and donating the profits to the cowboy crisis fund. My husband's a saddle-bronc rider. When he was hurt last year, some of that money kept us going."

Donovan seemed uncomfortable as he autographed the tape she handed him. When he gave it back, he asked how her husband was doing.

"He's fine now," she replied, glancing shyly at Bobbie before she thanked him. "He's riding this weekend in Amarillo."

Donovan told her to be sure to wish him luck and she thanked him again before she left with the tape.

"What was that you signed?" Bobbie asked curiously. "Don't tell me you've been recording country songs in your spare time."

He shrugged and pushed his eggs around his plate while her curiosity grew.

"It's a tape of cowboy poetry," he admitted finally. "The proceeds go into a fund that helps cowboys who get hurt while they're rodeoing. They can buy insurance, but it only pays so much."

Bobbie remained silent until he finally lifted his head and met her gaze. "That's nice," she said. "But I sure don't know where you found the time."

His grin was crooked. "Looking back, neither do I."

The man was certainly full of surprises, Bobbie thought, recalling their conversation as they deplaned in Boulder. Donovan's brother, Taylor, his wife and twin boys were driving down to the rodeo. Donovan was eager for them to meet their new cousin, and Rose was excited, too.

Asking herself where she fit in to all of this, Bobbie waited nervously while he secured his plane and spoke to an airport official.

"I like flying." Rose was balancing on one leg. "It's cool."

Bobbie realized she liked it, too. At first she had been nervous, but Donovan made a point to explain everything he was doing. Now she felt like a seasoned flyer.

"When's your family getting here?" she asked him as they walked across the tarmac to the terminal.

He was pushing a cart with their bags and giving Rose a piggyback ride as she wore his hat. "Hold tight to my Stetson," he told her.

His eyes were shielded by dark glasses. Even with Rose on his shoulders, her red cowboy boots resting on his chest and one of her small hands clutching the collar of his blue chambray shirt, he managed to look sexy. Next to the two of them, Bobbie felt almost dowdy in her pastel skirt and sleeveless blouse.

"They'll catch up with us at the arena later," he told her. "Taylor wanted to swing by a livestock auction first."

Bobbie remembered that Donovan's brother raised cattle in what he'd described as a cow and calf operation. She was curious about Taylor. Was he like Donovan? And what kind of woman had he married? All Bobbie knew was that she was a former rodeo barrel racer with a ranching background. When the time came, would Donovan, too, seek a mate who could ride, rope and brand cattle like a man? Or would a different type of woman catch his eye? Jealousy slithered through Bobbie like a garter snake through the grass.

Rose's stepmother! What an awful thought.

Part of Bobbie's curiosity was satisfied later that same afternoon when a big dark-haired man walked up behind Donovan outside the arena entrance and hooked a burly arm around his neck.

"Hey, bro," Donovan said without turning. "What's new?"

A pretty woman with long reddish blond hair and two little boys in tow followed the other man. While he and Donovan hugged each other, she bent down and spoke to Rose, who had ducked behind Bobbie.

"Hi. I'm your Aunt Ashley."

Rose glanced up at Bobbie, who smiled encouragingly. "That's right, honey. It's okay."

Ashley, who was bareheaded, straightened and stuck out her hand. "You must be Bobbie McBride."

Bobbie shook her hand briefly, returning her friendly smile. She was surprised that Donovan had bothered to mention her to them. After all, she was only the mother. "That's right, and this is Rose."

"What a little beauty," Donovan's brother said. "Hi, pumpkin." He tipped his black cowboy hat.

Rose giggled and let go of Bobbie's leg. Donovan performed the rest of the introductions and suggested they all go inside and get seats. Taylor didn't say much, but he studied Bobbie closely when she shook his hard, callused hand.

She wondered how much Donovan had told them about her and how they felt. Of course they would take his side, but did they condemn her as he did? Perhaps Ashley, having children of her own, would understand. If circumstances had been different, she and Bobbie might even have become friends.

When it was time for Donovan to head down to the locker room and gear up for his event, Taylor stood, as well.

"Might as well say hello to a few old friends," he said before he bent down to kiss Ashley soundly and remind the boys to mind their mom.

Donovan realized yet again how much Taylor had come out of his self-imposed shell since he and Ashley Gray had gotten together. He was still a quiet, contemplative man, but he had shucked the aloofness he'd once used to shield the emotions Donovan knew ran deep. Ashley's love had changed him—that and having a family of his own.

Donovan wondered if it canceled out the pain of losing their parents. The pain he still felt every day.

Now he swallowed his envy and leaned down to give Rose a hug. "See you later, princess."

"Good luck, Daddy."

As always, hearing her call him that moved him as little else could. He glanced over at Bobbie, who was sitting between Rose and Ashley. Her brown eyes were fixed on him, and a tiny frown pleated her forehead.

"Be careful."

Did she worry about his safety? He would have liked to give her a hug, too, or even a kiss, as Taylor had his wife. How would she react if he did?

Maybe he'd try it sometime when he wasn't surrounded by family to witness his certain humiliation when she belted him in retaliation.

"I'm always careful," he replied, aware that part of him was growing tired of being careful around her.

After Ashley had reminded him not to break anything crucial, like an arm or a leg, since they were all going to dinner later, he followed Taylor down the arena steps.

"What do you think of her?" Donovan asked when they got to the locker room. He was putting on the sturdy vest and chaps he wore to ride.

Taylor fastened Donovan's entry number on his back. "Rose or her mother?"

"My daughter," Donovan replied impatiently. "What do you think of my daughter?"

Taylor glanced around the familiar locker room, and Donovan wondered if his brother missed the steer roping that had given him the stake for his ranch. He hadn't achieved Donovan's level of success, but he had been one of the best. "She looks so much like Kirby that my heart almost stopped."

"I know," Donovan replied. "It's uncanny."

"Rose is a little doll in her own right," Taylor added. "So's her mom. It's not hard to see why you fell for her. I just can't understand why you let her go."

"It was never serious between us," Donovan mouthed the lie as he slammed his locker. He'd been a fool back then.

Taylor's brows rose. "Sharing a child can be serious. How's it working out, having them with you?" He and Ashley had traveled and competed together before she hurt her leg and he quit to buy the ranch. They had been married a short time later.

Donovan shrugged and removed his rigging from the duffel bag he'd brought with him. The rigging and his own determination were all that would keep him on the bull. "I like having them around." As he began working rosin into his rope, he wasn't about to confess that Bobbie's presence in the next room at night was interfering with his sleep. There were some things you didn't talk about, not even to your own brother.

Hormones, that's all it was. He hadn't been with a woman for months. There had been opportunities, but he had found out long before that sex without some emotional involvement was an empty exercise. He would rather lose a little sleep than indulge in something that did nothing more than scratch an itch.

"I fired the last investigator," Taylor said, changing the subject abruptly. "He came up empty."

Donovan knew Taylor was talking about the most recent P.I. they'd hired to find their sister, who had been adopted while the boys were still too young to prevent it.

"I'm sorry." Donovan wondered if it was time to give up. He almost said as much, but this wasn't the best place to discuss it. Taylor believed their parents had to be dead. Donovan disagreed. Both men wanted to find Kirby, but the trail was as cold as a night in the mountains, their only clues being that she was adopted in Idaho and the records were later lost or misplaced.

"I'll pay his bill," Donovan said. Taylor had enough expenses, with his family and the ranch. "Send it to Bill Crouch."

"You can pay half, as always." Taylor clapped him on the shoulder. "Someday she'll turn up, probably when we least expect it."

Donovan wished he could believe that. "Maybe so." He worked some more chip rosin into the heavy leather glove he would wear to grip the rigging. Guilt assailed him. He still felt responsible for their parents' disappearance.

He watched J. D. Reese open a locker several feet down from his own. As usual, the other bull rider ignored everyone else in the room.

"Is he still trailing your butt in the standings?" Taylor asked quietly.

"He's right on my butt. I wish to hell he'd take a southbound leap off a northbound bull," Donovan replied in an undertone. "He's good, though, I'll give him that. And about as friendly as a rattler with a toothache."

Reese glanced up, his expression unchanging, as if he knew they were discussing him.

"What did you hear from that clothing manufacturer?" Taylor asked. "Have they made you a firm offer yet?"

Donovan had told him on the phone that Rio Bravo Western Wear was looking for a rodeo cowboy to represent them in a new sales campaign.

Now Donovan glanced around cautiously. "Bill tells me they're talking seven figures for an exclusive contract if I can hang on to the title."

Taylor's eyes widened. He knew it was a good deal more than Donovan's other endorsements combined. "That's worth pursuing."

"Tell me about it." If Donovan could defend the bull-riding championship for the fifth time, the money would enable him to retire. Now that he had found Rose, he realized there was more to life than championship buckles.

"Having a rich brother might be nice," Taylor mused.

Donovan stuck his glove into his hip pocket. "I haven't won yet."

* * *

"Have Donovan bring you and Rose to the ranch," Ashley invited Bobbie as the two men said goodbye at the door to Donovan's suite. "I enjoyed meeting both of you."

Bobbie thanked her without bothering to explain that they were going back to Yuma in a couple of weeks. She liked the other couple a lot, although Taylor was nothing like his younger brother in either looks or temperament. He was a big, bulky man, attractive in his own rough-hewn way and slow to speak or smile. Next to him, Ashley chattered like a colorful bird.

After the rodeo, they had all gone to a spaghetti restaurant with a large play area for children. The twins had worn Rose out and now she was asleep in one of the bedrooms.

As soon as the other Buchanans left, Bobbie checked on her. When she walked back into the sitting room, Donovan took a beer from the fridge and held it up.

She shook her head. "No, thanks."

With a shrug, he twisted off the cap and took a long swig. Fascinated, she watched the muscles of his throat work. It had been a long day and exhaustion was making her vulnerable to him, she told herself. It wasn't even anything personal, just the fact that they spent so much time in each other's pockets and she'd cared for him once, that was all.

While she was running through the argument that was becoming entirely too familiar, she watched him. He lowered the bottle and stared back. His eyes had darkened, reminding her of a jungle at night—shadows and danger.

"See anything you like?" he asked softly as he crossed the room toward her like a puma on the prowl.

Startled, Bobbie froze, unable to look away. This was a side to him she'd been pretending didn't exist. Now she saw just how foolhardy that was. Donovan had been and still was immensely appealing to her. If he decided he was interested in her that way again, it would take all her strength to resist him.

And resist him she must. As he stopped before her and looked down into her face, she willed her voice to be steady.

"The only thing I want right now is a glass of water." Carefully, she stepped around him. "It's too bad you had to split first place with Reese," she continued when she'd filled a glass and added ice. It was impossible to gauge Donovan's mood. "You rode well."

"Thanks," he said absently as he continued to watch her.

Nervously, Bobbie took another sip of her water, aware of the faint drone of the air conditioner in the otherwise silent room. She set down the empty glass. "I guess I'll turn in."

Donovan shifted so he was blocking the door to the bedroom she shared with Rose. He raised his hand and curled his fingers around her chin, holding her head in place so her gaze was locked with his.

"It's still early." His voice was a velvety caress. "Wouldn't you rather keep me company for a little while?"

Her skin tingled dangerously where he touched her. Her gaze dropped to his mouth as she swayed toward him, wondering if his lips were still warm, still soft. He was so tempting. "I'm tired. All I want now is sleep."

"That's not true and we both know it," he said softly. "You want me, just as much as I want you." His eyes glittered. "Can you deny that you've been wondering?"

"Wondering what?" She blinked, struggling against the pull of his attraction and her own memories.

"Wondering if it would still be as good between us as it was before."

Chapter Seven

For a moment Bobbie was almost unbearably tempted. Just one taste, she thought, one taste of his lips to see if her memories of the way he kissed had become embellished over the years.

She gazed up at his mouth with longing, wondering if his mustache was as soft and silky as she remembered. He made a sound low in his throat and she saw that his eyes were hooded, hiding his feelings.

His *feelings!* Had she lost her mind? He had no feelings for her. She was here because of Rose and he was still the man who had turned his back on the two of them when they had needed him the most.

"No," Bobbie exclaimed. "The only thing I wonder about is whether you'll let us go when you said you would." Before he could reply, she brushed past him and opened the bedroom door. "And just for the record," she added softly,

"I remember what it was like before. It was damned painful. I cared about you and you left me."

When she would have slipped through the open door, he grabbed her arm. "I never lied to you." His voice was equally soft. Neither of them wanted to wake Rose. "I told you all along that I was going as soon as the finals were over."

Bobbie blinked away the sudden tears that filled her eyes. That much was true. He'd warned her he was leaving; it was her own feelings that had betrayed her. Her own belief that he, too, had fallen in love.

How could she have been so naive, to think he had to love her to sleep with her? Well, she wasn't naive anymore. She had learned her lesson well. This time it was Rose he wanted, not her.

Bobbie glared down at his hand, still wrapped around her arm. "I'm not lying, either," she said. "As soon as our month with you is up, we're going home. In the meantime, keep your hands and your *wants* to yourself."

His face was carefully blank when he released her, but his eyes seethed with emotion. If she hadn't known better, Bobbie might have thought it was hurt she saw shimmering in their emerald depths before he masked it with indifference.

Rejecting him after the cruel way he had rejected her should have been more satisfying. Instead, as she shut the door quietly behind her, she felt only the bitterness of regret.

As Donovan watched the door to the bedroom close, frustration poured through him. He was tempted to put his fist through a wall, but he resisted. The way his luck was running, he'd probably break his riding hand.

Fool! he thought. She brought out the worst in him. He had meant to coax her into letting down her guard and

kissing him so he could see if she felt any of the attraction
that was driving him crazy. Instead he had come across as
an arrogant, presumptuous ass. Now she would avoid him
more than ever.

Raking a hand through his hair, he went into the other
bedroom and flipped on a light. It looked like another cold
shower was in order, since his body was still complaining
about that aborted kiss.

Gulping in air, Bobbie leaned against the closed bedroom door and squeezed her eyes shut, willing her body to
stop shaking. Then she gazed down at her sleeping daughter in the soft glow from the bathroom light. Rose looked
like an angel with her blond hair swirling around her like a
tangle of gold threads and her dark lashes resting against
her rounded cheeks. Love rushed through Bobbie, reminding her what was really important.

Her heart was still pounding from what had nearly happened in the other room. How much longer was she going
to be able to resist Donovan, as well as her own growing
desire?

How relieved she would be when this ordeal was over and
she could return to her normal, quiet, predictable life. Un-
bidden, the thought rose that, compared to the hustle and
excitement of rodeo with its noise and dust and animals,
normal life was going to be pretty dull. She tried to convince herself that she'd had more than enough of cowboys
in general and Donovan in particular, but her heart wasn't
buying it.

The truth was that, despite his faults, she'd had far less
of Donovan than she wanted—even knowing how destructive an entanglement with him could be. She had barely
survived losing him once; this time she might not be so
lucky. He could destroy her. He could take Rose.

What Bobbie had to focus on was getting through the next couple of weeks without losing her mind, and her heart, all over again. Or, worst of all, her daughter.

"Oops, sorry." Donovan's grin was unrepentant as he brushed against Bobbie while he tossed their bags back into the plane. They had gotten to the rodeo in Oklahoma in time for him to check in and ride his bull; now they were headed to Fort Worth so he could do it all over again. The season was in full swing, the pace more frantic than ever. Bobbie's temper was fraying. Even Rose looked tired, but at least she could nap on the short plane ride.

Donovan reached out a hand to steady Bobbie, but she jerked away. "I'm okay."

If only he would quit touching her. If she hadn't known better, she might think he was doing it on purpose, but why would he bother? And how could she complain without admitting that contact with him threw her into an emotional tizzy and a physical storm of wanting she was finding more and more difficult to ignore? She'd sooner have a bull tattooed on her backside than admit anything like *that*.

Damn the man! He had won Rose over and now, unconsciously or not, he was laying siege to Bobbie's defenses like a band of renegades attacking a fort. She had been looking forward to going home to Yuma, and now the days with Donovan were flying by much too fast.

Bobbie's emotions were still in a tangle when she and Rose stood at the arena fence by the chutes and watched him ride that evening. The bull was an especially ugly one, with folds of skin that hung down like unholy robes.

She should have been immune by now, but Bobbie found herself biting her lip hard as Rose jumped up and down beside her, cheering happily.

At one point the bull followed a bone-jarring series of leaps with a dizzying spin and several quick direction changes that left Donovan leaning precariously the same way the bull was turning. Sheer strength of will and a powerful right arm were all that kept him on the animal's back.

Bobbie gasped with relief when he regained his seat; he'd told her a rider's hand got caught in the rigging more easily when he fell "into the well"—the way the bull was turning. She hated seeing a rider flopping helplessly, his hand tangled in his own rope as the bull battered him.

When the buzzer finally sounded, Donovan leaped from the beast's broad back. His hat flew off, he landed wrong and sprawled facedown in the dirt.

The bull dodged an arm-waving clown and charged. From her standpoint at the fence, Bobbie saw Donovan roll and twist, scrambling to escape the lethal horns and hooves. Swallowing a scream, she whirled her daughter away from the frightening sight and pressed Rose's face against her own trembling legs. Rose began to struggle. The clowns managed to distract the maddened bull. Miraculously, Donovan got to his feet while Bobbie choked on a sob.

"Daddy!" Rose wailed.

"He's okay," Bobbie said quickly. "Look!" She let Rose go and pointed as Donovan snagged his hat and climbed the fence. He didn't even limp. Tears burned Bobbie's eyes and she ducked her head. Realizing that she was trembling, she dredged up a shaky smile for her daughter.

Tears ran down Rose's face. "He isn't hurted?" she asked in a small voice.

"No, darling, I'm sure he's fine. We saw him climb the fence just like a monkey, didn't we?" Bobbie's heart was still thudding hard. "Come on," she exclaimed. "Let's find him." Hands clasped, she and Rose hurried around behind the stock pens, careful not to get in anyone's way. As soon as they saw Donovan, streaked with dirt and surrounded by a knot of other bull riders, Rose pulled free of Bobbie's hand.

"Daddy!" she cried, running to him. "We thought you were all broken!"

Donovan looked startled, and then he swooped her into his arms. Bobbie was right on Rose's heels and she didn't stop to think before she flung her arms around his waist and hugged him hard, squashing Rose between them.

"Are you all right?" she asked, breathing in the mingled scents of animal, dust and sweat. She had never smelled anything so wonderful in her life.

For a moment Donovan's free arm closed around her. Then she heard one of the men make a laughing remark about the risk being worth it. Self-consciously, she began to struggle.

Donovan's arm tightened before he released her. When she raised her head, his eyes were shadowed. Had he been hurt, after all?

Before she could ask again, his expression cleared and he smiled. "I'm fine. Looked worse than it was." He shifted Rose against him and nuzzled her neck. "Were you scared for your old dad?" he asked as Bobbie took another step back.

What a hell of a time to realize she'd done the most stupid thing possible. Despite the problems that lay between them, despite the danger of having her heart shattered, she'd fallen in love with him all over again.

Damn him. If he ever suspected, he'd use it as a weapon in their battle over Rose.

Donovan had been watching Bobbie for two days, trying to figure out what was going on. When she had run up and flung herself at him he'd figured they'd made some kind of breakthrough.

Since then, she had retreated behind a wall he couldn't penetrate. She had little to say unless she was talking to their daughter, and she refused to meet his gaze. Several times he had gotten her alone, when Rose was napping or after she had gone to bed, and demanded to know what was wrong. Bobbie only shook her bowed head and mumbled something about being tired or having a headache—all without looking at him.

She was pale and she picked at her food. Was she sick? Unhappy? Had he done something? He was wild to know what was wrong.

"Dammit!" he exclaimed, pounding the steering wheel in the car on the way back to the hotel from a bull-riders-only competition in Mesquite, making her jump in the seat next to him. "Tell me what I've done."

"Shh, you'll wake up Rose." Bobbie glanced into the back of the car, where their daughter was asleep after another long day. "I've told you before, you haven't done anything."

In his agitation, Donovan grabbed her hand where it lay between them on the center console. Her skin was warm and soft. His first impulse was to drag her hand to his mouth and kiss each separate finger. As he felt her attempt to pull out of his grasp, sanity took over and he freed her.

"You're as skittish as a range cow trapped in barbed wire," he growled.

She didn't answer.

When he stopped at a red light, he risked a glance in her direction. Her profile was to him, her chin raised and her lips pressed together.

"There's nothing wrong," she repeated tensely.

▲ FOLD ALONG DOTTED LINE AND DETACH CAREFULLY ▲

A Toast to You
Our Valued
Reader!

DETACH
SEAL
MOISTEN
AND
PLACE
INSIDE

EDITOR'S
SWEEPSTAKES
VALIDATION SEAL

N THE

A Toast t!

ing
ook
vels
ike
vith
ine

Dear Valued Reader,

A "Toast to You" for having chosen to kes
romance novels!

As a part of this special "Toast," and *for*
Editor's $1,000,000.00 Sweepstakes Valic *are*
Validation Seal, once returned by you, wil
personal sweepstakes numbers. These nu
will instantly qualify you for any and all ES.
chance and return your Validation Seal-- ltry
numbers is selected in our $1,000,000.0 REE
$1,000,000.00 Winner!

And that's not all...activating your
bring you an elegant long stemmed wine
toasts on those special occasions, and fc
well -- ABSOLUTELY FREE!

So go ahead and place your Editor'
spot provided and you can immediately
You" -- THE OPPORTUNITY TO WIN $1,C

Dara Gavin   Leslie Wayne   Ann

P.S. Validate our Editor's "Toast to You
PURCHASE NECESSARY -- be in o
and immediately receive your FR

With Our
Compliments!
The Editors

Your very own **set** of bookplates to make
each Special **Edi**tion Novel specially yours
Enjoy them **with** our compliments!

This Book Belongs to:

This Book Belongs to:

This Book Belongs to:

Before sealing, please be sure to...

1. Detach your Editor's Sweepstakes Validation Seal, moisten and place it in the space provided.

2. Fill-in your name and address.

3. Detach your Bookplates and make your favorite Special Edition Novels personally yours!

© 1994 HARLEQUIN ENTERPRISES LTD.
PRINTED IN U.S.A.

Frustrated, Donovan let the subject drop until they were back at the hotel and Rose was ready for sleep. At Bobbie's summons, he went in and sat down on the edge of the bed. For a moment he was reminded of the time he had first laid eyes on Rose back in the hospital. She had reminded him so much of Kirby.

Since then Rose had tangled herself around his heart like a runaway honeysuckle vine. How he loved her. For a moment he closed his eyes as gratitude poured through him. What could have turned into a tragedy had come out so well. The thought of truly losing her should have made him feel easier about the temporary separation when she returned to Yuma with Bobbie in a little more than a week. Instead, it made him feel worse.

So much could happen in the blink of an eye. All the time he was separated from his child was such a damned waste.

"What's the matter, Daddy?" Rose asked, bringing him back to the present. "Are you mad?"

Guiltily, he bent down and kissed her soft cheek. "No, honey, I'm just sad because you and your mom are going home soon," he blurted without thinking.

He heard a groan behind him. Before he could turn and ask Bobbie what was wrong, Rose's sweet little face crumpled like an empty paper bag and her eyes filled with tears. "I don't want to leave you," she cried, hurling her arms around his neck.

Holding her tight and making ineffectual shushing noises, he glanced helplessly over her shoulder. Bobbie had moved into his line of vision and was glaring down at him.

"Now you've done it," she grumbled. "It will take hours to get her to sleep."

"What did I do?" he asked, gently prying Rose's death grip from around his neck. "She knows you're leaving." With his thumb he wiped a tear from his daughter's cheek.

Then he dug a bandanna from his pocket and handed it to her.

"Blow," he instructed. Her expression was so woebegone he felt like crying himself.

What he needed was more time. Time with Rose and with Bobbie. Time, he realized with a jolt, to overcome Bobbie's distrust, to make amends for threatening to take her to court, to find out why she had lied about contacting him—and to win her back.

His gaze flew to hers. She appeared exasperated with him. The sweet little waitress who had captured his heart in Vegas had been usurped by a woman with a heart of stone and a will of steel—a woman as ferocious as a tiger with a cub. A woman he'd gone to great lengths to convince he'd do just about anything to take that cub away.

Now that he'd burned his bridges so thoroughly, Donovan realized that he found the new Bobbie even more captivating than the old.

If he told her how he felt, she would see it as another ploy to take Rose. He needed more time. Dammit, how was he going to keep them with him long enough to convince her he wanted the whole package and not just the child?

He'd done too good a job. She'd never believe it had all been a bluff.

"I don't want to go home," Rose repeated in a woeful little voice. "I want to stay with you and the rodeo. I want Mommy to stay, too."

Donovan glanced up at Bobbie, who had gone pale at Rose's announcement. He raised his eyebrows.

"Can't you—"

"Don't you dare make me the villain here," she warned him. "I know what you're going to suggest, but we can't stay any longer. I'll lose my job. Paul was adamant about that. The last time I talked to him, he told me Ann's managing, but she's getting married in a couple of weeks. He said if he has to break anyone else in, it will be a permanent replacement.''

Donovan's spirits sank. He knew that from where she stood, she couldn't risk losing her job. If the temp was getting married . . .

An idea took root. He stared at Bobbie until he realized she was frowning again. Had she expected him to suggest Rose stay with him while she went back to Arizona? Belatedly he knew that wasn't what he wanted at all.

Rose was patting his thigh insistently.

''Daddy,'' she said, and he realized it probably wasn't the first time she had spoken. ''I don't want to go home.''

''Mommy and I will talk about it,'' he promised rashly. ''You close your eyes and go to sleep, okay?''

''There's nothing to talk about.'' Bobbie spoke through clenched teeth. She leaned over to smooth Rose's hair away from her cheek. ''But we have a whole week before we need to leave, baby.''

''A week isn't very long,'' Rose grumbled as she lay back down.

Donovan felt a shiver of relief when she closed her eyes. Then they popped back open and she fixed him with a beseeching stare. ''You talk to Mommy,'' she said, sounding mature past her years as she shook her finger at him. ''You can make her stay if you talk really nice.''

''Rose . . .'' Bobbie began helplessly.

Donovan got to his feet, leaning over to kiss her again. ''We'll talk,'' he vowed. ''As soon as you go to sleep.''

He ignored Bobbie's exasperated sigh. Rose squeezed her eyes shut, making him smile despite his worry that Bobbie would go ballistic when she heard his idea. Somehow he had to buy enough time to win back her trust and convince her his growing feelings were sincere.

Turning off the light by the bed, she touched Rose's cheek. "Sweet dreams, honey. I'll be right in the next room," she said softly.

Donovan hoped her gentle tone was an indication that she wasn't too upset over his high-handed promise to their offspring. Meekly, he followed her from the bedroom.

As soon as they got to the sitting room and he had shut the door behind them, she turned on him like a spitting cat.

"What the *hell* do you think you were doing in there?" she demanded, eyes flashing with temper.

Distracted, Donovan found himself mesmerized by the sight of her flushed cheeks and the swirl of her dark hair as she tossed her head angrily. She had been pretty before, but maturity had given her a beauty that was almost more than he could resist. Her full lips, even pressed together as they were now, tempted him. Would they soften if he kissed her, or would she belt him?

He was afraid he knew the answer.

Still, only the warning gleam in her eyes kept him from hauling her into his arms and showing her how much he wanted her. That, and the knowledge that she would never believe him with all the misunderstandings that lay between them.

As he studied her, unsure just where to begin, she folded her arms across her rounded breasts and thrust out her chin. "Okay, cowboy," she challenged. "You told Rose we'd talk about our leaving, and you gave her false hope that we might be able to work something else out. So let's hear what you have to say."

If he had hoped she might listen to his idea with an open mind, he'd been wishing for the moon, he saw now. Clearly, logic wouldn't move her. Perhaps a surprise attack would.

He went over to her and looked deep into her eyes. Haughtily, her brows rose in silent query. Resisting the urge to tug nervously on his mustache, he took a deep breath and blurted, ''I want you to marry me.''

Chapter Eight

Donovan couldn't have said anything that would have surprised Bobbie more.

"M-marry you?" she echoed, incredulous. "Why would I do that?"

His gaze was penetrating. "I love Rose a great deal," he said quietly. "I don't want to lose her, and I'll never abandon her the way my parents did me."

There was pain in his voice that reminded Bobbie just how terrible an influence losing his parents at the age of ten must have been. No wonder he was so determined to hang on to Rose. To sacrifice his happiness in a loveless marriage for her.

Loveless on his side, of that Bobbie had no doubt. Her knees wobbled and she sank into one of the oversize chairs. If only some of the devotion he felt for Rose would spill over onto her. She'd accept that leftover love in a New York minute.

"You don't have to marry me to be a part of our daughter's life," she said. "A lot of unmarried parents manage to share a child. Divorced people do it all the time."

"I don't want that kind of life for my daughter," he protested. "Seeing her on weekends when I can steal time from my schedule and alternate holidays, having her visit for a few weeks in the summertime." He began to pace. His wide shoulders were hunched with tension.

Bobbie's first instinct was to massage away that strain. Her hands tingled at the idea of touching him. Then she remembered what was at stake, what he had proposed.

"I'm sure we could work out reasonable visitation." She chewed absently on her lower lip as he turned to give her a long look.

"You know what my life is like," he said. "Showing up in Yuma on short notice or canceling visits at the last minute. It's not fair to her or to you." He hesitated. "I owe you a debt of gratitude for being so understanding about that, though."

Her eyes widened. Was this the man who had threatened to take her to court? What was he up to? If they were to get married, could he somehow keep Rose and then get rid of Bobbie? Perhaps she needed to consult with that lawyer again. Just to be on the safe side.

"I didn't intend to keep you from Rose," she reminded Donovan, knowing he didn't believe her. "Remember that I lost my father, too. It was never my wish to raise a child alone."

Donovan came over to the chair where she was sitting and squatted down in front of her. The long muscles of his thighs strained against the worn denim, distracting her. Then he grabbed her hands. His palms were warm and callused, his grip capable and strong.

She looked into his eyes. Dependable? She wasn't sure, but part of her longed for someone to lean on when the responsibilities and worries became too much for one person.

Raising a child was an awesome task, despite its countless rewards. Even though Bobbie loved Rose fiercely, at times she felt so alone she could weep.

With a start she realized that, with his proposal, Donovan could very well intend to shoulder part of that responsibility. She studied his face, searching for clues.

He stared back candidly. Should she trust him? If she was wrong, she could lose her child.

"We can make it work," he urged when she remained silent. "Legally and financially, it would make everything a lot simpler, too."

"How do you mean?" she demanded, suspicions aroused.

One corner of his mouth hitched up in a lopsided grin. "We'd share custody. We'd both be there for her. My ranch would be our base, but you'd come with me whenever you could. Rose loves it on the road."

"What about school?" Bobbie asked. "She starts kindergarten next year."

He shrugged. "We'll work it out. Meanwhile, what's mine would be yours. And vice versa."

They both knew who'd be getting the better part of that deal. Bobbie wouldn't even be able to hold down a job if he expected them to travel with him. She opened her mouth to mention it, then realized they were skirting the big issues. Like how they felt about each other. She loved him, but she still had her pride.

And her price, she thought cynically. Financial security was a pretty tempting carrot, after some of the lean times she'd endured since Rose's birth.

Would Donovan really go so far as to saddle himself with a woman he didn't love for his child? She was dying to know, but the question stuck in her throat.

"What is it?" he asked.

Her cheeks flamed and she looked away. "Nothing."

He captured her chin in his hand and gently turned her head back so she was facing him. "Well?"

"How do you feel about me?" She lowered her lids so he couldn't read the emotion—the raw hope—that might show in her eyes. If he ever found out she loved him, he would either despise or pity her. She couldn't bear the thought of either and she wasn't sure which would be worse.

Surprised by the bluntness of her question, Donovan stared at the dark, curly lashes that screened her expressive eyes. Damn, but he wanted to tell her exactly how he felt.

He wanted both of them—his family. And he wanted to understand how Bobbie could have kept her secret from him for five years. And why. Maybe someday she'd own up to the truth and explain her reasons.

Too much rode on her answer to his proposal, so he didn't dare risk telling her how badly he wanted her. She'd never believe him. And, if she suspected how deep his feelings ran, she might bolt like a skittish filly.

"I have a lot of respect for you." He stumbled to a halt when her eyes flew open. "You've done a terrific job with Rose," he added hastily. "I know it hasn't always been easy." Seeing Bobbie's doubts, he cleared his throat and plunged on. "I think you and I would get along if we weren't on guard against each other."

"Whose fault is that?" she blazed.

"Just think about my offer." His gaze wandered to her breasts, their shape blurred by her navy blue shirt. It was tucked into jeans that hugged her body just the way he wanted to. Hell, was he too far gone or what?

She shifted restlessly. Realizing he was staring, he jerked his attention back to her face. And was distracted by that mole at the corner of her full mouth.

"We got along well enough before," he added on an edge of desperation.

"Before?"

"In Vegas."

She started to protest.

"I meant that we enjoyed talking to each other and spending time together," he amended. "You listened to me and made me feel, uh—" he was venturing onto dangerous ground here "—I liked our friendship," he finished lamely. "I liked *you*. I still do."

As a declaration of his feelings, it was laughably lame, she knew, but it was probably all she could hope for. Despite his stubborn refusal to believe she had written him about Rose, she'd be a fool not to consider his offer carefully. Respect, liking and a possible suspension of distrust were a foundation of sorts, even if they weren't as dazzling as eternal love.

Yeah, right.

She couldn't kid herself, though. Raising Rose alone was only going to get tougher in many ways. Even with the generous child support Donovan had already promised to pay, Bobbie would always have to work full-time.

That meant fewer hours to spend with Rose. Bobbie had dreamed of being available as her child grew up—available with a willing ear for childish confidences and problems, with time and money for Rose's interests, whether they were sports or Girl Scouts or music lessons. To volunteer in the classroom, to carpool on field trips and bake treats for school celebrations.

All the things that were difficult to pull off, if not impossible, for a single working mother with limited time and money.

"Bobbie?"

She blinked and focused misty eyes on Donovan. "Huh?"

"What are you thinking?"

She was thinking she must be crazy to consider his unorthodox offer for even a moment. What chance did she have of gaining or holding the interest of a man like Big D, even if she lived with him and wore his ring? She had seen the kind of women he was used to, watched the way they looked at him. Glamorous and sophisticated or athletic and sexy, with healthy hair, gleaming teeth and the confidence to go after what they wanted. The competition was formidable.

That brought Bobbie up against something else she hadn't the nerve to ask him about. What were his expectations of her as a wife? Was it a marriage in name only that he envisioned, or a relationship that was more...intimate?

She swallowed dryly, knowing she should find out—and sure the question would stick like a spur in her throat. "I need to think this over," she told him instead.

Frustrated, Donovan dragged in a deep breath and caught her hands in his. At least she hadn't turned him down.

"I love Rose. I'll be a good father and I'll take care of you both," he vowed. He wanted to tell Bobbie that he would give her time to adjust, to get to know him all over again before he expected anything from her—anything personal—but he wasn't sure how long he could wait for her.

Once she was his wife... His hands trembled and he let hers go.

"It's a big decision," she said.

"Of course," he muttered. "Think it over." He got to his feet and braced his empty, itchy hands on his hips.

He thought about kissing her gently, persuasively, but he was too scared that once he had his mouth on her, he wouldn't be able to stop until she was well and truly branded. He'd seen the way she watched him when she thought he didn't notice. And he remembered how she'd thrown herself at him after that bull had tried to grind him into hamburger. For the brief moment he had held her tight against him, he'd felt her heart thudding out of control.

He could build on that, he was sure of it. If only he could make use of that tense thrum of attraction she tried to hide; but he was too afraid he'd spook her or that his own ragged control would shatter like glass.

Hell, he thought, gazing down at her clouded expression. *Say yes, Bobbie,* he entreated her silently. *For all our sakes, say yes.*

Bobbie couldn't sleep. From the other bed, the sound of Rose's even breathing washed over her like an incoming tide as she lifted her head and stared at the clock. Two in the morning.

Restlessly she thumped her pillow, yanked on her covers and turned over, wondering if Donovan was sleeping peacefully.

As clear as if it had just happened, she could remember that last night back in Vegas, when she had still thought he was just another rodeo bum trying to scratch out a living. The rodeo was ending and he was leaving in the morning, but he had asked her to go with him to some dinner that evening.

When her shift was over at the diner, she had changed into her good black dress, its thin straps baring her shoulders and its flirty skirt swirling well above her knees when she walked. She redid her makeup, adding smoky shadow and a smudge of liner to her usual mascara and lip gloss, brushed and sprayed her short hair and put on dangly gold earrings. She was squeezing the essentials into a black beaded bag from the thrift store when she heard Ruby's excited voice calling her from out front.

"Bobbie, come here! You gotta see this."

Puzzled, she hurried around behind the counter to where the other waitress was standing, arms akimbo, staring up at the TV. Bobbie glanced at the screen.

"Isn't that your cowboy?" Ruby asked, reaching for the volume knob.

Together they watched Donovan, face streaked with dust and sweat, as the interviewer rambled on excitedly, calling him "Big D" and praising him for capturing the world bull-riding title.

Bobbie closed her gaping mouth and swallowed. The world championship? She'd had no idea. While Donovan shifted uncomfortably on the screen, the interviewer named a dollar amount well into six figures—Donovan's winnings for the year. He went on to mention a lucrative endorsement contract with a big-name clothing manufacturer.

Bobbie stared at the TV, stunned, as the picture cut to a shot of Donovan riding a huge bull. From the interviewer's deference, she could tell that the man she assumed to be a drifter was really a celebrity, a champion in his field. Big D. A wealthy, successful figure whose circle of acquaintances no doubt didn't normally run to waitresses in pink nylon uniforms.

A chill swept over her as the announcer went on to describe the exclusive celebration taking place that evening in one of the newest, most glamorous hotels in town. A camera panned the huge empty banquet room being readied for the party, dripping in gilt and crystal chandeliers and filled with round, linen-draped tables. A voice-over commented that tickets to the dinner were as scarce as a royal flush and worth nearly as much.

"Wow," Ruby muttered, awestruck. "I had no idea."

"Neither did I." Bobbie blinked away tears of disappointment. He had won the world title. What were the chances of Big D, champion bull rider, spokesman for boots and saddles and Western clothing, remembering a last-minute, no doubt impulsive, date he'd made with a waitress?

Sadly, she glanced down at the dress she had been so proud of sewing herself and the secondhand purse dangling from her arm. Most disappointing was the certainty that she had lost the chance to tell him goodbye.

As she turned down the television, the bell over the front door jangled cheerfully. From force of habit, she glanced around.

There stood Donovan framed in the doorway, big and blond and sexy. He was clad in a cream-colored Western suit that had to have been custom tailored. On his head was a spotless white Stetson. He was grinning from ear to ear and he looked for all the world like a conquering hero back from the war. A wide, ornately tooled leather belt was slung over his shoulder, topped with a huge oval gold buckle, and he held a single red rose in his hand.

"Be still my galloping heart," Ruby muttered.

When Donovan spotted Bobbie behind the counter, his grin widened and he ambled slowly toward her.

"Come on, darlin'," he coaxed, looking her up and down as he held out the rose. "You're so beautiful, I can hardly wait to show you off."

Now Bobbie struggled to shut out the memories that followed, memories of the magical night she had spent in his loving arms. As hard as she tried to banish it, Donovan's image refused to fade completely.

Restlessly she wondered if he was sound asleep in his room tonight, or was he lying awake, too, waiting for her answer? She slipped out of bed and put on her robe. The flowered fabric was thin, but it covered her shortie pajamas with complete modesty. Moving quietly through the shadowy room, she peeked at herself in the bathroom mirror. Her hair was in a tangle, so she worked a brush through it until it fell straight to her shoulders. Then she rinsed her mouth.

The only way she was going to get any sleep tonight was to tell him what she'd decided. Watching Rose for any signs of wakefulness, Bobbie tiptoed out to the sitting room, where a wall sconce glowed faintly.

Before she could reconsider, she was standing in front of the closed door to the other bedroom. She pressed her ear to the heavy panel, but she heard nothing. Taking a deep breath, she raised her hand to knock lightly. If he didn't answer, she'd just go back to—

"Looking for me?" A dark figure separated itself from the shadows near the bay window.

Jumping, Bobbie bit back a squeak of fright as he stepped into the lamplight. The only thing he had on was his jeans. They rode low on his hips, the fly gapping open where he hadn't bothered to fasten the top two snaps.

As she lifted her gaze to his beautifully sculptured torso, dusted with hair, Bobbie's nervousness was erased by a different but equally compelling emotion.

Heat suffused her as she continued to stare at his lean muscles and silken skin. At the latent male power of his shoulders and arms. At his shadowed face, the soft glow from the wall light turning his mustache and sideburns to burnished bronze.

Moving as sinuously as a big mountain cat, he glided over to where she stood trembling. "What's wrong? Is Rose sick?"

Looking into his eyes, breathing in his scent, Bobbie felt her courage draining away. How could she trust her heart to this man and risk her own destruction, even for her baby?

"She's fine." To Bobbie's ears, her voice sounded like a bungee cord that had been stretched too thin. "Do you still want to marry me?"

"Yes, ma'am, I do."

His reply was so emphatic that for a moment she let herself believe it was her he truly wanted.

"Okay," she said, turning away from the potent sight of him. "I accept your offer."

Donovan wanted to wrap her in his arms and bury his mouth in hers, to scoop her into his arms and carry her back to his lair, to show her there the feelings he couldn't yet put into words. Not until they trusted each other.

Was he being as clever as he thought he was, or was he just a pathetic fool she'd let down all over again? Right now, gazing at the shadowy cleavage nestled into the deep V of her robe and the outline of her nipples pressed against its thin folds, he didn't much care which he was—foolish or clever. He cared only that she and Rose were both going to be his.

"Well," he said, clearing his throat, "that's good. When we leave Salt Lake City on Friday, we'll slip over the border into Nevada. Is that okay with you?"

Looking slightly shell-shocked, she nodded. "Okay."

"Is there anyone you want to call? To be there?"

She shook her head. "I guess not."

"Fine." Absently he smoothed his mustache. "Shall we tell Rose our news over breakfast?"

"That would be a good idea." Bobbie fiddled with the tie of her robe, tightening it around her narrow waist. "Well, I guess I'll go back to bed."

"Yeah. Me, too," he said, reaching for her. With a sudden, glaring realization of what he was doing, he shifted the direction of his hands and rubbed them self-consciously against his bare chest instead.

Just one kiss, a voice inside his head whispered insidiously. He knew beyond a shadow of a doubt where that one kiss would lead and he was fairly confident he could lure her into sharing his bed—at least for tonight.

And then in the morning she would grab Rose and run like a field mouse in a barn full of cats.

"Good night," he said instead, turning his back on temptation before he could do what his overloaded senses were clamoring for, and to hell with the consequences.

Bobbie watched him go, unable to tear her eyes from the sight of his long, lean back even as disappointment washed over her.

What had she expected, for him to be deliriously happy at her announcement? To take her into his arms and pour out his heart?

Right. Blinking away bitter tears, she padded back to her own bed. She'd better remember why she had agreed to this ludicrous marriage. Not for her own galloping hormones, but for the child who meant everything to her. Any other reasons had best be banished to a dark secret place in her heart and left there to wither in silence.

Bobbie didn't think she would be able to sleep for worrying about Rose's reaction to their announcement in the morning, but the next thing she knew, the alarm clock was dragging her from some dream that lingered at the edge of her consciousness.

"Mommy, open your eyes!" Rose exclaimed, scrambling up onto Bobbie's bed and bouncing. "It's time to wake up."

Bobbie stretched and yawned, then grabbed Rose and nuzzled her neck. Her shriek of laughter was reassuring. Despite the serious threat to Bobbie's own happiness, she was doing the right thing.

"You make a beautiful bride," Ashley said as she stared at Bobbie's reflection in the motel-room mirror. "Donnie's tongue will be on the floor when he sees you."

She and Taylor had come to the tiny Nevada border town for the ceremony. Now Bobbie wondered just how much Donovan had told them about the reasons behind the sudden marriage.

At first she had been self-conscious around Ashley. It was so obvious that the other woman was madly in love with her husband, even after being married for over half a decade.

"Do I look pretty, too?" Rose asked, twirling so the skirt of her new purple dress belled out.

"Yes, honey, you look like a princess," Ashley replied warmly. She was wearing a primrose yellow sheath that turned her hair to fire.

How would she feel toward Bobbie if the truth came out that she was marrying Donovan for financial security? What would Taylor think? So far he had treated her with nothing but courtesy.

That could change in a heartbeat. Were the two of them really fooled into thinking this was a love match?

A discreet knock sounded on the door.

"I'll get that," Ashley said, turning away from the mirror.

"Thanks." Bobbie continued to stare at her reflection, at the lavender dress Donovan had suggested she buy back in Salt Lake City. It was sleeveless, with a rounded neck and a fitted bodice above a full skirt. Donovan hadn't actually seen the dress yet, but he had given her his credit card and insisted she and Rose go shopping. Rose's dress was similar in style to her own except for tiny puffed sleeves. Matching purple ribbons bound her twin blond ponytails.

Bobbie's hair, worn in its usual long, straight style, was topped by a puff of ribbon and lace shaded from the pale lavender of her dress to the darker purple of her daughter's. With the outfit she wore tiny amethyst earrings that had been a gift from her mother on her sixteenth birthday. She had tucked them into her luggage more as a good luck token than because she thought she'd be wearing them.

"The florist sent these," Ashley announced when she came back from answering the door. She was carrying three white boxes.

"Ooh, let me see," Rose exclaimed. At least she was enjoying this. She'd been bubbling with excitement since Donovan and Bobbie had broken the news of their wedding to her three mornings before.

Ashley handed Rose a square box with her name written on the top. "Open it carefully, sweetie."

Rose lifted the lid while Bobbie looked on, pleasantly surprised that Donovan had thought to order flowers. She had assumed they would walk into a wedding chapel, recite their vows and leave before the ink on their marriage certificate was dry.

"Mommy, look," Rose exclaimed, lifting out a tiny wrist corsage. A perfect white rosebud was trimmed with lavender netting and a purple bow. Carefully, Bobbie slid the corsage onto Rose's wrist, where it fit perfectly.

"Lovely," Ashley proclaimed. "Let's see what's in the other boxes.

The second one held her corsage, yellow and white carnations and baby's breath. Bobbie helped her pin it on and then she lifted the lid on the last box. Nestled inside was a spray of sterling silver roses, their velvety lavender petals surrounded by greenery and tied with a white bow.

When she took the corsage from the box, Bobbie saw something sparkle in the center of the bow. She looked closer and gasped softly, almost dropping the flowers in her surprise.

"Oh, how pretty," Ashley exclaimed as Bobbie picked up a pear-shaped amethyst pendant framed by diamonds and suspended from a thin gold chain. "It'll be perfect with your dress."

"And how did he know that?" Bobbie asked with a mock frown. Under the circumstances, she hadn't expected anything like this.

"He told me he needed to know your colors for the flowers," Ashley replied with an innocent smile. "Of course, I had to tell him."

"It's all lovely," Bobbie murmured, deeply touched. Despite the circumstances surrounding their unconventional wedding, Donovan had managed to make it special for her. She wondered whether he had any idea how much these extra touches meant or if he was only doing what he thought was right.

For a moment her happiness dimmed and then she looked at the pendant again. The deep purple stone surrounded by tiny diamonds had to be more than an empty gesture.

"Let me fasten it around your neck," Ashley offered. "And then we'd better get going."

Immediately butterflies the size of helicopters began dive-bombing Bobbie's stomach. With a shaky smile, she bowed her head and bared her neck.

"You look as handsome as a blooded bull calf," Taylor told Donovan with an unsympathetic chuckle.

Donovan alternated between fiddling with the bow of his black string tie and jingling the change in his pocket. He and Taylor were waiting for the ladies in the foyer of the Happily Ever After Wedding Chapel. The light from the tall amber windows across the front bathed the room with a golden glow.

"I never thought I'd see the day when a woman could ruin my baby brother's composure," Taylor continued. "Can't say I mind, either."

Donovan glared and then went back to checking his appearance in one of the long gilt-framed mirrors that bracketed the carved double front doors. He would rather be riding Twister with both hands tied behind him, he thought grimly. Hell, he'd rather be riding him backward with a bag over his head.

He was wearing a charcoal gray Western-cut suit with a white shirt and the tie he'd nearly mangled. Spit-shined black boots were on his feet and he held a new white beaver-belly Stetson in one sweaty hand. "I'm glad you find this so enjoyable," he growled.

"Allow me my one chance to feel superior." His brother reached up to straighten the single lavender rosebud Donovan wore in his buttonhole. A matching boutonniere adorned Taylor's own light gray suit jacket. "I was as steady as a rock at my wedding."

Distracted by the outright lie, Donovan guffawed and slapped Taylor on his wide back. "You were a wreck," he contradicted. "I thought you'd pass out from pure fright."

Briefly, Taylor's gray eyes danced and then his face so-
bered. "You know I wish you all the happiness in the
world," he said gruffly.

Donovan remembered the days when Taylor kept his
feelings buried beneath a stony facade and thanked God for
Ashley's influence on him. She had freed his soul and
brought him a wealth of happiness.

Donovan tried not to envy him. "Thanks," he said, voice
rough with emotion he didn't bother to hide. Before he
could say anything more, the front door opened and Ashley stuck in her head.

"Are you boys ready for this?"

A sudden knot the size of a hay bale stuck in Donovan's
throat. Realizing he was crumpling the brim of his expen-
sive new hat, he quickly relaxed his grip. "Ready as I'll ever
be," he muttered as Taylor poked him with an elbow.

"Grit your teeth," he whispered. "The wedding night
will make all this fuss worthwhile."

His comment didn't help. The door opened wider and
Rose glided inside, her dancing eyes and bobbing curls be-
lying her attempt at adult sophistication.

"Hi, Daddy," she said, smiling. Ashley whispered
something to her and she stepped aside, turning toward the
door expectantly.

Donovan's mouth went dry with anticipation. Slowly,
Bobbie stepped through the doorway.

His heart lurched in his chest. She was stunning. He
noted with relief that the amethyst pendant hung around
her neck. Swallowing, he lifted his eyes and met her gaze.

Her smile trembled at the edges. When he realized how
nervous and frightened she must be, he quickly crossed the
thick white pile carpet and reached out his hand.

"Come on, honey," he said, barely noticing the endearment as his fingers clung to hers. "Let's get hitched."

* * *

Bobbie managed to keep her emotions tightly under wraps until Reverend Patterson, the spiritual shepherd of some obscure denomination, asked for the ring. She'd never given it a thought!

Had Donovan remembered? He had certainly taken care of everything else. Taylor stepped forward and winked at her as if he could read her thoughts as he handed something to his brother. Bobbie jumped nervously when Ashley touched her arm.

"Here," she whispered, holding out a broad gold band on the flat of her hand.

Flushing as she realized that Donovan had bought himself a ring, too, she took it with fingers that trembled.

"I hope you don't mind," he whispered in her ear. "I got us matching bands."

She had never dreamed he'd want to wear a wedding ring. Confused, she shook her head without looking up. "Thank you for taking care of it."

Her eyes misted as she struggled against the impulse to think of this as a real wedding for all the usual reasons. Could it be that this marriage meant more to him than he was letting on?

Fostering false hopes would lead to disaster, she reminded herself sternly as the minister droned on. If Donovan wanted to fool Taylor and Ashley, that was up to him. Just as long as Bobbie didn't allow her own imagination to run off with her common sense, she didn't care what anyone else thought.

Keeping her smile firmly in place, she got through the rest of the ceremony without losing her composure. Only at the end, when Reverend Patterson invited Donovan to kiss his new bride, was there an awkward moment. He hesitated, looking deep into her eyes, and then he bent his head and pecked her cheek. His mustache brushed her skin like an angel's wing.

Forgetting her new sophistication, Rose giggled and applauded loudly.

"I can see I need to have a talk with you, little brother," Taylor drawled.

Everyone except Rose chuckled at his comment. Bobbie felt herself blush as the moment of awkwardness was shattered. She bent to give her daughter a hug and a kiss while Reverend Patterson pumped her new husband's hand.

"I love you, baby," she whispered to Rose.

Donovan and Taylor slapped each other's backs as Bobbie thanked Ashley for helping.

"Come to the ranch soon," her new sister-in-law invited. "You're family now."

Bobbie barely had time to blink away her sudden tears at being so warmly accepted when Taylor enveloped her in a strong hug. "Take care of him," he rumbled in her ear.

Pulling away, she thought she saw understanding in his somber gaze. Were her feelings toward Donovan so easy to read?

She had no time to worry about it as he dropped an arm around her shoulders and they followed the others outside. When they got to the front steps, Ashley and Rose pelted them with confetti.

The next thing Bobbie knew, Donovan had settled her into his rental car, a white convertible, and slid behind the wheel.

"What about Rose?" she asked as he started the engine and backed out of the slot.

"Taylor and Ashley are taking her for the night so we can have some privacy. You don't mind, do you?"

"Why can't we keep Rose with us?" She knew she was being awkward, but she couldn't help it. The idea of spending the night with Donovan was setting off alarms all along her nerve endings. He was her husband now and she had no idea what he wanted from her. Had he, too, read her feelings in her face and assumed she expected him to perform his husbandly duties?

The thought that he might pity his poor, besotted bride brought with it a crushing wave of humiliation.

He glanced at her and then returned his attention to the road. "They offered to take her," he said quietly. "How was I to explain that we didn't want or need the privacy, Mrs. Buchanan?"

Oh, she hadn't thought about that. "I see your point."

"They're happy for us," he continued. "I didn't want to disillusion them, at least not right away." There was an underlying thread of anger in his tone, making her wonder if her reluctance to be alone with him had disappointed him in some way.

What *did* he expect from this marriage? She should have found out before she ever agreed to the whole crazy scheme. Now it was too late and her husband's grim profile didn't bode well for a civil start to their life together.

Chapter Nine

"Are you hungry?" Donovan asked Bobbie as he trailed after her into the lobby of their Nevada hotel. She hadn't said anything since he'd explained why he'd accepted Ashley's offer to keep Rose overnight.

Now Bobbie glanced up. Despite the strain he could see on her face, she was still beautiful, still desirable. And—he resisted the urge to clench his fists with frustration—now she was also his wife.

"I guess I could eat something," she said, and he wondered if she'd grabbed his offer as a way to postpone the inevitable. "If you want to."

His appetite for food was nonexistent, but he recognized the need to take a break from the awareness building between them.

"Would you like to go somewhere or eat in the suite?" he asked.

"We could go out..." Her voice trailed off as she stared up at him with a frown. "What do you want to do?"

He managed a smile. "Darlin'," he drawled, "it's your wedding day. I'm all yours."

Clearly it was the wrong thing to say. Her eyes widened and her cheeks went pink.

Relenting, he caught her hand in his, holding it loosely. It was small and fine-boned, but he could feel the strength there, too, and the capability. He'd seen those hands brushing Rose's hair, drying her tears. He thought of them touching his own body, and his temperature spiked.

"Let's get out of these clothes and have something sent up," he suggested.

Her blush deepened and she took a hasty step back. "I don't—"

Realizing what he'd said, he swore under his breath and released her to yank at his tie. Did she think he was going to pounce on her the moment they were alone?

Struggling to hang on to his growing impatience, he tried again. "You look worn-out. All I meant was that we should relax and have something to eat. Okay?" Glancing around at the deserted lobby, he lowered his voice. "I wouldn't ravish a starving woman before she'd had a chance to eat dinner and regain her strength."

His last outrageous remark finally brought an answering spark to her dark, wary eyes.

"Too weak from hunger to manage it?" she asked.

Donovan grinned down at her and cupped her elbow lightly. "Come on. I can't wait to climb out of this suit and back into a pair of jeans."

"But you look so nice," she exclaimed.

His expression sharpened. "So do you, sweetheart. You look pretty enough to gobble right up."

Beside him, Bobbie took a steadying breath and led the way to the bank of elevators. His comment did nothing to reassure her, nor did his wolfish expression.

Just because they'd exchanged wedding vows didn't mean he had undergone some kind of wicked transformation, she reminded herself as she waited for the elevator. He was still the same cowboy she had been with for weeks. Now he had what he wanted, his daughter. There was no reason for Bobbie to act like a nervous virgin and worry that he'd set his sights on anything else she had.

By the time they had changed out of their wedding finery and the little round table in the sitting room of their suite had been set with the steaks and fries they'd both ordered, her tension had dissipated.

As soon as the waiter uncorked the champagne Donovan had ordered with the meal, he dismissed the man with a healthy tip.

After the waiter wished them a pleasant evening and left, Donovan poured the chilled champagne into two fluted glasses. He handed one to Bobbie and raised the other. "Here's to new beginnings."

Resisting the temptation to analyze his words to death, she acknowledged his toast and took a sip. The dry champagne danced on her tongue.

By the time they were done with dinner, she had finished her glass and declined a refill. Together, they loaded up the room-service cart and Donovan wheeled it out into the hall.

Before their food had come, he'd exchanged his gray suit for worn black jeans and a matching shirt he'd only partially fastened. The sleeves were rolled halfway up his forearms, revealing strong wrists and a dusting of gold hairs. On his left hand gleamed his new wedding band.

Touching her matching ring as if it were a talisman, she admired the way the black denim hugged his firm male buttocks as he pushed the cart from the room. In the dark clothes he looked dashing, dangerous and infinitely appealing.

While she waited, bemused, he came back inside, shutting the door behind him and leaning against it. His eyes were hooded as he studied her. The sight of him was unbearably tempting, making her wonder why she'd been so nervous earlier.

"What do you feel like doing now?" he asked, tone light. "Should we see if there's a movie on pay-TV?"

Perversely, Bobbie found herself wishing theirs was a real marriage and this a real wedding night. If only he cared for her, she would welcome him eagerly into her arms and her bed.

Something of her feelings must have shown on her face, because he crossed the room and leaned down to study her closely.

As she met his inquisitive gaze, she heard his breath catch. Her response to his nearness was like the blast from a furnace, melting her even as it seared away a good deal of her common sense.

She wanted him. Only her uncertainty about his feelings kept her from going into his arms.

"Or we could find something else to occupy us." His voice was suddenly rougher, thicker, his gaze narrowing. "It occurs to me that I haven't yet had a chance to kiss my bride."

"You kissed me at the chapel," she reminded him breathlessly.

"Only a peck on the cheek."

Her heart was thundering so hard she wondered if he could hear its rapid tattoo. "That was your choice."

He reached for her then, his long fingers wrapping around her bare arms below the sleeves of her T-shirt as he dragged her to her feet. "I wasn't about to kiss you for the first time in five years in front of an audience," he growled, lowering his head.

Bobbie could no more resist him than a shoreline resisted the incoming tide. Lifting her head to meet his descending mouth, she rested her hands against his hard chest. The spicy cologne he had worn to the ceremony, fainter but still enticing, filled her nostrils. His hand shifted, capturing her jaw as his gaze settled on her lips like a brand.

Her last coherent thought was that she could feel his heart beneath her palm and it was beating as frantically as her own.

Donovan skipped tentative, brushed aside gentle and went straight to hot and hungry. His open mouth covered hers, searing, melding, as his tongue sought entrance and swept boldly inside. Heat flamed around her as he demanded the response she'd been dying to give. Unconditional surrender.

He was starving for her, a dim part of his brain realized, and now her dark sweet taste threatened to explode the last of his control. Bending her back over his arm, he took the kiss he had dreamed of. He laid siege to her defenses. The more he drank from her honeyed mouth, the more his hunger grew. The more she responded, clinging to him, opening for him, purring deep in her throat, the more he burned for her. His body shook with the effort not to rip off her clothes and bury himself inside her.

Echoes of his heartbeat slammed in his ears as hot blood surged from his head to pool decidedly lower, pulsating and insistent. She moaned and he dragged her closer, curving one hand around the firm swell of her behind as he trailed hot kisses across her jaw and down her pale, exposed throat. Pressing his lips to a pulse that fluttered just below her fragrant skin, he was vaguely aware that one of her hands had slid around his neck and was buried in his hair; the other had settled in the gaping neckline of his shirt. Her palm skated across his burning skin, her fingers brushing his nipple. His body nearly jackknifed in response.

Feeling one of his hard thighs nudge her trembling knees apart, Bobbie gasped for breath and crowded closer.

His pulsating response surged against her.

"Oh, yes," she moaned. Her body had been asleep for aeons and now he was waking her, searing away her icy cocoon with the fiery heat of his hunger. Beneath her seeking fingers, his nipple drew into an intriguing nub.

Intimately, his arousal nudged the cradle of her passion. Wild as an electrical storm, his need surrounded her, overwhelmed her, driving her higher in a swirling maelstrom of hunger and love.

She was ready to give him everything, to grant any wish he might make, when he began to draw away from her, like molten lava that had started to cool.

First his lips left the sensitive area below her jaw. Then his hand, splayed against her buttocks, relaxed. The muscular thigh she'd been riding slipped from between her knees, causing her to stagger.

Groaning, bereft, she let her fingers slide from the silken hair at his nape to clutch at the fabric of his shirt as she wrenched open her eyes.

Donovan's face was flushed with passion, the skin stretched taut across his cheekbones. His eyes gleamed through the screen of his short, thick lashes, and his moist lips still curved invitingly below his mustache.

"Don't stop." She barely recognized her own voice. It was smoky with longing.

"Just in case you were under the impression that you wanted some cardboard copy of a real marriage," he said grimly as he straightened and pulled her up with him, "now you know better."

When he grabbed her hand and began easing away from her, she realized she was still plastered down the length of his body. Gaze locked on hers, he drew her hand downward and pressed it to the bulge under his fly. "Neither of us wants that."

"I—" Abruptly, her throat closed. Surely he was aware of her response to him, as well. Would he think she had been swept away by passion and champagne, or would he realize there was more to her feelings than mere liquor and lust? She would die of mortification if he suspected, but she could hide nothing from him when he held her in his arms.

She struggled and he let her go abruptly.

"You're wrong," she said. "I never realized you wanted this marriage to be real, as you so politely put it."

His expression was incredulous. "You want me," he insisted. "I know you do."

She lifted her chin, struggled for cool indifference. "I admit that you kiss well," she began.

A dull flush ran over his cheekbones and his eyes flashed like the eerie green lights in a dark, dangerous storm cloud. "Kiss well?" he echoed. "You make me sound like a clever adolescent who's learned a new skill."

She shrugged, willing her body not to tremble.

Before she even saw his hand move, he grasped the back of her head. "You want me," he rasped, "even if you don't have the courage to admit it." He stared thoughtfully. "Tell you what." He dipped his head until less than a breath separated his lips from hers. His mustache tickled. "Next time, you come to me."

Her eyes widened.

"That's right," he whispered, and she could feel the air stir against her mouth. "It's your move, sweetheart. I'll be waiting."

Watching her absorb his challenge, Donovan wondered if he could really make himself let her go. Her confusion came at him in waves. He didn't want to break her, but he had his pride, too. He was a man, not just Rose's father.

Dammit, he'd felt Bobbie's response when he'd kissed her. She had all but burst into flames. Now merely seducing her into being with him wasn't enough; only her total capitulation would satisfy him.

Before she could throw his challenge back into his face, Donovan untangled his fingers from her hair and released her. She watched him silently and he wished he could read her expression.

"Good night," he said softly, gratified by her surprise. It was cold comfort when he went to bed alone.

The crowd applauded with approval as Donovan leaped from the bull's back and tipped his hat to Rose, seated with Bobbie and Taylor in the stands. Bobbie and Rose had gotten back from packing up their apartment and putting everything in storage down in Yuma a few days before. The elder Buchanan brother had flown in for a cattle auction in Wichita and now he was keeping Donovan's family company during the rodeo.

"Yea, Daddy!" Rose cried, clapping madly.

Bobbie applauded and Taylor waved his hat. "Watch out for the bull, bro," he said under his breath as Donovan's score was announced. An eighty-three was high enough to hang on to first or second place.

As soon as Donovan climbed the rail and disappeared, Taylor turned to Bobbie and studied her carefully. Until now their conversation had been sporadic.

"Being on the road agrees with you," he said as she shifted self-consciously. "Or is it being married that makes you smile?"

Bobbie wasn't about to satisfy his curiosity. "Perhaps it's both."

He touched the brim of his hat in acknowledgment of her reply. "Rose looks happy."

They both turned to her, seated on Bobbie's other side so she could talk to a little girl she'd met in Dallas named Sarah. Sarah's father was a saddle-bronc rider and she traveled with her parents in a motor home. Bobbie had been delighted to see Sarah and her mother outside the rodeo office here in Wichita.

"I think Rose is happier than she's ever been," Bobbie admitted, watching her daughter whisper to her new friend. "She loves her daddy very much."

"And he loves her."

As soon as the last bull rider hit the dirt, Taylor got to his feet. "Ready to go?"

Bobbie nodded, mouthing a goodbye to Sarah's mother and waiting while the two little girls hugged.

"Sarah's my best friend," Rose said as they went down the steps. "Do you think we'll see her again soon?"

"I'm sure we'll run into her somewhere," Bobbie replied as she followed Taylor's broad back around to the locker room where Donovan would soon appear.

Despite the underlying strain from his challenge on their wedding night, she and her new husband had been getting along fairly well. Some nights it was almost more than she could do to leave him and bunk with her daughter, but her feelings were too mixed-up for her to make the first move.

"If you ever want a break, you and Rose can always come to the ranch without him," Taylor said as they waited outside the dressing-room door. "Ashley would love to see you again."

"Thank you."

Taylor rubbed a finger along one dark sideburn. "Is everything okay?" he asked.

The question surprised her. Although he'd been kind, Taylor was still her husband's brother.

"Everything's fine." Her voice was emphatic.

"I know you don't have anyone else," he said gruffly. "I just want you to know you always have a place to go if you need to." He closed a big hand over her shoulder and gave it a gentle squeeze. "Donnie might be my brother, but you and half-pint here are family now, too. We're all on the same side."

Bobbie was moved by his speech, a long one for him. "I appreciate that." She wondered if he suspected there was more—or was it less?—to their marriage than it seemed. "You don't resent me for keeping Rose from her father?" she had to ask.

Taylor shrugged. "That's between you and Donnie." He glanced down at Rose, who was too busy looking around to pay any attention to the adult conversation. "She's happy enough now, and so's my bro."

Bobbie wondered if Taylor was right. Was Donovan happy? Sometimes the two of them got along well, talking and laughing over something their daughter said or did. His questions about her first four years were endless, but Bobbie answered them as best she could. At other times she caught him watching her as if he was waiting for a sign. Then awareness always flooded her and she wished she had the courage to break the stalemate between them.

Fear of destroying their uneasy peace always held her back. That and the knowledge that he'd let her down once and he could do it again.

Finally Donovan came out of the dressing room. He shook hands with his brother, gave Bobbie a peck she had to remind herself was only for show and swept Rose into his arms.

"Hi, sweetheart."

"Did you see me clapping?" she demanded.

His grin deepened the lines in his cheeks, making Bobbie's breath catch. "Sure, I saw you," he drawled.

"Good ride," Bobbie told him. He'd finished second by only two points, but she had learned enough to blame the bull for a lackluster performance.

"Reese drew that bull last night and only got a sixty-eight," he replied. Since the bull earned half the points, its performance was crucial. No cowboy wanted to draw one that didn't buck.

"Reese isn't the bull rider you are." Her comment earned a wink from Donovan and a chuckle from his brother.

"Ain't she gettin' to be a good little rodeo wife?" Donovan asked Taylor. "Knows just the right thing to say to a man whose aspirations have fallen short."

Taylor glanced from one of them to the other. "I suspect she's better for you than you've even realized yet."

Donovan's eyes narrowed and he gave her a long, assessing look as they walked from the arena. "You keeping something from me, honey?" he asked in a teasing voice.

Predictably, Bobbie blushed at his question. "That's for me to know and you to find out," she managed to reply.

He turned away, but not before she thought she heard him mutter, "I aim to," under his breath.

The half-understood words sent a bolt of longing through her that left her feeling lonely and sad. Was she only a challenge to him, or were his feelings more complex than that?

* * *

It was a couple of weeks later that they ran into Sarah and her parents again at a rodeo in Kansas. When her mother, Mary Pat Perkins, heard they were staying until the next day, she invited Rose to spend the night in their motor home at the campground behind the arena.

"Can I, Mommy?" Rose asked, jumping up and down.

Bobbie glanced helplessly at Donovan. How could she say no, just because their daughter had been a buffer against intimacy? It wouldn't be fair.

"What do you think?" Donovan asked. "We'll be within walking distance, if she gets homesick during the night." Their motel was across the road from the rodeo complex.

Bobbie chewed her lip, torn between being pleased Rose had made a friend and worried that the unexpected privacy with her husband would prove the last straw to her willpower.

"Please, Mommy," Rose said again. "Sarah is my best friend in the whole world."

Bobbie and Mary Pat exchanged amused glances.

"She'd be no trouble," the other woman said. "They can play together in the morning and I'll bring her to the show later, or you can pick her up if you'd rather. We aren't heading down the road until after Danny rides."

Bobbie knew when she was cornered. "If you're sure—" she began.

Sarah and Rose joined hands and began dancing around in a circle.

"We'll be at the campground all evening," Mary Pat said. "Bring her by anytime." She gave Bobbie directions to their motor home.

"I'll walk her over after the show," Bobbie replied. "Thanks again."

"Won't she need pajamas and her toothbrush?" Donovan asked.

Bobbie's cheeks flamed. She had been too busy worrying about the night ahead with her husband. "We'll be over after I've packed her a bag at the motel," she amended.

"We'll both come," Donovan corrected her. "Tell that husband of yours to have a cold beer ready for me."

By the time the three of them walked over to the motor home Sarah shared with her parents, Rose was skipping with excitement. As soon as she saw her friend, she kissed Bobbie and then Donovan, grabbed her bag and followed Sarah inside.

Dodging the girls, Danny brought Donovan a beer and offered one to Bobbie.

"No, thanks, I'm fine." She knew she'd need her wits about her this evening if she hoped to withstand her attraction to the handsome blond cowboy at her side.

Mary Pat came out and the four of them sat in lawn chairs beneath an awning. As the men drank their beers and discussed that day's rodeo results, Rose and Sarah rushed back outside, chattering like magpies.

"Rose sure looks a lot like you," Danny said when the two girls began chasing each other around the picnic table.

"She's my daughter," Donovan replied, crossing one booted ankle over the other.

Danny scratched his chin as Donovan's meaning sank in. "I thought you two just got hitched." Mary Pat reached over to give his arm a shove.

"We did." After Donovan's reply, an awkward silence fell.

Bobbie tried to think of something else to say, but she drew a blank. The last thing she wanted was to have to explain the last few years.

Donovan took another drink of his beer and she began to wish she hadn't turned one down. "It's a long story," he said, breaking the silence.

"And none of our business." Mary Pat sent her husband a quelling look.

"I'm sorry." Danny was obviously uncomfortable. "I didn't mean to get personal."

"Don't worry about it." Donovan tipped his head back and drained the beer bottle while Bobbie watched the muscles of his throat work. When Danny offered him another, he shook his head.

"I'd ask you to stay and visit," Mary Pat said, getting to her feet, "but I bet you newlyweds don't want to spend the evening hanging around with old married folks."

Donovan rose and grabbed Bobbie's hand, pulling her up beside him. "We can't wait to be alone, can we, sweetheart?" he asked, sliding his arm around her waist.

She resisted the urge to kick him in the shin. Instead, she returned his smile and snuggled closer. "No, baby, we sure can't," she replied, batting her eyelids.

Accidentally, her breast bumped his arm. She heard his soft, indrawn breath, and he must have felt her stiffen, because he tightened his grip on her waist. His scent and the feel of him all down the length of her body fired her imagination. For a moment she was tempted to throw caution to the wind and indulge herself.

"Now I wish we'd driven the car over." His tone was teasing, but his eyes promised retribution for the way she had flirted with him.

"Walk fast," Danny kidded as Mary Pat rolled her eyes.

Very deliberately, Donovan let his gaze drop to Bobbie's mouth. Her lips burned as if he had actually touched them. Sheer bravado made her pucker up and blow him a kiss.

Donovan's eyes widened and then his expression grew thoughtful. "You're playing with fire," he murmured for her ears alone.

Feeling as if she had just tweaked a tiger's tail, Bobbie tried not to let his words intimidate her. He was the one who had said the next move was hers. He wouldn't touch her tonight unless she initiated it. "Getting too hot for you?" she purred, swallowing a yelp when he pinched her.

Without answering, he set down his empty beer bottle. "Thanks for taking Rose," he told the other couple. "We'll be back in the morning to pick her up."

"Not too early," Danny warned. "Even old married people like to sleep in."

Donovan's grin was cocky. "No chance of that."

He gave the appearance of a man eager to spend the night with his wife. Calling Rose over, Bobbie hugged her tight.

"Have a good time and mind Rose's parents," Bobbie said. "Daddy and I will be back for you tomorrow morning."

For a moment Rose's arms tightened and Bobbie wondered if she would back out. Then she let Bobbie go and reached for Donovan.

"Bye, Daddy."

When he and Bobbie had walked halfway back to the motel, an unexpected shower began spattering them with moisture.

"Maybe this will cool you off," she commented, tipping back her head so the rain bathed her warm face.

To her surprise, Donovan ran a finger down her cheek. "Think I need cooling off?" he challenged, leaning closer.

"I don't know," she replied honestly.

"Want to find out?" His voice was husky, daring her.

She felt as though she were walking on quicksand. Her bravado disappeared. "I'm not sure."

"Now's not the time for uncertainty."

They had both stopped walking, and Bobbie was only marginally aware that the rain was coming down harder, soaking their clothes. "Then what is it time for?"

His eyes had darkened. "I think it's finally time for us," he said slowly, gripping her shoulders.

Bobbie swayed toward him, all the reasons why this wasn't a good idea seeping away. Then a car drove by, horn blaring, and shattered the spell.

Abruptly Donovan lifted his head, water running off the brim of his hat. "Come on." He released her shoulders and shackled her wrist instead, pulling her along behind him. She was almost running to keep up.

"Where's the fire?" she panted. One look at his face as he glanced down and she didn't bother with any more questions. A shiver that had nothing to do with the rain's coolness went through her. She had indeed tweaked the tiger's tail and now he was fully wakened.

Wordlessly, Donovan hurried her across the motel lobby and into a waiting elevator. As the doors glided shut, enclosing them in the small cubicle, he was tempted to hit the stop button, back her against the wall and kiss her senseless.

He resisted the impulse. Once he got her into his arms, they might not make it to their rooms—even if the two-bedroom unit was more private and much more comfortable than the floor of the elevator.

When the doors opened onto the second floor, he began digging the key from his jeans pocket as he pulled her along behind him. The denim was damp, making him swear with frustration.

Only when they were inside, the door locked behind them, did he dare look at her.

Long strands of soggy dark hair clung to her damp cheeks. Her white shirt was almost transparent from the rain. Through the wet fabric, he could see her bra and the outline of her nipples.

"You should get those wet clothes off," he told her, breath jamming in his throat.

She stared back at him. "So should you, before you catch cold."

Cold, hell. He was burning up. When Bobbie turned to go into the next room, he caught her arm and propelled her back around to face him. "This probably isn't a good idea," he began, staring at her moist, sexy mouth.

"No, it probably isn't." Her voice was hushed as she lifted her soggy hair away from her upturned face. In the wet shirt, her breasts rose and fell, tempting him to bend his head and press his mouth to her beaded nipple through the white fabric.

Helpless against the desire surging through him, he curled his hands into fists and willed them to remain at his sides. Shaking with need, he leaned forward and touched his mouth to hers.

Her lips were cool, like satin, but they heated quickly and softened against his. Swallowing a groan, he traced them with the tip of his tongue. When they parted, coaxing him inside, he could have wept with relief. Instead, he wrapped his fingers around her wrists, the bones as delicate as a bird's. His tongue explored the inner contours of her mouth as he drew her hands to his chest.

"Do you want me to stop?" he whispered. "Are you cold? Do you want to go back to your room and shower?" He felt as if he would go up in flames if she left him now.

She shook her head, her reply only a breath of sound. "No, no and no."

With her palms flat against him, soaking up his warmth, feeling the steady beat of his heart, Bobbie absorbed the taste and textures of his mouth beneath the soft brush of his mustache. When she stroked her tongue along his, he groaned, a low rumble deep in his throat. His hands settled at her waist and he dragged in a ragged breath, chest expanding to graze her breasts. He froze and then he shifted, rubbing against her nipples lightly. His hands tightened and he drew her closer.

Her fingers curled into his shirt and then she slid her arms up around his neck. The scent and the taste of him were all that she remembered them to be, and more. As he continued to tease her with his lips and tongue, her natural caution started to unravel, rational thought ebbing away. Her fingers tunneled through the warm silk of his hair as he nibbled a path along her jaw.

His hands slid down her hips, urging her closer; her body melted into his.

Way too soon, he lifted his mouth. Chilled by his withdrawal, she dragged her eyes open and collided with the smoky green of his.

"I don't think I can let you go," he rasped.

His admission washed over her, dissolving the last of her restraint. She tightened her arms around his neck and pressed against his hard body. "Then don't let me go."

A shudder went through him and a hot light flared in his eyes. "Do you know what you're saying?" he demanded. "If I take you now, this marriage is going to get very real, very quickly."

It was her turn to ask what he meant. As she did, she tried to pull back, but her body didn't listen. She stayed pressed against him, feeling his strength, his heat, the power of his arousal.

His fingers curved around her chin, holding it still while his gaze bored into her. "Don't think I can make love with you and then let you go back to Rose's room," he said, answering her. "I've spent too many restless nights as it is, thinking of you just beyond that door. Five-year-old memories are painful enough to deal with. If you don't want our relationship to change irrevocably, don't stay with me now.''

His fingers gripped her jaw and his expression was grim. She wanted him to seduce her into forgetting everything but him, to sweep away her doubts on a tide of passion. Instead, he was forcing her to make a choice.

When she pulled back, his heart sank. His hand dropped, his gut clenched with raw need. She bowed her head and her damp hair fell forward. Why the hell hadn't he kissed her into mindless agreement rather than presenting her with such an ultimatum?

He had told her he didn't think he could let her go, and he wasn't sure that he could. He had never forced himself on a woman and he wasn't about to start now, but damn, if he wasn't tempted to try changing her mind.

Before he could turn away from her, she lifted her head. Her brown eyes were moist with tears, her lips parted. Suddenly he couldn't bear to hear her speak the words that would surely kill him.

Bobbie was about to admit that she didn't want to leave when Donovan's eyes narrowed with intent and his face went taut with some dark emotion she couldn't read. Before she could utter a sound, she was back in his arms.

''Too late,'' he muttered, and then his mouth covered hers in a scorching kiss, as driven as the other had been tender. All she could do was absorb his unleashed passion and meet it with her own. When he felt her response, he groaned and his desperate embrace relaxed slightly. Together, they surrendered to the hunger that had been building between them since she'd first walked back into his life. In the face of his obvious need, Bobbie's defenses had crumbled. No matter the outcome, she couldn't turn away from him now. For too long she had dreamed of sharing herself with him once again. She wasn't about to let any of the doubts or mistrust between them get in the way now.

She had no idea when the rain stopped, too lost in her husband's arms to pay any attention to the elements outside their room. All she knew was that his need matched her own. After ducking into the bathroom for his shaving kit and dropping it beside the bed, he once again gathered her into his arms.

"It seems as if I've wanted you forever," he said, voice rough.

Her throat filled with emotion, leaving her unable to reply. All she could do was reach up and cradle his jaw against her palm.

Tenderly, he helped her remove her wet clothing and stripped away his, swearing as he struggled with his boots and jeans. Then he drew her with him beneath the covers on the bed. As the room grew darker, the heat of his body warmed her and the passion of his touch ignited her desires. His kisses and the soft sweep of his mustache melted away her doubts as the sure strokes of his hands drove her higher. Mindless, she explored him, as well. His arms tightened and his breathing grew rapid, shallow.

Even as he rose above her, she was begging him to take her. As soon as he had assured himself that she was ready for him, he reached into his shaving kit. Then he came back and claimed her in the most elemental way men had been claiming their women since time began.

Chapter Ten

When Bobbie woke up the next morning, she lay perfectly still and kept her eyes squeezed shut as she struggled to remember the dream hovering at the edge of her consciousness. Despite her best efforts, awareness intruded and, with it, the realization that she wasn't alone. A warm, muscular arm lay heavily across her waist. Holding her breath, she opened one eye.

"Good morning, Mrs. Buchanan. Sleep okay?" The deep, familiar voice drifted up from the pillow beside her head.

Now she'd done it. Last night she had succumbed to temptations of the flesh. If she didn't keep her emotions under control, she could pay dearly for the lapse.

"I dunno," she muttered, turning her head to look at her husband. "Someone kept waking me."

His green eyes sparkled as he propped his shaggy blond head on one hand. "That was me," he murmured. Even with his hair rumpled and bronze whiskers sprouting on his tanned cheeks, Donovan made her breath catch. "I was about to wake you again when you opened your eyes."

His nearness and the expression on his face, sleepy contentment edged with desire, was enough to reawaken the sensual side of her nature. Last night he had proved that her memories of their lovemaking were no fluke. If she didn't already love him, she would have fallen for him when he wrapped her in his arms and took her on a rocket ride to heaven—not once but several times.

Bobbie knew she had to think about what had happened between them, and they needed to talk. Later. For now, all she wanted was to melt into his embrace and recapture the passion that had flared between them. From the way his hand had tunneled beneath the covers to stroke the sensitive skin of her hip and stomach before wandering lower, she assumed that Donovan wanted the same thing. Caught up in the spell his fingers were weaving, she rolled toward him.

By the time her breathing and her heart rate had finally slowed to normal again, Donovan had managed to pull himself up to a sitting position beside her and was running his fingers through her tangled hair.

"I wouldn't mind waking up this way every day," he said lightly as he leaned over her and studied her face.

Bobbie wished she knew what he was thinking. Was sleeping with her just an added bonus to having his daughter with him, or did he genuinely care? Several times since their wedding, she'd caught him watching her with an unreadable expression on his face, but he hadn't said a word. She wished she had the courage to demand a few answers before he broke her heart again, but she was too afraid the cold truth would shatter the tiny bud of happiness that had begun to grow the night before.

He wanted her; he'd admitted that much. Was she deceiving herself to think that his obvious desire could be the foundation of a fresh start for them?

"How about some coffee?" he asked when she didn't reply to his comment. "I'll call room service."

Holding the sheet against her breasts, she gazed up at him. "Coffee would be nice." Her attention shifted to the clock on the bleached-oak nightstand. "I suppose we'd better think about picking up Rose. I wonder if she had a good time." It was the first time Rose had spent the night away from family, unless one counted the hospital stay. There had been a couple of times when Bobbie had succumbed to exhaustion and the doctor's urging that she go home and grab a few hours' sleep before continuing her vigil in her daughter's room.

"There's no hurry," Donovan replied as he flipped the cover aside and casually pulled on a pair of white cotton briefs while Bobbie resisted the urge to trail kisses down his spine. "Danny told us not to come over too early."

"That was before he spent the night with a couple of four-year-old girls," Bobbie reminded him. As he sat on the edge of the bed and called room service, she lay back and admired the rippling muscles of his shoulders. Several scars marred the satiny surface and she wanted to hear how he'd gotten each one.

He completed the call and hung up the phone. "Fifteen minutes," he said. When he noticed the way she was looking at him, his expression sharpened. He leaned over and kissed her hard.

"What was that for?" she asked, lips tingling from the press of his.

Ignoring her question, he asked one of his own. "Do you want the shower first while I sign for the coffee?"

She stretched lazily and the sheet started to slide down, stopping right before it would have bared her nipples to his avid gaze. "What's my other option?" she asked, catching the sheet and shifting onto her side.

"Sharing a shower with me later."

Unable to resist him, she lifted a corner of the covers in silent invitation. Quicker than she could have said "Yes, please," Donovan stripped off his shorts and joined her. He rolled her onto her back as her arms came around him, claimed her mouth in a kiss that sent her temperature soaring and then he slid inside her.

Her last thought before her mind emptied was that waking up to him was infinitely more delicious than the best coffee in the world.

"Oh, Bobbie, I'm so glad you could come!" Ashley exclaimed as the two women embraced. "You, too, sweetie," she told Rose, bending to hug her, as well. "The boys will be so happy to see you again."

Bobbie breathed in the good Colorado air and watched her husband and his brother pound each other on the back. Donovan had managed to carve three precious days from his hectic schedule so they could visit Taylor's ranch. The same morning that Bobbie had first woken up in his bed, he had decided they needed the change.

"We're glad to be here," she told Ashley, who had burst out the back door as soon as they'd pulled up behind the sprawling yellow rambler with white shutters and trim. Donovan had buzzed the house before they landed on his brother's private airstrip, and then Taylor picked them up in his truck.

"Aunt Ashley," Rose asked, "where are my cousins now?"

"They're probably at the barn," she replied. "I'm sure your dad and Uncle Taylor won't mind walking you down there."

Donovan raised his head. "You bet, princess. I'm dying to see the new bull your uncle's been bragging about." He turned to Bobbie and raised his brows in query. "That okay with you?"

Her breath caught at the promise smoldering in his gaze. "It's fine," she managed, keenly aware of their audience.

"Thought you would've had your fill of bulls," Taylor commented dryly.

"This one's different." Donovan's grin was lopsided. "I don't have to ride him. Let's get our gear inside and find those little cowpokes of yours."

His comment about the bull made Bobbie wonder if he ever tired of the danger, the abuse to his body, the race to ride one more bull than his competition. Although he did his best to hide the occasional limp or aching muscle, she had seen the scars and the bruises, the braces and surgical tape. She always shared his sadness over news of a fallen comrade. She knew him too well to think he got high on risking his life, as some men did. Would he retire as his brother had, burned-out and content with a quieter life, or would he keep on until the horns or hooves of a rank bull made the decision for him?

"Come on into the kitchen," Ashley invited. "I've made cookies and there's fresh lemonade."

A plump teenage girl with black hair was arranging cookies on a plate. She looked up and smiled when they all trooped inside.

"This is Jennifer," Ashley said, introducing them in turn. "Her mother usually helps me out three days a week, but Jennifer's filling in while June visits her sister."

Jennifer's smile was rather shy, but Bobbie noticed that she offered Rose a cookie before setting the plate on the island in the middle of the room.

In a few moments the men had carried the bags to the other end of the house and come back to the kitchen, laughing over some shared joke.

"Take some cookies out to the boys." Ashley gave Rose a stack wrapped in a paper napkin, then slapped at Taylor's hand when he filched a few more.

"I was getting them for Donnie," he protested, then belied his own words by devouring one in two bites. "Mmm, good."

Laughing, Ashley offered Donovan the plate and then shooed them from the kitchen. "Don't let your dad and your uncle eat the cookies I'm sending Jeff and Jay," she cautioned Rose.

"We put her in the bedroom next to yours," Ashley told Bobbie after the others had left and Jennifer excused herself. "Will that be okay?"

"Perfect." Bobbie collapsed into a kitchen chair and thanked Ashley again for having them. "Donovan needs this break," she said. A shiver of longing went through her when she recalled the reason neither of them had been getting much sleep lately. How many hours until bedtime?

"I suspect you all do," Ashley replied as she poured lemonade. "And I bet you'd like a minute to catch your breath right now."

"I think that would take a year." Bobbie took a satisfying swallow, savoring the blend of sweet and tart tastes. Then she remembered that her new sister-in-law had plenty of experience on the circuit. She'd been a barrel racer before a knee injury had sidelined her. "I mean, I love it, but—"

"I know what you meant," Ashley interrupted. "You can love the pace and still get bushed if you don't get away from it once in a while." She pushed the plate of cookies closer and slid into an empty chair. "Besides that, you've got a child to care for. Believe me, I know how tiring that can be."

"But you've got twins," Bobbie exclaimed. "That must be twice the work."

"At least." Ashley rolled her eyes. Then her smile widened and she leaned forward conspiratorially. "Actually, make that closer to three children than two."

Bobbie was puzzled until she realized what her sister-in-law was saying. "You're pregnant?"

Ashley nodded, obviously pleased. "Taylor is the only other one who knows, but I suppose he's telling Donovan as we speak."

As Bobbie voiced her congratulations and asked when the baby was due, she felt a sharp stab of envy. Donovan had been careful to use birth control every time they made love. After Rose's unexpected appearance and the way she had affected his life, Bobbie couldn't really blame him, but she would love to be carrying a child whose existence she could share with him from the start.

"We haven't told the boys yet," Ashley was saying, "but we'll have to pretty soon." She patted her still-flat stomach.

"Except for the glow in your cheeks, I would never have suspected," Bobbie said. In her dark jeans and cropped knit top, Ashley was still as trim as a teenager.

She grinned and selected a cookie. "You know just what to say," she teased. "Eat these before I devour them, would you? I'd know I was pregnant just from the chocolate cravings I've had. I'm lucky I haven't gained a hundred pounds."

When she got up to check on the dinner preparations, Bobbie insisted on helping. Jennifer had gone to another part of the house, no doubt to give them a little privacy.

Bobbie was slicing raw zucchini for the salad to have with the steaks Taylor was planning to grill for dinner when she heard shrieks of childish laughter from outside. They were punctuated by the deeper voices of the two adults. Ashley glanced out the window.

"Husbands and children sighted at four o'clock," she announced. "I'll remind Taylor to get the coals started."

Bobbie followed her to the back door and stood watching Rose as she chased after one of the twins. Bobbie wasn't sure which one. The boys were identical and looked more like their father than Ashley, with dark hair and gray eyes.

Rose shrieked when her cousin ducked away from her outstretched arms. Her round cheeks were flushed and one of her braids had come loose. It made Bobbie's heart ache with happiness to see her having so much fun.

Donovan had been good for Rose, Bobbie realized. Without him, she wouldn't have met her extended family here at the ranch, nor would she have made friends with Sarah or so many of the other rodeo folk she and Bobbie had gotten to know over the past few weeks. Despite her reservations, Bobbie was forced to admit, at least to herself, that Donovan had provided a dimension to Rose's life that Bobbie could never have given her. For that alone, she was in his debt.

She watched his long-legged stride carry him to the deck that ran across the back of the house and she savored his wildly attractive grin as he exchanged some comment with Taylor. It was more than gratitude that she felt toward him. Remembering the way he made her pulse leap when they were alone, heat poured through her.

Was that why Donovan had abruptly decided to visit the ranch now? Because they had begun sharing a room and he wouldn't have to make awkward explanations?

She wanted to believe he really had just wanted to take a break from the schedule he must find exhausting. Before calling Taylor, he had mentioned how eager he was for her to see the ranch and get to know his family better. She had been looking forward to a few days of sharing him with a minimum of other people instead of the usual multitude. She pictured moonlit walks and other times for just the two of them. Her longing for him sharpened. Traveling with a young child left little more than nighttime for privacy, but here on the ranch the possibilities were endless.

While Taylor and Donovan stood on the deck and discussed the new bull, Ashley came outside with a cold beer in each hand. For a long time Donovan had envied his brother's obvious contentment. Now he found himself wondering instead if Bobbie was alone inside the house.

"Honey, would you start the grill?" Ashley asked Taylor as she handed a long-necked bottle, dripping with condensation, to each man.

While he busied himself with the bag of charcoal, Donovan hooked an arm around her shoulders. "Taylor told me your news," he said quietly as he gave her a gentle squeeze.

If Donovan didn't love her for herself, he would have for Taylor's sake. She'd cleared the shadows from his brother's eyes. She'd given him a family to replace the one he and Donovan had lost and had eased the burden of guilt Donovan carried for driving their parents away. For that, he was more grateful than he could have ever admitted.

"He swears this baby's a girl," Ashley said, sending her husband a look brimming with love. His back was to them as he squirted lighter fluid on the briquettes and he didn't notice, but Donovan did—and wondered if Bobbie would ever look at him that way. Not as Rose's father or the one who signed the checks, but simply as her mate, her other half.

"How are you feeling?" he thought to ask Ashley, remembering his brother's pale face and tormented expression during the delivery of the boys. Compared to their father, she had come through the ordeal with flying colors. Thinking about that made him wonder who, if anyone, had been with Bobbie when she had Rose.

"Does being pregnant put any added strain on your knee?" he asked Ashley. She had hurt it badly when her horse threw her while circling a barrel. Taylor had told him it sometimes ached in the cold weather.

"Are you implying I've gained weight?" she demanded now, slipping out from under his arm to prop her hands on her slim hips and fixing him with a mock glare.

"No, but you gained a little with the twins."

Her wide mouth curved into a smile. "I gained a ton with the twins," she admitted, "but my leg held up okay. If this is a delicate little girl, it'll be a cinch after carrying those future steer wrestlers that man fathered." She pointed an accusing finger as Taylor straightened. Traditionally, steer wrestlers were big, powerful men, and he was no exception.

"Who, me?" he asked with a tender look as he came over and leaned down to kiss his wife. Donovan noticed the way her lips clung before she let him go. It reminded him of the way Bobbie had kissed him early that morning, changing his mind about getting out of bed for another half hour.

Reaction surged through him like a stampeding bull, making him struggle to focus on what Taylor was saying.

"This one's a girl. I just know it," he insisted, laying his splayed hand over the apron covering Ashley's stomach.

"Say that when I've gained thirty pounds," she told him. "Meanwhile, everything's ready but the steaks and we're all hungry."

Still grinning, Taylor shook his head and winked at Donovan. "I swear, you want anything done around here, you have to do it yourself."

Lightly, Ashley punched his arm. "The meat's in the fridge, marinating," she told him. "If it was up to you, it would still be in the freezer, rock hard."

Just like I'm going to be if I keep mooning about last night, Donovan thought as he spotted Bobbie through the kitchen window. To distract himself, he picked up a spongy ball that someone had left in a lawn chair and asked the kids if they wanted to play a game of catch.

Bobbie had been right about the chance to grab a little time alone with her husband. In the two days they'd been in Colorado, Donovan had ridden out early each morning with Taylor, who still had a ranch to run, while she kept Ashley company and played with the children. Jennifer helped with them, too, teaching them games and songs.

On the first evening, the women cleaned up from dinner while the men supervised the exhausted children's bath time. Then the four adults tucked them into bed and lingered over coffee at the picnic table until Donovan rose abruptly.

When he bid the other couple good-night and led Bobbie away, she heard Taylor remark in a patently innocent tone that the country air must have tired them out. The second night, though, when the kitchen was cleaned up and the children settled in front of videos on the VCR, Donovan folded Bobbie's hand into his and took her on a long walk.

She assumed he would show her the outbuildings and the original ranch house where Taylor and Ashley had lived for the first six months. Now the foreman and his family lived there.

Instead, Donovan led her in the other direction, walking down the long slope from the new house and through a grove of aspens.

"It's beautiful here," Bobbie said, gazing at the sea of drying grass before them and the faint outline of the mountains in the distance. The sun had disappeared behind the uneven horizon, and the colors streaking across the sky—pink, coral and lavender—were fading.

She turned in a slow circle, noticing that the house was now hidden by the grove of aspens. Except for the muted sounds the cattle made, the two of them were completely alone.

She became more keenly aware of her husband strolling beside her. He stopped and took a deep breath that expanded his chest. Letting it out slowly, he pushed back the baseball cap he wore on his head and stared at the lingering sunset.

"I'm glad you like it here. The land I bought looks a lot like this."

"Is it close by?" she asked, wondering how much her opinion really mattered. A breeze stirred her hair, a pleasant change from the heat of the day. Taylor had commented at dinner that the weather had been perfect for the haying that was underway. Both men had been streaked with sweat and dust when they'd come back to the house to eat.

"My spread is about twenty miles south of here," Donovan replied, lowering himself to the tall grass and patting a spot beside him. "I don't have this much land, but there are rumors that one of my neighbors might be getting ready to sell out. It would double my acreage."

"Are you going to buy it?" she asked, sitting cross-legged beside him and selecting a long weed to chew absently. He removed his hat and stretched his legs out in front of him, propping himself on his elbows. Every cell of Bobbie's body was aware of him sprawled out like a big golden cat less than two feet away.

He'd been looking straight ahead, but now he turned to her. "If certain things work out, I'll probably buy it."

She wanted to ask what things he meant. Before she could formulate the question, he pulled her down and rolled her beneath him in one smooth move.

She could only stare up at him in wonder. This handsome cowboy was her husband, the father of her child. For once she refused to let her doubts about his true feelings for her intrude. The tall grass surrounded them in a cocoon of privacy and his eyes gleamed with desire. For now, that was enough.

"I missed you today," she admitted, reaching up to settle her hands on either side of his collar. She could feel the corded muscles there.

His eyes narrowed and his gaze slid to her mouth. He was braced above her on one arm. With his free hand, he traced the shape of her lips. When she nibbled his thumb, he groaned and lowered his head. He blotted out the sky so that all she could see was him.

When she tipped back her head to meet his descending mouth, Donovan's breath caught in his throat. Desire licked at him like tongues of fire. Her scent and the sound of her moan swirled together in his head as he caught her chin with his hand and held her still for his kiss.

Resting his weight on his elbows, he slid one leg possessively across both of hers as his heated blood pooled in his groin, leaving him light-headed. Still kissing her, he freed her chin and stroked his hand down her body to pull her hips closer.

Her mouth clung to his and her fingers slid through his hair, nails scraping lightly against his scalp. How did she do it? One kiss and he wanted her more than he'd ever wanted anyone or anything in his life. One taste of her and he was so aroused that he ached.

Control slipped another notch as he pressed his hardness against her. Dimly, he was aware that she arched beneath him, rubbing his thigh.

When he'd brought her out here, he'd intended no more than a few private kisses to set the scene for later in the guest room they shared. Now he abandoned the plan to wait. A drive far stronger than his common sense compelled him to bury himself deep inside her. Caution rose feebly, reminding him that he was unprepared. He managed to lift his head, breaking the kiss. Bending one knee, he began levering himself away from temptation.

He was about to warn her that his pockets were empty when she snaked a hand between them to stroke his length through his jeans. Donovan groaned, afraid he was about to lose all control and explode like an inexperienced teenager. Rolling to his back, he dragged her with him so she straddled his hips. With hands that shook, he stripped off her T-shirt and bra, replacing them with his hands on her breasts. He brushed his thumbs over their dark tips, watching her face tighten with desire. She squirmed against him and he nearly levitated off the ground.

Catching her close, he shifted again until they were side by side.

"Is the grass too prickly?" he managed to ask.

She blinked clouded eyes and shook her head. He struggled to a sitting position and stripped off his shirt, spreading it flat and laying her on it even as her hands stroked his bare chest. A lusty smile curved her mouth. Her fingers skimmed over his abdomen, making his muscles dance as he sucked in his gut. His automatic reaction made room for her to slip her hand down farther, beneath his belt and the waist of his jeans. With the last bit of control he possessed, he clamped a hand around her wrist, keeping her from her ultimate goal, while his body throbbed a protest.

"I don't have anything with me," he gasped. Could he find the unselfishness to give her satisfaction without claiming it himself? He wouldn't mind another child in the least, but she might not feel the same.

"Let me take care of you," he offered, whispering raggedly as he rose up to unfasten her jeans.

As she tried to calculate her own intimate schedule, it was Bobbie's turn to still his hand. "Together," she demanded, voice hoarse. She arched her back, thrusting her bare breasts at him in a blatant attempt at seduction. "I want you inside me."

"But I can't—" he began.

"It's okay," she interrupted, biting her lip. "I should be safe." Was she, or did she only hope that was true? Her mind was clouded with hunger, slow and clumsy.

His hand slid over her bare stomach, the calluses and rough skin of his palm deliciously abrasive, and settled against the underside of her breast.

"Should be?" he echoed, frowning.

Aware of his fingers circling her nipple, she gave up trying to think. "Pretty sure." Would it be so bad? a tiny voice murmured insidiously within her brain. Another child would bind him closer.

The thought shocked her, but before she had a chance to react, he leaned over and buried his face in her neck. His lips nibbled at the sensitive skin. "I'll stop if you think we should." His voice sounded thin, as if his throat muscles were squeezed tight. Beneath her hands, he was rigid with tension.

Her body felt so empty, so bereft without him that it began to cramp. She could only imagine what he was going through. There were other ways, she knew, but only one that would truly satisfy her.

"No," she gasped on a sudden impulse. "Don't stop." Maybe, if she had known when he first kissed her, she could have dredged up the fortitude to deny him, but now it was too late.

Then he kissed her again, pulling her jeans and panties down to bury his fingers between her legs, and the capability for thought fled. Only after he had slowly filled her, stalling until they were both wild with need, and then taken them over the edge, did a tiny doubt return to plague her.

Donovan shifted his weight, still joined to her intimately, and whispered her name like a prayer. Even that last nagging thought dissolved.

It was all Donovan could do to leave his sleeping wife in bed alone as dawn broke the next morning, but he wanted to help with the haying and they had to leave early the next day for Wyoming. Bobbie stirred as he sat on the edge of the bed and rubbed one hand over his face, but she didn't wake up.

Studying her tempting mouth and the way her eyelashes curled at the tips, he thought of the night before. It was no wonder that she needed her sleep. Making love to her in the field hadn't been nearly enough for him. When they had come back to the house, they had turned down Ashley's offer of pie and coffee.

Donovan had answered her grin of understanding with a wink over the top of his wife's head before they checked on Rose and hurried to their room, hand in hand. There he had begun a leisurely exploration of her body that culminated in a fiery mutual conflagration.

At least that time his supply of protection had been close by. When his brain was functioning on more than one cylinder, he understood that there were still too many problems between them for another pregnancy to be a good idea. At least if they had created a baby together, though, he was here to lend his emotional and financial support—whether she wanted it or not.

While Donovan stood beneath the shower's chilly spray and gradually became more awake, he pictured Bobbie round with his child planted deep inside her. Her next pregnancy, no matter when it occurred, was not something he was going to miss, he vowed silently as he dried off with an oversize bath towel.

Perhaps by then they would have managed to overcome the barrier of mistrust that still lingered between them, as destructive as a barbed wire fence.

All that day, using hay hooks to position the bales on the stack as they came off the conveyer, Donovan was too busy to think much about his problems with Bobbie. When dinner was finished and the children attended to, Taylor asked him to come to his office. Curious, Donovan followed his older brother down the hallway toward the back of the house.

When they got to the office, Taylor pushed the door closed, pointed to a leather chair that was a twin to the one he settled into and poured them each a measure of brandy in a balloon glass.

"How's the master plan going?" he asked after they had sampled the potent liquor. "Do you think you'll get that big endorsement contract?" He was the only one besides Donovan's business agent who knew about the lucrative offer hinging on his retaining the championship for another year.

He stared into his glass as if it held the secrets to his future. "If wanting would get it for me, I'd be a sure winner," he confessed ruefully. He hadn't yet mentioned his plan to retire if the contract became a reality, but now he did.

Outside in the hall, Bobbie had been about to knock on the partially closed door to see if the brothers wanted coffee. When she heard Donovan say something about leaving the circuit at the end of this season, her hand froze in midair. Her heart leaped at the possibility and then she wondered why he had never mentioned retiring in the near future to her.

Conscience squirming with guilt, she listened while he outlined the plans he had for his ranch. Not once did her name come up, making her wonder if he intended to stay married to her. He hadn't said he loved her; he had walked away from her once before and he could do it again. Had he figured out some way to strengthen his custody case so that he could divorce Bobbie and still get Rose? Was he capable of doing something that underhanded or was she seeing bogeymen who didn't exist?

What about Rose? Was it possible Donovan was becoming disillusioned with fatherhood after all? Rose would be crushed if he abandoned her now. Bobbie's own father had left her and never came back. Could Donovan do the same? By his own admission, he had been raised by a foster parent who had showed little affection and inspired even less.

Was Donovan even capable of the deep love that lasted a lifetime? She didn't want to believe any of the possibilities, but once she acknowledged them, they grew and multiplied like the most virulent of the new viruses.

While she stood outside the door, sickened by her own doubts, the men's conversation shifted to a discussion of the various breeds of beef cattle. Afraid she'd be caught eavesdropping, Bobbie tiptoed back down the hall, one hand pressed to her churning stomach. The worst part was that she couldn't even confront him without admitting that she had overheard.

Inside Taylor's office, Donovan was in the middle of a question about crossbreeding when his brother interrupted.

"Are you happy?" he asked abruptly.

"Yeah, sure. Why wouldn't I be?" As close as the two of them had always been, Donovan still had to adjust to Taylor's more recent penchant for discussing things he would have avoided before. Unwilling to talk about his own feelings for years, Taylor hadn't been one to pry into Donovan's personal business, either. Now he wasn't so sure he liked Taylor's new willingness to ask questions to which Donovan hadn't yet worked out the answers.

Taylor was studying him over his nearly empty brandy snifter, and Donovan could almost see him organizing his thoughts.

"I like Bobbie," he said finally.

"I'm glad." Donovan squelched his impatience, knowing Taylor would get to the point in his own time.

"You didn't know about Rose until recently." It wasn't a question; Taylor knew the situation because Donovan had called him from the hospital in Yuma. "Are you okay with that?" Taylor asked.

Donovan was about to reply that of course he was and keep his lingering doubts to himself, but then he hesitated.

Taylor had always been there for him, even when keeping his own feelings behind a protective wall—even when they had argued about their parents' disappearance. Taylor had insisted they had to be dead after all these years, while Donovan still believed deep inside that his misbehaving had been the reason for their desertion and they were alive. He refused to let himself off the hook by accepting Taylor's explanation that they would have tried to get in touch before now. It was too easy, too tempting to shift the guilt away from himself.

Still, he owed his brother a truthful answer about his feelings for Rose. Haltingly at first, Donovan recited the events that had led up to her conception and those that had kept her out of his life until a couple of months ago.

"Bobbie never tried to contact you?" Taylor asked when Donovan was done talking.

He had skimmed over that part of the story, but now frustration rose inside him and clamored to get out.

"Hell," he said, rising to pace the small room, "I don't know what to believe. She claims she tried to notify me. She even acted hurt that I'd supposedly ignored the news."

"What does that mean?" Taylor asked, setting down his empty snifter to pick up a paper clip and form it absently into another shape. "You'd both know whether or not she told you."

"She said she tried calling and then wrote to me," Donovan admitted, still annoyed by the absurdity of her claim.

"Letters get lost," Taylor pointed out.

"Yeah, one letter might, but not two."

Taylor put aside the paper clip that now resembled a tiny lariat and raised his dark brows. "She claims both letters were lost?" he repeated, his skepticism obvious. "That's harder to swallow." Contemplating the situation, he rubbed the side of his nose. "What address did she use? I suppose there's a possibility they both got lost, the way you move around, but you'd think she would have gotten at least one of them back."

Donovan could see that his brother was having trouble accepting the idea that Bobbie might be the kind of woman who could lie and deceive the father of her child. Taylor liked her and he wanted Donovan to be happy.

"This is what's even more absurd," Donovan told him. "She told me she sent one in care of your ranch, and the other through the PRCA. Now do you understand why I still don't completely buy her story?" He drained the rest of his brandy in one swig. "Not only does she expect me to believe her, but she had the nerve to accuse *me* of lying about getting the letters to cover my own lack of interest when I heard she was pregnant."

Taylor was frowning thoughtfully, paper clips forgotten. "I don't remember whether or not I've ever gotten mail for you. When does she claim to have written?" he asked.

Donovan raked a hand through his hair and calculated in his mind. When he reeled off the estimated dates, Taylor picked up another paper clip, but he didn't uncurl it.

"Isn't that about the same time you had to fire that personal secretary you'd hired to handle your correspondence, the one who made such a pest of herself because she had a crush on you?"

His question stopped Donovan cold. "You mean Joyce? What does she have to do with anything?"

Taylor sat back in his chair. "If you were on the circuit and I didn't think I was going to see you right away, I would have forwarded to Joyce any mail I got," he said with a gleam of triumph in his eyes. "Wouldn't the PRCA have done exactly the same thing? And what do you think a jealous woman would do with a letter from an old girl-friend who claimed you were about to become a father?"

Chapter Eleven

Donovan stared hard at Taylor, who was still sprawled in the leather executive chair behind his big desk. Taylor returned his stare with a level one of his own. Only his eyes revealed his feelings. They gleamed with interest.

Taylor was right. Before Donovan had switched to Bill Crouch, his present business manager, he had employed a secretary to handle his mail, help with his schedule on the road and take care of other bothersome details he didn't have the time for. Joyce had worked for him for only a few months before he'd had to replace her because of the embarrassing crush she had on him.

Now he remembered how, more than once, she had shown up at a rodeo with some lame excuse that could have been dealt with over the phone. When she failed to pass on a couple of messages from the woman he was seeing at the time, he had let Joyce go.

"I'd forgotten all about her," he told Taylor, who nodded with satisfaction. "After I fired her, Mrs. Patten took over until I hired Bill." She had been a retired office manager who treated him more like a son than a prospective lover. The most personal thing she'd ever done was to send him homemade cookies on his birthday.

"What would have prevented Joyce from reading and then destroying a letter or two from any woman she saw as a threat?" Taylor asked.

"There's no way to find out now," Donovan replied. "Even if I tracked her down, she probably wouldn't admit anything."

Taylor leaned back in his chair, leather creaking, and stacked his booted feet on the corner of his desk. "All I'm saying is that something like that could have happened," he pointed out. "Are you willing to bet your marriage that it didn't?"

Donovan allowed himself one unprintable expletive as he raked his fingers through his hair. "I climbed all over Bobbie when she gave me that story about the letters," he remembered out loud, jumping to his feet to pace the length of the small room. "And I really came unglued when she accused me of ignoring my own child." His chest contracted painfully as he pictured her, alone and pregnant, waiting for a reply to her plea that never came. And then he, arrogant ass that he was, had asked with a sneer why she hadn't just come after him.

Sick at heart, he curled one hand into a fist and slammed it into the steel front of a tall file cabinet.

"That your riding hand?" Taylor asked quietly, distracting him from his self-flagellation.

"I've got to talk to Bobbie." She'd probably throw his apology back in his face, but he needed to try—for his own sake, if for no other reason.

It was Taylor's turn for caution. "We don't know for sure that's what happened."

The urgency leaked from Donovan like the air from a punctured tire. More confused than ever, he sank heavily back into his chair. "You're right," he grumbled. What bothered him the most was his immediate desire to grab at any excuse to absolve his wife from guilt. When had it become so important to explain away her alleged lies? Was it when he'd married her, when he had first taken her to bed or when he realized he still loved her? God, what a mess.

Another city, another rodeo, another strange hotel. Donovan stood with his back to the window, draperies open to the moonlight, and watched his wife. She lay sleeping in the big bed they shared, one hand cushioning her cheek.

Earlier that night he had made love to her again. As usual, once his immediate satisfaction had begun to fade, his hunger for her had returned, as steady and unrelenting as his own heartbeat.

Even now as he stood in the dark room, he wondered whether he would ever get enough of her. Wondered, too, if she would ever return the feelings he'd given up denying, at least to himself. She might open her arms willingly enough and respond to him so ardently that she stole his breath, but she hadn't said a word about her emotions.

Was it the excitement of the circuit and his celebrity status she had come to enjoy? If so, what would happen when he retired to the quiet and predictability of ranch life? How she felt about him was only one of the worries that kept him from going back to sleep tonight.

Perhaps he hadn't always made the best choices in life, but he wouldn't have thought of himself as a coward. But a coward he was.

In the days since they had left Taylor's ranch and resumed the whirl of rodeos, interviews and public appearances, he still hadn't admitted to Bobbie that he had a good idea what might have become of the letters she insisted she wrote.

He hadn't been able to figure out a way to tell her how sorry he was for doubting her. The more he had mulled over the scenario Taylor had painted so realistically, the more he believed in its likelihood. His brother was right about one thing: they would never know for sure. Donovan, on the other hand, had come to know his wife pretty well since he had all but blackmailed her into joining him.

Well enough to see that deception wasn't a part of her nature.

Now Donovan bowed his head and pinched the bridge of his nose as he remembered how cold-bloodedly he had threatened to take away her child. And what had she done in retaliation? Turned Rose against him? Upset his busy schedule? Made his life hell?

No. Despite himself, he smiled at her sleeping form, bathed in silver by the moonlight streaming into the room. Instead of taking revenge, she had given him the space to forge a relationship with his daughter; she had shown him how best to deal with a four-year-old; and she had generously shared Rose's love without a hint of jealousy. And then, when he had pushed her again, she had married him and let his family think their union was a love match.

Donovan rubbed his smarting eyes with the heels of his hands. Last of all, she had taken him into her bed and responded to him as no other woman ever had. She'd given him a child and had somehow restored the faith in himself he hadn't even realized he'd lost. And while he was busy exploiting every one of her favors, all he had given her in return was distrust.

Even today, she had astounded him with her generosity. After he rode a mean little bull misnamed Grasshopper that spun him like a top and nearly succeeded in yanking his riding arm from its socket, his shoulder ached like a sore tooth. He'd tried to ignore the pain, but Bobbie must have noticed him favoring that arm.

As soon as they had eaten and bid Rose good-night, Bobbie sent him to the shower with instructions to let the hot water beat on his shoulder for a good five minutes. When he had finally come out with a towel draped around his hips, he found her in a red satin nightie that barely brushed the tops of her thighs. Its scoop neck revealed more of her curves than it covered. Her expression was one of thoughtful concentration, making him wonder how fast he could distract her.

"Lie down on your stomach." As she waved him toward the bed, she stole his towel.

"You sound pretty bossy," he teased with a crooked smile. "Got a whip hidden somewhere? Are you going to pull out handcuffs when you have me where you want me?"

She let her approving gaze drift down his body. "Lie down and find out," she purred.

Immediately he responded to the sensual promise smoldering in her eyes as the blood drained from his head. It left him dizzy. Lying down seemed like a good idea. Obediently, he did as she asked.

The mattress gave as she knelt beside him. Her perfume filled his senses and he started to rise, biting back a groan when he lifted his sore shoulder. Before he could try to move again, she straddled his hips.

The satin gown was the only thing she wore. He could feel her moist heat caressing his bare skin. Lucky the mattress was soft or he might have been seriously maimed when she leaned down, her breath tickling his ear. Her satin-covered breasts stroked his back as sweetly as a courtesan's knowing hands.

"You're going to enjoy this." Bobbie snuggled closer, sending his pulse into overdrive.

If he could have spoken with the sudden lump in his throat, he would have agreed, but all he managed was a ragged groan.

She began smoothing lotion over his aching muscles. His thought processes evaporated. She started with his arms, spreading the lotion from biceps to fingertip. Working patiently, she kept up the subtle attack until the protesting aches and knots were loose and warm and his bones had turned to water. Somewhere during her ministrations, his groans had become moans of pleasure.

"Oh, that feels good," he managed to say as she administered to him. He tried to wiggle his fingers and chuckled softly when they responded sluggishly to his silent command.

Meanwhile, she'd moved on to his shoulders. He must have dozed off while she was easing away his tension. The next thing he knew, she was kneeling on the mattress at his side, kneading his buttocks and the backs of his thighs. More relaxed than he'd been in weeks, he realized dazedly that if there had been a hotel fire at that moment, they would have had to haul him out in a wheelbarrow. He doubted his legs would support him.

By the time Bobbie had massaged down to his feet and back up past his knees, the nerve endings along the insides of his thighs were sending him a frantic message.

At some point, her touch had altered slightly. As her hand made one more stroke up his leg, wandering ever closer to the part of him recovering the fastest from his limp state, he finally found the strength to turn onto his back.

Bobbie murmured a protest.

Naked as he was, hiding his reaction to her touch wasn't an option. When her gaze wandered over him, her mouth curved into the kind of smile he'd once seen a prospector give a gold nugget. Struggling for control, Donovan curled his hands into fists at his sides and watched through slitted eyes to see what she would do next. Every muscle in his body was twice as rigid as it had been before the sensual massage.

"And I wanted to relax you," she cooed with false regret as his arousal grew so hard he was sure he could have split a diamond with no trouble.

"You did relax me," he managed to reply before she bent her head, dark hair falling forward in a silken curtain, and his voice went the way of his brain and his self-control. If she did what her intent expression suggested, he'd erupt like a new volcano. He felt her breath and then the brush of her lips against his straining flesh as he jerked into a sitting position and grabbed for her.

"How's your shoulder?" she gasped right before he whirled her onto her back and covered her mouth in a kiss of pure possession and raw need.

"My shoulder's fine," he growled, breaking the seal of their lips as he made a place for himself between her thighs. Before he could test her readiness with his hand, her legs were wrapped around his waist. She arched against him.

"Now," she pleaded. "Donovan, please."

A loaded gun couldn't have stopped him.

Almost immediately, he felt her climax. Groaning her name, he followed her into oblivion.

After his heart rate had finally returned to a semblance of normality and his breathing had slowed, he'd begun a stumbling apology for refusing to believe she had written him about Rose. The only problem was that when he risked a quick peek to gauge her reaction, he saw instead that she had fallen asleep. It would have taken a harder heart than his—and a braver one—to awaken her.

Now as he stood by the window and watched her sleep, he remembered the sensation of being gloved so snugly within her. His body tightened once again in mindless reaction. Then he remembered all the barriers that still lay between them and wondered if they would ever find lasting happiness in each other's arms.

The sun beat down on Bobbie's bare head as she locked the car and hurried through the arena parking lot, weaving between the rows of vehicles as she headed toward the back entrance where she was supposed to meet her husband and their daughter.

Jennifer, who had come on the road with them to help take care of Rose, had the morning off. Donovan had brought Rose down early while Bobbie finished writing a couple of letters. Now she spotted him standing with a group of cowboys. Rose was holding his hand as she looked around, probably bored by the adult conversation.

Bobbie waved, but Rose was looking in the other direction. Her friend, Sarah, waved and shouted something Bobbie was too far away to hear.

Rose pulled on Donovan's hand, but he appeared deep in conversation with one of the bullfighters. She tugged again and he leaned down just as a burst of masculine laughter distracted him. Sarah shouted again and Rose let go of him.

What happened next took place so fast that Bobbie didn't have time to take it in until it was over. An approaching pickup sent up a plume of dust as Rose darted out between two parked cars.

A scream was ripped from Bobbie's throat. Sarah's father shouted a warning and Donovan spun around to see where Rose had gone. Before either he or Bobbie could move, there was a screech of brakes. A choking cloud of dust went up and someone dove into the path of the truck.

Sobbing, Bobbie began to run. When she got to Rose, lying in the gravel, Donovan was kneeling beside her.

"Honey, are you okay?" he demanded. "Oh, God, let her be all right."

"I hurt my hands," Rose sobbed as she sat up in the dirt. "Ow, ow, they're stinging." The knees of her tiny blue jeans were dirty and one was ripped.

"Did the truck hit her?" Bobbie could hardly believe that her baby was still alive. Tears of relief threatened to choke her.

Donovan scooped Rose into his arms, his face chalky. "Someone pushed her out of the way."

His words didn't make sense. Bobbie had seen the truck, had seen Rose right in front of it. In her mind, she could still see it.

She fell to her knees, barely feeling the rocky ground. There were angry red scrapes on the palms of Rose's hands. Her face was streaked with dirt and tears. Nausea surged in Bobbie's throat and she lifted her baby from Donovan's arms. Holding her close and rocking her, she recited a soundless prayer of gratitude.

"I'm sorry," Donovan gasped, face tormented. "It happened so fast. I should have been watching her more closely."

"It's okay, baby," Bobbie murmured to Rose. "Shh, it's okay." She offered Donovan a smile that trembled around the edges.

"I've got to check on the other guy," he said, getting to his feet.

"Someone call the medics," a masculine voice shouted. "This man's hurt bad."

Bobbie whirled around, still clutching Rose tightly. A knot of men were all bending over someone lying in the gravel by the car. His long, tangled hair hid his face. A black cowboy hat lay crumpled in the dust.

"It's Reese!" a calf roper she knew exclaimed. "He needs help."

"I've got a phone in my car." A short, thin man hurried away as Bobbie stared, horrified, at the crumpled, still body.

Oh, God, was he dead?

"He jumped right in front of the pickup and pushed your little girl out of the way," said a bullfighter Bobbie recognized. "Bravest thing I ever saw."

"Pitched him over the hood," said someone else, spitting a long stream of tobacco. "I was standing right here, saw the whole thing. See that broken windshield? He hit it with his shoulder."

Bobbie felt ill.

Nearby, Donovan knelt over Reese's still body. "J.D., can you hear me? Are you okay?"

Reese didn't reply and his eyes remained closed. He was breathing and Donovan didn't see any bleeding.

"Thanks, man," he said, taking J.D.'s limp hand. After a few moments he saw a sheriff's deputy. An aid car pulled up, lights flashing. Two medics jumped out and pushed past the group of spectators that had already gathered.

A muscle jerked in Donovan's cheek as he squeezed J.D.'s hand and then released it. He knew the other bull rider had probably saved his daughter's life. But at what price to J.D.'s own?

His eyes were closed and his face was lined with pain. From the way his body was twisted, Donovan suspected his leg might be broken.

"Move back, please. Let us take care of this man." The paramedics knelt beside J.D.'s prone body.

Donovan moved back to where the deputy was already questioning witnesses. The driver of the truck, a young kid who looked as if he wanted to cry, was talking earnestly to him.

"I didn't even see them. The little girl came out of nowhere. I was hitting my brakes when the cowboy ran in front of the truck. There was nothing I could do, I swear."

He looked no more than twenty. His freckles stood out on his white face beneath a hat with an elaborate feather hatband.

"You were going a mite fast," someone told him while Donovan looked back at Reese. The paramedics were checking his vitals. Thank God he'd been there. Taking a deep, shaky breath, Donovan sent up a silent prayer that Reese would be okay.

"How is he?" Donovan asked one of the paramedics.

"His leg's broken, maybe his pelvis. Don't know about his back."

A chill slid down Donovan's spine. What would this do to Reese's season? He'd been so close all month that Donovan would have sworn he could feel J.D.'s breath on the back of his neck.

"How do you feel?" the paramedic asked.

J.D.'s eyes opened, his expression stoic. "Like a bull stomped me." The skin around his mouth was white with pain. He shifted his head and saw Donovan.

"Is she—?"

"Don't try to talk," one of the paramedics told him while the other started an IV.

Donovan had to clear his throat before he could answer. "She's fine, because of you. I can't thank—"

J.D. turned his head and closed his eyes as Donovan felt a hand on his shoulder. He glanced around to see the deputy.

"I have a few questions," he said. "Would you come over to my car so I can make out a report?"

"Yeah, sure." Donovan followed him to his cruiser and told him what he knew.

The deputy pushed back his hat as he glanced over at J.D. The paramedics had taped his injured leg to his other one and fastened a cervical collar around his neck.

"Hell of a thing for him to do," the deputy muttered. "Was your little girl hurt?"

"Just her hands where she fell in the gravel." Donovan looked for Bobbie and saw that Mary Pat was with her. Danny was headed over to where Donovan stood with the deputy.

The paramedics had slid a board under J.D. and were lifting him onto a stretcher. As soon as he was loaded into the aid car, it pulled away, siren wailing.

"We'll take Bobbie and Rose back to your hotel," Danny said. "That okay with you?"

"I appreciate it," Donovan replied as he raised his hand to Bobbie. Guilt and remorse washed over him like an icy wave as she signaled him back.

"I can stay with Rose," Bobbie told Donovan as he sat in their suite with their daughter on his lap. "Jennifer's here, too." Bobbie smiled at the other girl before she spoke again to Donovan. "You should go to the hospital and see J.D."

By the time Donovan had finished answering the deputy's questions and come back to the hotel to check on his daughter and his wife, Bobbie and Jennifer had already taken care of Rose's hands and calmed her down. Now his arms tightened around her and he touched his cheek to hers.

"I'm sorry, Daddy," she said anxiously. "I didn't mean to run away from you."

"It's okay, princess." His heart was still thudding anxiously. "I'm glad you weren't badly hurt."

"But the truck hit that man." There was worry in her dark eyes. "I was mad at him when he pushed me, but then he got hurt. Do you think he knows I'm not mad anymore?"

"I'm sure he understands." Donovan glanced at Bobbie. "I'd better go to the hospital."

Her heart went out to him. His expression was grim and she knew he blamed himself for everything. She, too, was still badly shaken by what had only missed being a tragedy by the narrowest of margins.

"Maybe Mr. Reese isn't too badly hurt after all," Jennifer said with a hopeful expression.

"I know his leg's broken," Donovan replied. "I want to make sure he has everything he needs and that his family's been notified. It's the least I can do for now."

"Good idea," Bobbie said. "And see that he understands how grateful we are. Tell him I'll be by tomorrow to thank him myself."

Giving Rose a kiss before he shifted her off his lap, Donovan got to his feet. The paleness had finally left his face, but his gaze was still haunted, his mouth a bitter line beneath his mustache.

With sudden insight, Bobbie put her arms around him. He hauled her close and bent his head to rest his cheek against her hair. A shudder went through him.

"Bobbie, I'm—"

"It's okay," she murmured, knowing how badly he needed the words. "It could have happened when she was with anyone."

Briefly, his arms tightened. She felt his kiss against her hair and then he let her go. Gratitude flashed in his eyes and his brief smile was crooked.

"I'll be back as soon as I can," he promised. "Or I'll call you." As he turned to say goodbye to Rose and Jennifer, Bobbie sent up another silent prayer of thanks for her daughter and then added one for J. D. Reese. If he was badly hurt, he was going to need all the prayers he could get.

"He's still in surgery," a young woman told Donovan when he got to the hospital and asked about J.D. "If you go to the surgical waiting room, the doctor will speak to you there when she's done."

Donovan got some coffee he didn't want from the vending machine and went down the hall to a small room containing several chairs, a stack of magazines and a partially finished jigsaw puzzle on a round table. He was surprised to find the room empty. He'd thought some of J.D.'s friends would be there, but then he glanced at his watch and realized the afternoon show was still in progress.

For once, Donovan hadn't given a thought to missing his ride. Apparently no one else was willing to miss theirs for a loner like J.D.

If it wasn't for Rose, Donovan wouldn't have been here, either, he acknowledged to himself with a twinge of guilt—but then neither would Reese. Donovan had given up on being friendly toward him, as had most of the other bull riders. Now Donovan owed him a debt he could never begin to repay.

Not only had Reese saved Rose, but he might very well have forfeited his chance at the National Finals to do so.

Donovan took a swallow of the lukewarm, bitter coffee. Grimacing, he got to his feet to toss the rest. Just then, the door to the waiting room flew open, admitting a small Asian woman in surgical scrubs.

"I'm Dr. Kee," she said. "Are you here for Mr. Reese?"

Donovan's boots and Stetson must have tipped her off. "That's right. How is he?"

"We just set his leg and his hip. The socket was crushed and his femur is broken. That's the long bone in the thigh. I'm more worried about his hip. Other than that, he has a badly bruised shoulder and a sprained wrist. No sign of any internal injuries, but we'll watch him pretty closely for a while." Her black eyes were somber. "Are you a relative?"

"Friend," Donovan corrected, realizing suddenly that it was true. No matter how he'd felt about Reese in the past, all that was now changed.

The surgeon nodded with apparent satisfaction. "Well, he's still sedated and he'll be in recovery for another hour or so. You can wait in his room if you'd like. Oh, would you stop by the office on your way? Perhaps you could give them some information about him."

"Sure." Donovan wasn't about to admit that all he knew about his "friend" was his name and his occupation.

"If you have any questions, I'll be around." Dr. Kee turned to leave.

"There is one thing," Donovan said. "J.D.'s a bull rider. How long will he be laid up?"

She frowned thoughtfully. "I would think for a few months, at least."

Donovan's heart sank at the news. "That's what I was afraid of." How was Reese going to manage? Rodeo cow-

boys had no sick leave. When they didn't work—and win—
they didn't get paid.

After Donovan had thanked the doctor, he went to the
business office. The woman there was obviously disappointed that he knew no one in J.D.'s family to contact.
Then her eyes widened when he told her he was taking responsibility for the other man's account and handed her his
ID.

"Just send the whole thing to my business manager,"
Donovan said, giving her Bill Crouch's business card.
"He'll take care of anything J.D. needs."

If she wondered why Donovan was paying the bills for a
man whose age or address he didn't even know, she kept it
to herself.

When he was through, Donovan located Reese's room.
He had just settled his tall frame into an uncomfortable
molded plastic chair when a nurse poked in her head and
asked if he wanted some coffee.

Remembering his last cup, he hastily shook his head.

"It's not from the vending machine," she replied with a
smile. "We make our own right at the desk. Sure you won't
change your mind?"

"Thanks, I will." He asked if he could use the phone on
the nightstand to call Bobbie. By the time the nurse came
back with the coffee, he'd passed on what he knew and
asked about Rose. When he heard that she seemed to have
recovered from her scare, he settled back to wait.

It was a couple of hours later by the time Bobbie heard
Donovan's key in the door. When he came in, she put a
finger to her lips. After a bowl of soup and half a grilled-
cheese sandwich provided by room service, Rose had finally fallen asleep. Jennifer was sitting with her in the other
room and Bobbie didn't want to wake her.

"How's J.D.?" she asked quietly.

Donovan hauled her into his arms and held her tight for a moment as worry skittered down her spine. It wasn't right that J.D. had to suffer for doing something so unselfish.

"He's feeling well enough to be as ornery as a rattler with a skin rash," Donovan drawled disgustedly. "As soon as a couple of his buddies showed up, he made no bones about kicking me out."

"Did you tell him how grateful we are?" Bobbie demanded. She intended to thank him herself before they left the next day, unless Donovan changed his plans.

"I tried." He was scowling. "I told him I wanted to pay his medical bills, to call anyone he wanted notified, to take care of his rig and the rest of his stuff, but he made it real clear he had no use for my help. Just kept insisting that he'd manage." Head bowed, Donovan sighed and rubbed his hand across the back of his neck.

"What about family?" Bobbie asked. "Had they been called?"

"One of his buddies said he didn't think Reese has anyone but his mother, and she's too ill to travel."

"We'll just have to do what we can for him without his cooperation," Bobbie replied, determined.

Donovan chuckled humorlessly. "You don't know Reese."

Bobbie's determination wavered the next morning when she left Rose in Jennifer's capable hands and went to the hospital with some magazines and a potted plant, only to see a No Visitors sign posted on Reese's hospital room door. She explained to the nurse who she was, but the younger woman shook her head.

"I'm sorry, but he was adamant. No visitors."

After a failed attempt to find his doctor, Bobbie gave up and went back to the hotel. She and Donovan discussed the situation and he, too, tried to visit Reese again. When he was equally unsuccessful, he left J.D. a note with Bill Crouch's phone number and a plea for Reese to let them help. Then he and Bobbie decided that no purpose would be served by hanging around. In a couple more hours they were in the air on their way to South Dakota.

"Rose will be fine with me," Donovan argued. Bobbie had mentioned wanting to get her hair trimmed, and Jennifer was at the laundry, but now Bobbie seemed reluctant to go. It had been a week since the accident and she had hardly let Rose out of her sight. He was beginning to realize it was him she no longer trusted with their little girl. The knowledge was eating a hole right through him.

"Bobbie," he said quietly, gripping her arm and looking into her face, "you know how sorry I am about what happened. I swear I won't be so careless again. Let me prove it to you."

She studied his face, nibbling her lip with even white teeth as she played with her hair.

"It's okay," she said. "I really don't need to have it cut yet. I can probably go a couple more weeks."

Frustration rose within him, but he fought it down. Anger wouldn't help. "Whatever you think," he muttered, defeated. She still didn't understand how he felt about Rose and about her. How could she, when he was afraid to tell her? And how could he expect her to, when she had such a fresh reason to disbelieve him? Would Bobbie ever trust him with Rose again, or with her own heart?

Chapter Twelve

"Mr. J. D. Reese's room, please." Donovan had phoned the hospital every day for the last three weeks, but not once had the man taken his calls. The nurses told Donovan precious little about J.D.'s condition, only that he was doing as well as could be expected.

"Mr. Reese is no longer a patient here. He's been released," came the voice over the phone.

"Where did he go?" Donovan demanded.

"I'm sorry, sir, but I don't have that information."

Frustrated by Reese's obstinacy, Donovan gripped the receiver tighter when something else occurred to him. "Has his bill been paid?"

"I'll have to transfer you." The line clicked and he was treated to elevator music for several seconds before another disembodied voice came on the line.

Donovan repeated his question.

"Are you a relative?" asked the masculine voice.

"No, I'm—" He took a deep breath. "Forget it. Thanks, anyway." He replaced the receiver with exaggerated care, resisting the urge to slam it down in sheer frustration. He checked with Bill, but his business manager had received nothing about Reese's account from the hospital. It figured.

Maybe one of J.D.'s buddies would know where he'd gone. Meanwhile, Donovan had a bull to ride.

Now that his main rival was out of the running, at least temporarily, Donovan had a clear lead in the standings. Even so, it was too late in the season for complacency. A lot could still happen.

"Did you find out anything about J.D.?" Bobbie asked when Donovan exited the arena dressing room to join her and Rose.

"I asked a couple of his buddies, but no one's talking. I even told them I wanted to pay his medical bills. Bud Hawk said he's too all-fired stubborn to accept help from anyone." Donovan chuckled humorlessly. "As if I hadn't already figured that out."

He shifted his gear bag from one hand to the other and slapped his Stetson against his thigh to remove any lingering arena dust. Considering the bull he'd drawn today, he was lucky all he'd lost was his hat.

"I guess J.D. just doesn't want to be found," Bobbie commented as they wove their way through the crowd to the exit.

Donovan had to agree. Perhaps he had managed to sock away enough of his earnings from the last few years that he didn't need Donovan's help.

Well, he'd done all he could to find J.D. short of hiring a private investigator. After their spectacular lack of success in finding a trace of his own missing parents or his sister, Donovan wasn't about to throw away any more money looking for a bull rider who didn't want to be found. Sooner or later J.D. would turn up on the circuit. Until then, Donovan had other things to think about.

They dropped Jennifer off at her mother's on their way to the partially remodeled house on the land he was slowly turning back into a working ranch. The house was fairly small, with two bedrooms and a bathroom with a claw-foot tub upstairs, and a kitchen, living room and remodeled bath on the main floor.

"It's beautiful here," Bobbie said as she looked out the bay window in the living room. The two of them had just tucked Rose into her new twin bed upstairs. There was a matching dresser and a nightstand, as well. Donovan had arranged for the set to be delivered while they were on the road.

The furniture was a little girl's dream, painted palest yellow and decorated with sprays of daisies and buttercups. Rose had loved it on sight and so had Bobbie. Trust Donovan to know the way to a little girl's heart, she thought now as she gazed through the tall window at the twilight beyond.

Remembering back to those first awkward hamburger dates in Yuma, she could scarcely believe how far he had come as a father. She was even beginning to trust that he intended to stay in Rose's life for the long haul.

As far as her own life and their marriage went, she wasn't so sure. She knew the routines of her body well, and a suspicion had begun to form that she had no intentions of sharing with her husband until she was able to get to a drugstore. Time enough for him to know after she made sure there was really news to tell.

"I'm glad you like it here," he said as he joined her at the window. He had showered earlier and she could smell the subtle after-shave he favored. He had worn the same one for years and it still brought back memories of the first time she had noticed it. If she'd had a crystal ball back then to see the future, would she have done anything differently?

She thought of Rose. No, probably not.

Now Donovan slid an arm around her shoulders. "Let's turn in," he suggested in a husky tone that sparked a response along her nerve endings.

As Bobbie rested her head against his chest and sighed, he was tempted to ask what had been troubling her the last few days. He knew she'd had something on her mind because she was distracted, even around Rose.

It wasn't like her. From the way she responded to him in bed, he knew the horror of Rose's near accident in Houston had finally begun to fade. If Bobbie blamed him, she would never have been able to make love with him the way she did. She was too honest for that. There would have been a barrier between them that he would have sensed when he took her in his arms.

Now he tightened his embrace, wishing she would confide in him. Instead, he let her pull away and then he took one of her hands in his.

"Come on," he urged. "I know you're tired." They had spent most of the day since their arrival traipsing around the ranch as he described his plans—right there would go the new brood-mare barn, while the existing stable would house the stallions and riding stock. The big corral would make a dandy outdoor arena. Out farther were the outbuildings and pastures. In the other direction was the site where he wanted to build a larger house.

She had listened indulgently as he described in great detail everything he saw so clearly in his mind's eye. Rose skipped along beside them or collected rocks from the edge of the creek that wandered through the property. By the time they returned to the old ranch house, Donovan's pockets were bulging with lucky pebbles.

Only after the three of them had eaten dinner—a simple meal of hot dogs cooked on a small barbecue, beans and chips—did he realize that, as avid a listener as Bobbie had been, she'd had precious little to say except for an occasional suggestion. Nor had she spoken much for the last few days, now that he thought about it.

"Is anything wrong?" he asked now as they went arm in arm to the stairway. "Rose isn't sick, is she?" She had seemed okay to him, but perhaps Bobbie's motherly radar had picked up something he missed. "Does she really like the ranch? Do you?" Perhaps that was it. Bobbie was just being polite.

She turned and faced him, and he saw the tension around her dark eyes. "Rose is fine. She loves it here and so do I. It's a wonderful change from the pressure of being on the road so much."

"If there's anything you don't like, I can change it," he offered rashly. This would be her home, too, and he wanted her to be happy here.

Bobbie shook her head. "It all sounds terrific. Throw in a hot tub on the deck and I'll be a happy woman."

Her lighthearted words failed to ease his mind as long as he could see the stress on her face, feel it humming along her nerves when he touched her.

"Honey, what's wrong?" he asked again, much later that night when he woke to find her slipping out of bed. "Did you hear Rose?" Usually their daughter slept like a rock, but her slightest muffled whimper could have Bobbie on her feet. No doubt being a single parent for all those years had honed her parental awareness to an advanced degree.

"Too much iced tea before bed," she said now as she padded toward the door. "When I was pregnant with Rose, I never slept through the night."

By the time her comment had soaked into Donovan's sleep-saturated brain and had him sitting bolt upright in bed, she had already disappeared down the hall.

Hands shaking, Donovan pulled on his shorts and got to his feet. Suddenly he was too restless to stay in bed.

Had he heard right? Pregnant? Was it really a possibility? They had been so careful, except for that one time at his brother's. And then she'd been sure it was safe.

Not that any of it mattered now. What did matter was how she felt about bearing another of his children, and how he did, and what it would do to a relationship already strained by circumstances.

He paced the length of the room impatiently, waiting for her return from the bathroom. Then he stopped, a silly grin spreading across his face.

Another child. A little boy or maybe another girl he could help raise from the start. His gut reaction was one of sheer pleasure. No matter how else the news might affect his relationship with Bobbie, he wanted another child. And he wanted that child with her.

At last, her head poked around the open door of the bedroom and her gaze tracked him from the empty bed to where he stood, feet braced apart, arms folded across his wide chest.

Damn, but it was going to hurt if she wasn't anticipating the possibility with as much enthusiasm as he was.

"Mind explaining your parting shot?" he asked lightly, fighting the urge to scoop her up and cover her face with kisses. And not daring. Not until he saw how she felt about all this. And how she felt about him for bringing it on her once again.

From where Bobbie stood in the doorway, he looked like a tawny-haired outlaw. All he needed to complete the picture was a set of six-shooters in leather holsters.

Her unguarded response to all that masculinity pulled her back into the room. Closing the door behind her, she contemplated his question and the suspicion she hadn't meant to share until or unless it became a reality.

"I don't know anything for sure," she said quickly. "The possibility just slipped out."

"And you didn't mean to tell me, did you?" he guessed, smile fading.

Her chin went up. "Do you blame me? There's really nothing to tell."

He stared hard, and then he sighed. "What I want to know is how you feel about the possibility."

It was her turn to stare. "How I feel?" she echoed dumbly.

"Yeah." He took a few restless steps around the end of the bed until he was standing in front of her. Close enough to touch, her senses mused. "During your first pregnancy, you were alone, money was tight and you had a lot of decisions to make." His brow quirked and he glanced down at her flat stomach, hidden by her short flowered gown. "You had to decide about keeping the baby, maybe whether you'd even have it. How'm I doing so far?"

She swallowed, opened her mouth, but didn't say anything. While she'd been in the bathroom, he must have been giving this some thought.

"By the way," he said more gently, "did I ever thank you for having Rose, for keeping her instead of giving her to strangers? If I haven't, I'm thanking you now." His expression was tender, making her breath catch.

As he often did, he managed to touch something buried inside her. "You're welcome." Her voice sounded scratchy to her own ears.

"Anyway, if you really are pregnant," he continued as if he hadn't been sidetracked, "how will you feel?"

Pressing her palms together as if she were about to pray, Bobbie turned away from him. "I'm not sure." It wasn't a totally honest response, but it was all she could share without laying her feelings completely bare.

"Honest enough." His tone was light again, and it occurred to her that he was taking risks, as well. "When will you know?" he asked. "I mean, whether you are or not."

"As soon as I get to a drugstore and buy one of those home pregnancy tests," she replied. "Probably on the way down to Boulder."

His smile was as relaxed as if that wasn't three days away. "Will you tell me as soon as you find out?"

She blushed. "Of course." It wouldn't be fair to ask how he felt about the possibility, since she hadn't really answered his question, but she was still tempted. He loved Rose, she knew, but would another child make him even happier or would he feel doubly trapped?

"Come to bed," he invited, distracting her. In the shadowy room, she could just make out the width of his sculpted chest. Without warning, desire that was hot and strong rose up within her.

"Yes," she murmured with deceptive docility. She slid beneath the covers and turned to watch him pull down his shorts.

His gaze locked on hers as his hands went to the waistband. Before he could strip them off, she heard the sound of an engine coming down the long driveway. They both froze and she glanced at the clock.

Two-thirty. It had to be bad news.

Donovan went to the window and peered out. "That looks like Taylor's truck," he said as he grabbed his jeans and sat on the edge of the bed to don them and his boots. "Something must be wrong, but why didn't he just pick up the phone?"

Bobbie had no answer as she switched on the bedside lamp. Her chest was tight with worry. She had come to love Donovan's brother, as well as his wife and the twins. *Dear Lord*, she prayed, *don't let it be Ashley or the baby she's expecting.*

"It can't be anyone in the family, or he'd be with them," she reasoned aloud. "I can't imagine—" She broke off abruptly as she scrambled from the bed and slipped into the cotton robe that matched her thin nightie. At least the robe, with its short, puffed sleeves, buttons and demure knee-length hem, was fairly modest. "I'm coming with you," she said unnecessarily.

Donovan waited in the doorway, teeth clenched so tight she could see a muscle ticking along his jaw. She touched the rigid muscle of his arm in a silent attempt at comfort and then followed him as he hurried downstairs.

Before he got to the bottom of the stairs, they heard knocking on the front door. In a few more strides, Donovan had the lights on and the door open.

Bobbie hovered behind him, trying to read the expression on Taylor's face as he stepped inside. His eyes were dark and stormy, the lines bracketing his mouth and nose deeper than the last time she'd seen him. For once he was hatless and his dark hair was mussed as if he'd repeatedly raked it with his fingers.

"What is it?" Donovan asked him without preamble, gut twisted with a premonition of disaster. When he had first recognized Taylor's pickup, he'd hoped it was some wonderful news that wouldn't keep till morning. Now that he'd seen his brother's eyes, he knew better.

Taylor gave him a tired smile and then he glanced at Bobbie. "I'm sorry to get you both up like this. Could you make some coffee?"

"Of course. It will only take a minute." She disappeared silently.

"Are you okay?" Donovan asked, leading the way to the kitchen.

"It's been a long night," Taylor replied. "I need the caffeine."

In the kitchen, Donovan pulled out a chair.

Taylor shook his head. "I'd rather stand. You might want to sit down, though."

"The coffee will be ready in a minute," Bobbie said softly. "Can I get you a glass of water?"

"No, thanks." Taylor's gaze remained riveted on Donovan, making him want a cigarette for the first time in years. "There's no easy way to say this, bro. The sheriff came to see me this evening. He had a call from the Idaho State Police."

Donovan was more puzzled than ever. He and Taylor had grown up in Idaho. Except for a few local rodeos during their early days on the road, they hadn't been back.

The coffee was done and Bobbie handed Taylor a cup, then poured more for Donovan and herself.

Taylor thanked her and took a sip. "A crew of fire fighters was battling a forest fire near Twin Falls."

Some dark premonition wrenched at Donovan's gut. Twin Falls was where they had lived with Kirby and their parents.

"In a deep, overgrown ravine near the road, they found the wreckage of a car." Taylor's voice faltered and he rubbed his hand over his face. "God, I can't believe this," he muttered, blinking rapidly.

Nothing could have shaken Donovan as deeply as the sight of his older brother struggling for composure. "Was it our parents' car?" he asked. "Are they alive? Where are they now?" Vaguely, he was aware of Bobbie's hand braced against his back in silent support.

Taylor shook his head, jaw clenched, and moisture filled his eyes. "The sheriff told me they traced the license plate and confirmed the IDs they found inside. They checked the dental records, too."

Donovan shook his head in confusion. "IDs? Dental records? What are you trying to tell me?"

Tears spilled down Taylor's weathered cheeks. "The wreck is over twenty years old," he said slowly. "The remains they found inside have been verified as those of our parents. The police think they've most likely been dead since the night we last saw them."

Chapter Thirteen

Donovan swayed and Taylor pulled out a chair for him. Without protest, Donovan sank into it as he tried to absorb the news his brother had given him. Taylor squatted in front of him, forehead creased in a worried frown.

"I know it's a shock," he said. "You always insisted that our parents were still alive."

Dazed, Donovan shook his head and swiped at his burning eyes. He had never let himself believe, as Taylor had, that their mother and father must be dead or they would have gotten in touch by now.

"The wreck has been there for twenty years?" Donovan asked aloud. "All the time we waited and wondered, their bodies were lying in some ravine?" A great sadness swept over him, pressing down on his chest and squeezing out the air like a giant hand.

Taylor dragged out a bandanna and mopped at his tear-streaked face while Donovan pretended not to notice.

"When I told the sheriff the circumstances behind their disappearance, he said it was likely the wreck happened the night they left. That would explain why there was no trace of them after that." He sipped his coffee while Donovan stared down at his trembling hands.

"Whether someone ran them off the road or Dad lost control," Taylor continued, "their car was hidden in that ravine all these years, until a forest fire led someone to find it."

"Was there any way to tell whether, uh, they died right away?" Donovan asked, nearly choking on the sadness lodged in his throat. "Or if they—" His voice broke and he bowed his head, hating to think of them injured and waiting for help that never came.

Gently, Bobbie stroked his hand, which gripped the arm of his chair. Her soothing touch slowed the wild racing of his heart.

"No," Taylor replied emphatically. "They didn't suffer. Apparently, from the condition of the bodies..." He faltered and then pressed on. "The medical examiner could tell that both of them died instantly."

Donovan swallowed hard as another thought began tormenting him. "Was the car burned?" For some reason, the idea that the fire might have touched them, even after they had been dead for more than two decades, was still upsetting.

Taylor shook his head. "From what the sheriff told me, it burned away the brush that hid the wreck from sight, but the fire leaped over the ravine itself. It's just bare rock, I guess. The car was wedged in pretty tight."

There was a long silence in the room.

"Damn," Donovan finally muttered. "All these years..." His voice trailed off.

"Do you know what this means?" Taylor asked him as he rubbed his throbbing temple.

"Yeah," Donovan replied, suddenly exhausted. "It means they didn't plan on deserting us."

"That's right," Taylor agreed. "They didn't leave because of anything you did. Their disappearance was never your fault."

"Your fault?" Bobbie repeated, shocked. She shifted so she was looking down at her husband's slumped form. "Why would it be your fault? You were only a child."

Donovan looked up, but it was Taylor who answered her question. "Donnie always insisted they took off because he was such a little brat," he said baldly. "Of course, he was wrong. We were normal kids, scrapping with each other and getting in trouble on a pretty regular basis. Our father wasn't exactly an easy man to live with. Actually, he was pretty strict with us, and he wasn't demonstrative. I can't remember him ever kissing or hugging either of us, not even when we got hurt. It was different with Kirby, though. He adored her."

Donovan made a sound of agreement.

"I always suspected," Taylor continued, "that Donnie's theory of them leaving because he didn't do what he was told was a lot of hooey." For the first time since he'd arrived on their doorstep, Taylor managed a crooked grin. "Turns out I was right," he said softly.

Bobbie was too concerned about her husband to smile back. Good Lord, but he must have been carrying around a huge load of guilt all these years.

"Taylor *is* right," she told him, touching his cheek to get his attention. "They would never have deserted you on purpose. This has all been a terrible tragedy, but not in the way you believed for so long." She blinked back tears of her own at the confusion on Donovan's face. "I'm sure they're resting easier now, knowing the truth has finally come out." She held her breath, wondering if he would accept her attempt at comfort.

To her relief, he grabbed her hand and squeezed it. "That could be true," he admitted, voice hoarse. "Wherever they are, they're probably relieved that we know what really happened." He glanced up at Taylor, who had risen to pour himself more coffee.

"What do we do now?" Donovan asked him. "I mean, there must be arrangements that have to be made."

"We're supposed to call Lieutenant Twyman's office in Twin Falls first thing in the morning to let him know what we want to do. I have his number at home." He rubbed his jaw consideringly. "I thought we might get them a plot back there somewhere and have a small, private service. Will you go to Idaho with me?"

Donovan nodded. "Yeah, that sounds fine." He sighed. "Too bad we haven't found Kirby. It would have been nice to have her there, too. She must have wondered all these years why she was given up for adoption."

"We'll find her," Taylor told him. "I haven't given up yet."

"Neither have I."

As Bobbie looked on, Donovan reached for his brother and they hugged each other hard, two big, tough men sharing a deep emotion neither of them made any attempt to hide. Then Donovan reached out his arm and pulled her close so that she, too, was part of their circle.

"The guys should be here soon," Ashley said as Bobbie looked out the kitchen window yet again. Taylor and Donovan had been gone for three days, their commercial flight due back at the Denver airport almost two hours ago. "I wonder how it went. Taylor didn't really say much when he called. Just that everything was taken care of and when to have Buck pick them up."

"Donovan didn't say, either," Bobbie replied as she sat back down and began fiddling with her teacup. "He sounded different on the phone, though. Maybe he's relieved that the mystery has finally been solved, since he felt so guilty."

"Of course," Ashley said calmly as she made another tiny stitch in the baby bib she was embroidering. "From what Taylor told me, Donovan always blamed himself for their disappearance. Just like kids blame themselves when their parents get a divorce." She shook her head sadly and took another tiny stitch. "Your husband managed to hide a lot of emotion behind that killer smile of his."

Bobbie was about to agree when she saw a cloud of dust and then a dirty pickup coming down the road. Protective of his wife's delicate condition even though Ashley insisted she was as strong as a horse, Taylor had forbidden her to make the trip to the busy airport. Ashley had confided in Bobbie that she'd only let his high-handedness pass without comment because his concern for her health was so sweet and because she hated the new airport anyway.

Bobbie and Rose had been staying at the ranch while the men were in Idaho. As impatient as Bobbie was to see Donovan the minute he set foot on Colorado soil, she had agreed to wait at the house with her sister-in-law instead.

"They're here!" she said now as she hurried to the back door. Ashley was right behind her.

"Daddy's home!" one of the twins yelled as he, his brother and Rose all came running from the barn, where they'd been watching a new litter of kittens under Jennifer's careful supervision.

"Daddy, Daddy!" Rose chanted, her chubby legs pumping beneath her shorts, arms flailing as she did her best to keep up with the bigger boys.

As usual, one of her braids had come loose and there was a smear of dirt on her cheek. She looked so happy that sudden tears came to Bobbie's eyes.

All this was because of Donovan, she reminded herself. Even if he did deny getting the letters she wrote him about her pregnancy, he had more than made up for it since. Something in her heart turned over and she realized that his actions of five years before were no longer important. He had given her and their daughter a home, a family and a future with him. What more could Bobbie hope for?

Love, her heart whispered. She still hoped that someday he would come to love her as she loved him.

Bobbie still felt the same when she watched Donovan riding in the NFR, the season finale, in Las Vegas. Ever since he and Taylor had come back from Idaho, he'd been acting as if a tremendous burden had been lifted, and not because she wasn't pregnant.

When she had seen the negative results of the home pregnancy test she'd used the morning after his return, her feelings were decidedly mixed. He hadn't seemed as relieved over the false alarm as she'd expected, either.

"It's okay," he'd murmured, hugging her gently. "We have plenty of time."

She had wanted to ask him what he meant, but Rose chose that moment to interrupt. The intimate mood had been shattered. Neither Bobbie nor Donovan had brought up the subject since, but she still puzzled over his words. They sounded more like comfort than celebration.

Now she watched the chute as her husband lowered himself carefully to the back of a seventeen-hundred-pound bull. It was the eighth round of the final ten, and he'd scored on every ride so far. He was ahead in the average and he was the leading money winner by a comfortable margin.

The chute boss waited for Donovan's signal. Bobbie knew her husband was rubbing the heavily rosined rigging to heat it, then wrapping it around his gloved riding hand. She tried to remain calm while he positioned himself on the thrashing bull.

Bobbie always hated this part. As the gate opened, she pressed a hand to her stomach. As usual, the knot of fear that twisted inside her whenever he rode pulled tight. Until the buzzer sounded and he was safe, she always had to make a conscious effort to breathe. Otherwise, when the eight seconds were up, she would be light-headed from holding her breath.

Rose was seated between her and Taylor, who was there with his boys to cheer Donovan on. Jennifer had gone home to take a full-time job. It was Bobbie's first time at the championships, but coming back to this city brought with it powerful memories.

She watched Donovan stick on the heaving, twisting bull. Watched and counted the seconds. As the buzzer finally signaled the end of the ride, he swung his leg over the animal's wide back and jumped off. At the same time, the bull spun into him. His hand got caught in the rigging and he struggled to free himself as the bull continued to buck and spin.

Bobbie watched, a scream trapped in her throat, as Donovan was flung against the beast repeatedly, as helpless as a rag doll. Both bullfighters came running, one trying to distract the animal as the other did his best to release Donovan's riding hand.

It wasn't easy, since the bull was determined to keep bucking. Endless seconds went by. Finally the rope came loose, freeing Donovan, and slid to the ground.

Donovan stumbled, trying to get his legs under him. Enraged, the bull swung its massive head his way. Bobbie's heart stopped as he was knocked to the ground. The bull ran right over him, Donovan trying to dodge the wicked horns and pounding hooves.

Blindly, Bobbie reached for Rose and hugged her tight, hiding her face. Would this be the time she saw her father's blood spill onto the dirt of the arena?

Even as the thought surfaced, one of the clowns managed to distract the bull by moving dangerously close while the other pulled Donovan to his feet and shoved him toward the fence. As soon as he hit the bottom rung and other hands reached down to pull him to safety, the bullfighter turned back to help his partner. Bobbie was too busy watching Donovan clear the top rail to notice his score.

Donovan was still shaking when he hit the ground on the other side of the fence, barely aware of the applause that followed him or the men who slapped his back. He'd felt the ground vibrate beneath the bull's hooves.

Someone shouted and he turned around in time to take his dirty Stetson and his rigging from the clown. At this particular moment, Donovan wouldn't have gone back into that arena for either. He was still wondering whether it was past time for him to retire when Bobbie hurried to his side.

"We need to talk," she said. Her pupils were dilated, making her normally soft brown eyes appear almost black, and her cheeks were pale.

"Where's Rose?" he asked, glancing around for his daughter. Had the near disaster frightened her?

"She's okay. I left her with your brother."

Donovan barely had time to wonder if it was his ride that had shaken Bobbie up or something else when she herded him into an empty corner near the grandstand as efficiently as a sheepdog with a pregnant ewe. He was tempted to steal a kiss, but something glittering in her expression warned him that this wasn't the time.

"Are you all right?" she asked. "Your arm? Your shoulder? Did you get kicked?" Without waiting for an answer, she spun him around, running her hands over his leather vest in search of injuries. Donovan caught the eye of a passing judge and grinned self-consciously.

"I'm fine," he told Bobbie as he pulled away. Then he saw the tears welling up in her eyes.

"What's wrong?"

"I want you to quit," she burst out as the first tear spilled over and ran down her cheek. "I can't take this anymore. I don't want to watch you die." More tears followed the first one and she wiped at them impatiently.

Donovan stared at her, stunned. He knew she worried. All the wives did, but she'd never acted like this before—overwhelmed by the fear she must have been fighting all along. She must care for him, at least a little.

"I'm not planning on getting hurt," he said reasonably.

She gave him a look that told him how ridiculous his statement sounded. "No kidding." Her voice was dry. "Does anyone?"

"I can't quit," he said in a low voice. "There's a million-dollar endorsement contract on the line if I can win the championship one more time. It's enough to retire on and set up the ranch the way I want." Surely that kind of money would make an impression.

To his surprise, she barely seemed to hear him. "I don't care about the damned money. It won't do you any good if you're not here to spend it," she snapped.

And he'd worried she might miss the fat paychecks and the excitement. Though deeply moved, Donovan knew she couldn't dissuade him. Their whole future rode on his winning. "I can't quit yet," he said bluntly.

"You mean you won't."

"If that's the way you want to see it." When the finals were behind him, they'd sort this all out. So far, his luck had held. All he needed was another good day, a couple more rides.

"Tell you what," he said. "As soon as this is all over, we'll talk. I promise."

Her fingers curled into the edges of his flak jacket and she gave him a hard shake, making his eyes widen.

"Tell you what," she echoed. "When this is over, you retire, win or lose."

The determination in her tone surprised him.

"We'll see." He gave her his most charming smile, the one that deepened the dimple in his cheek.

Bobbie gave him back a baleful glare before she released him and started walking away, toward the dressing room where he had left his equipment bag and extra clothes. When he didn't immediately follow, she turned and motioned impatiently. Suddenly lighthearted although he wasn't sure why, he hurried to catch up with her.

With Bobbie at his side, retirement didn't sound so boring, after all.

Chapter Fourteen

"Did he win?" Rose demanded, pulling on Bobbie's arm. "Did Daddy win the championship?"

Bobbie was almost too busy cheering and clapping to reply. "Yes, honey," she said when she finally realized what her daughter was asking. "Daddy won the whole thing, the National Finals bull-riding title."

On Bobbie's other side, Taylor gave her a thumbs-up and a wink. "Told you he was unbeatable."

As Donovan took his victory ride, circling the arena on a borrowed horse, a palomino as golden as his own hair, the crowd got to its feet and applauded wildly. Not only had he won the title, he had done it by scoring on every one of the ten wild, dangerous bulls he'd drawn during the NFR, a feat very few other bull riders before him had managed to accomplish.

Bobbie watched him waving his hat at the crowd, her heart bursting with the love that had grown since he'd come back into her life. Now that the immediate danger was past, the momentum that had sustained her suddenly drained away, leaving her as vulnerable as an open wound.

Before she faced him, she had to get her emotions back under control. Perhaps one way to get a handle on what she was feeling was to go back where everything had begun, before her common sense had been stampeded by a rodeo bum with a killer grin and her own runaway heart.

"Taylor," she asked over the roar of the crowd, "would you keep Rose with you? I just remembered something I have to do."

He looked surprised. "Now?" he asked. "Are you okay? Is there anything I can help you with?"

Her smile faltered as she struggled for control, tempted to ask if he had any advice on how to deal with a heart that was hoping for a miracle. She knew her heart was what she was risking, loving Donovan so much when he still didn't trust her. When he didn't return her feelings. Wordlessly, she shook her head.

"No, thanks anyway."

No doubt Taylor saw the tears filling her eyes, because his frown increased as he studied her. "It will be okay," he said quietly, reaching past Rose to give her shoulder a brotherly squeeze. "You don't see how he looks at you. Just give him a little more time. He's had a lot to deal with lately."

Bobbie saw that her daughter was watching them intently. Blinking away her tears, she gave her head a shake. "I know that." Her smile wobbled precariously. "I'll catch up with you later."

Before he could say any more, she bent and gave Rose a quick hug. "Stay with Uncle Taylor," she said, kissing her daughter's cheek. "Daddy will be here before you know it."

Rose's chubby face brightened. "Okay, Mommy," she said obediently.

With one last glance at Donovan's brother, Bobbie left her seat and joined the crowd streaming to the exits. She didn't slow down until she was outside, and then she hurried across the parking lot to the car.

Donovan paced the hotel room restlessly, stopping only to glance again at his watch. He had showered and changed his clothes and now he was dying for something to eat.

"Where the hell is she?" he demanded. "Did she say how long she'd be?"

A hotel baby-sitter was watching the children in the suite Taylor had booked for the night, and Donovan was restless. Somehow, his victory didn't seem real until he shared it with his wife, but she hadn't even waited around to congratulate him.

Taylor shrugged. "I told you, all she said was that she had something to do. That was a while ago now. From her expression when she asked me to keep an eye on Rose, I had a bad feeling, but I couldn't very well refuse. Did you two have some kind of argument?"

Donovan shook his head. "Not really. I wonder if being in Vegas again brought back some painful memories for her—I told you we first met during the finals five years ago. She didn't seem to mind when we came here for The Pro Bull Riders' Championship in October, though, so I didn't give it a thought." He shrugged restlessly. "After I got hung up in the rigging, she wanted me to quit whether I won tonight or not, so it isn't the idea of my retiring that upset her," he concluded. "I wish to hell she'd get back here."

"She must love you a heck of a lot," Taylor commented. "To want to trade all this for a dusty old ranch in Colorado." He indicated the opulent suite with his hand.

Even as Donovan discounted his brother's observation, his brain was telling him Taylor had a valid point. He'd been in tight spots before, but this time the threat of danger in the arena had genuinely upset her.

Was it possible he'd misread her feelings? Had she quit blaming him for abandoning her when she was pregnant? Was she finally starting to understand how he felt about his daughter and about her?

"I wish I knew where she was," he said aloud.

Taylor looked thoughtful. "Would she have gone back to some old haunt?" he asked. "Or to visit a friend? What about where you kissed her for the first time or someplace like that? You know how sentimental women can be."

Donovan tugged on one end of his mustache. Would she have? He didn't know. "She may have gone to visit one of the other waitresses from the diner where she worked when we first met. It was torn down a while back." He'd been by there himself, but he wasn't about to admit it. "I don't know about the place where she lived. It was just an old apartment building. She said she didn't know her neighbors very well." There was the hotel where he'd been staying at the time, the place where they had first made love. No, she wouldn't have gone there.

He had first kissed her on the street in front of the diner. He could still remember how sweet she had tasted. Another dead end, though.

Taylor looked puzzled. "All I do know is that there was more going on with her than a simple errand. Unless I miss my guess, she was running away from something."

Donovan grabbed his hat. "I think I'll go check out a few places. You mind?"

"Want me to go with you?"

Donovan shook his head. "Just lend me your truck and tell me where you'll be later."

Taylor tossed him the keys. "It's parked right out front, in about the third row. I think I'll mosey on downstairs and get a beer. Ought to be a few people I remember hanging around the bar."

Donovan pocketed the keys and slapped his brother's back. "Keep your ears open for any news about J. D. Reese," he said. "No one seems to know what happened to him. I'll catch up with you after I find Bobbie."

"Let me know if you need any help," Taylor said as Donovan shut the door behind him.

First he drove by Bobbie's old apartment house, but he didn't spot their rental car, so he went down the street where the diner used to be. Cruising by the Western-wear shop that had replaced it, he drove past the grill where he had taken her for hamburgers.

He slowed, looking through the big front windows, but he didn't see Bobbie. Swearing under his breath, he turned down a side street. There, tucked behind a van, was their car.

He must have missed her in the restaurant. It took him five more minutes to find a place to park Taylor's truck. Finally he left it in a small lot behind the Western store, hoping it wouldn't get towed. Pulse racing, he hurried back to the restaurant, but she wasn't there. He even asked the waitress if there was anyone in the ladies' room. She gave him an odd look, but she shook her head.

"The woman I'm looking for is about this tall," he told her, holding up his hand. "She has long dark hair and she's really pretty."

The waitress, an older woman with short gray hair and bright blue eyes, tipped her head to one side, giving him the once-over. She must have decided he didn't look like a serial killer, because she finally cracked a smile.

"Lost her, did you?"

He returned her grin with a rueful one of his own. He hoped to hell he hadn't. "Let's just say that I temporarily misplaced her."

"I been working since noon and no one like that's been in," the waitress replied. "Were you supposed to meet her here? Maybe one of you misunderstood."

"It's a long story." One he wasn't willing to go into now. Some instinct deep in his gut was urging him to find Bobbie, telling him something important was going on. "Thanks, anyway."

She gave him an appreciative glance. "Good luck."

Touching the brim of his hat with two fingers, he hurried back out the door. Now where?

Two noisy couples in citified Western dress, complete with embroidered satin shirts, designer jeans and boots with silver toes, were coming down the street. One carried a bag from the nearby Western-wear boutique.

A light went on inside Donovan's head. Could Bobbie have returned to the scene of their first meeting for some reason he didn't understand, even if that scene had changed drastically?

Scarcely daring to hope, he walked down the street to Cactus Sam's Western Clothiers and went inside. The place was jam-packed with circular racks of shirts in every fabric and color of the rainbow. Shelves displayed boots made of exotic leathers. Stetsons in a variety of shapes and shades covered two walls. Ornate buckles and bolo ties filled a glass display case by the door. The shop was full of people looking for something to buy, or just looking.

Nowhere did Donovan see anyone who resembled either Bobbie or a genuine cowboy. Even Donovan's new jeans, brightly striped shirt and black leather vest were drab in contrast to the other customers' plumage. Despite his celebrity, he drew few glances as he worked his way through the crowd.

He was about to leave when a knot of patrons shifted and a dark head caught his eye. Mouth going dry, he walked slowly toward the back corner of the store. There, in a chair by the dressing rooms, sat his wife.

As Donovan watched her, he noticed that she had a wistful expression on her face. She was staring at the carpet in front of her, oblivious to everyone, and her fingers were laced so tightly together that her knuckles were white. Moving closer, Donovan saw a tear trembling on her lashes.

He wanted nothing more than to go to her and gather her into his arms. He was just about to when he had second thoughts.

She'd come here for a reason and it wasn't to replenish her wardrobe. Why, then? Melting back into the crowd, he studied her as he pretended to look at a rack of fringed suede jackets. Someone bumped him and muttered an automatic apology. A country song with a driving beat played in the background.

Could their first meeting possibly mean so much to Bobbie that she had come back here to recapture something they had since lost? Was he kidding himself to think she might return some of the feelings he'd been struggling so hard to control?

Did she love him? There was only one way to find out, but first he decided to try giving her back a little of the magic they'd first found on this very spot.

He went over to the glass case of Western buckles and silver jewelry. "Can I borrow that for a few minutes?" he asked a clerk, pointing through the glass. "I won't take it out of the store."

The clerk touched a huge oval buckle, shining like a solid-gold dinner plate as it rested on a bed of black velvet.

"Yeah, that one. Got a wide belt I could put it on?"

Expression curious, the clerk handed him what he'd asked for.

"Thanks," Donovan said. "I'll be back in a minute." Slinging the belt with its elaborate buckle over his shoulder, just as he had his championship belt so long ago, he took a deep breath. What else did he need?

Oh, yeah, he remembered, a long-stemmed red rose. Glancing around, he didn't see any roses. He thought of finding a flower shop and then abandoned the idea. She might disappear while he was gone. Frustrated, he walked over to the front window. At the edge of the holiday display of fringed leather chaps and vests was a red plastic poinsettia in a pot. Feeling slightly foolish, Donovan glanced around and then carefully pulled the flower free.

Artificial poinsettia in hand, he went back toward the corner of the store where Bobbie was still sitting.

"There you are, darlin'," he said as he walked up to her, aware of several other heads turning. "And don't you look as pretty as a newborn foal. I can't wait to show you off."

Bobbie glanced up and then did a double-take as her eyes widened. "Donovan," she whispered, getting to her feet. "How did you find me here?" Now that he had, she felt silly for thinking he might—for hoping it would mean something if he did manage to track her down.

No doubt he was annoyed at the way she'd taken off.

He didn't look annoyed. In truth, he looked as handsome as sin as he stood in front of her wearing his killer smile. There was a light gleaming in his green eyes, a light she hadn't seen since their wedding and one she'd discounted then as a reflection from the chandelier overhead.

Puzzled, she stared at the plastic poinsettia he held in one hand. Where on earth had he gotten that? Then she spotted the ornate gold buckle and the belt slung over his shoulder. Her heart stuttered and then began again, thumping hard inside her chest. Was it possible that he understood after all, that he was trying to give her a message?

Before she could ask, he set down the poinsettia and came over to take her hand in his. Dimly, she was aware that people around them had stopped to watch and that the noise had died down so she could hear music in the background.

"How did I find you?" he asked, repeating her question. "Darlin', I just followed my heart."

As she gaped, speechless with shock, he swept off his hat and bent her back over one arm. The kiss he gave her set her head to spinning and her heart soaring right into her throat. When he finally released her to clapping and cheers, she could only stare.

"Have I forgotten to tell you how very much I love you?" he asked in a soft, husky voice meant for her ears alone.

A woman standing close enough to hear him sighed loudly and pressed a hand to her throat, breaking the spell.

"You do?" Bobbie asked dumbly.

He released her and put his hat back on. Then he crooked his elbow invitingly. "Why don't you come with me and we'll talk about it."

When Bobbie hesitated, the same woman who had sighed said, "Go for it, honey!"

Still recovering from his kiss and his declaration of love, Bobbie slipped her arm through his and followed him mutely on legs that trembled, past the cheering crowd. Word about the tableau must have spread to the front of the store because everyone moved aside for them. At the counter, Donovan slipped the belt from his shoulder.

"Thanks for the loan," he told the wide-eyed clerk.

It dawned on Bobbie then that he really did understand why she'd come back here. Anticipation began to sing along her veins as he led her silently through a narrow alley to a small parking lot at the back of the store.

The lot was deserted except for a couple of cars and Taylor's pickup. Donovan led her over to it, then turned and leaned against the door. She noticed that his smile had been replaced by a more solemn expression.

"There are a couple of things I've been wanting to tell you for a while now," he began, taking her hand.

"There's something I want to tell you, too," she interrupted, eager now for him to know just how she felt.

"Me first, okay?" The ghost of a grin softened his firm mouth beneath his thick mustache.

Remembering the silky sweep of it against her skin when his warm lips were kissing her, she suppressed a shiver of longing and a burst of impatience. "Okay, shoot."

He surprised her by dropping her hand and tossing his hat into the bed of Taylor's truck. Then he hooked both of his thumbs into his belt as he tipped back his head and gazed up at the sky, as if he was searching for something.

Courage, perhaps? Whatever he was about to tell her was obviously difficult for him to say.

She reached out and touched his arm. "Tell me," she coaxed. "It can't be any harder than what you told me in the store."

He let out a long breath and shifted, so he was again leaning against the truck. "I guess you're right. Taylor and I figured out what probably happened to your letters."

His announcement was a shock. As he explained, Bobbie found herself running through a whole gamut of emotions, from anger to relief to dismay. Why couldn't he just have taken her word that she had written those letters, instead of finally believing her when he had a more obvious explanation?

Then she remembered how quick she had been to assume he must have lied about getting them, and she felt the heat of embarrassment spread across her face. She had hung on to that belief long after he'd shown her he was too good a father to callously ignore the news that he had a child.

She had wronged him as surely as he had her.

"None of that really matters now," he said. "It was just an excuse for me to hide from my feelings. Can you forgive me for doubting you?" His voice was husky.

"I will if you'll forgive me," she replied. "I did my own share of doubting, if you remember right." She took a deep breath, fighting the sudden emotion that had boiled up inside her. "It's just that I was so sure I'd hear from you. I waited—" Her voice broke and she turned away, struggling for control. She had so hoped he had fallen for her, too, and that her news would bring him back.

Now she felt his hands on her shoulders and then his warm breath on the side of her cheek. "I've thought a lot about that," he said softly. "Pictured you alone and pregnant. Cursed my own stubborn stupidity in running away in the first place. I don't know if I can ever forgive myself for disappointing you."

"Then why did you leave?" she muttered, voice wavering.

He tipped his head back and squeezed his eyes shut tight. "You made me feel things that terrified me, things I'd sworn I'd never let myself feel." He opened his eyes and looked deep into hers. "Remember that I'd lost both of my parents and my sister. I blamed myself for that. I knew how bad love could hurt and I wanted no part of it ever again. When I started to fall for you, I was scared to death. All I could think of was escape.''

''I guess I understand,'' she said slowly. ''You told me from the start that you were leaving as soon as the rodeo was over. Part of me wanted to hate you, but part of me knew you hadn't done anything you didn't warn me about.''

''Anything except leave you carrying my baby,'' he said grimly.

''But you used protection,'' she reminded him. ''And we only slept together that one night.''

''But we made love three times,'' he whispered, grinning when she looked away, embarrassed. ''I remember everything about that night. You were fantastic.''

Her blush deepened. ''So were you.''

''Where did you go when the diner closed down?'' he asked suddenly.

''Go?'' she repeated, confused by his abrupt change of subject.

''Yeah. You didn't stay in Vegas.''

''How do you know?''

It was his turn to look uncomfortable. ''Because I came back for you,'' he confessed. ''About two months after I'd left, I got sick of losing sleep, not being able to concentrate, missing the one woman I'd fallen head over heels for, despite my own hardheaded ideas. I realized I didn't want to live without you—that the risk of maybe being hurt someday didn't compare to the hurt I was going through then.'' He took her hand again, his thumb caressing her knuckles.

''I came back here to ask you to come on the road with me, but the diner was closed and I couldn't find anyone who knew you. The manager at your apartment looked at me like I was a snake fresh out from under some rock and wouldn't tell me anything.''

"Mrs. Otis," Bobbie exclaimed, remembering the gruff old lady. "She probably thought she was protecting me.''

"I figured she knew more than she let on," he said with a grim smile of satisfaction.

"I went to my mother's in Arizona," Bobbie explained. "When I lost my job at the diner, I already had morning sickness a lot. I couldn't find a steady job.''

Donovan's face reflected his pain over her stark words.

"I stayed with Mom until I had Rose, but her emphysema was getting worse all the time. Eventually I landed another waitressing job and got a place of my own.''

"God, I'm so sorry," Donovan burst out. "If only I could have found you. I turned Nevada upside down, but you'd vanished without a trace.''

"The only person I kept in touch with was Ruby," Bobbie admitted. "Do you remember her from the diner?''

He nodded hesitantly. "I do now. Everyone else from the diner had scattered. Your boss was in Sacramento and the owner had gone to Toronto. Neither of them knew what had happened to you.''

"No, they didn't." Bobbie was amazed at the lengths he'd gone to in order to find her. How different both their lives would have been, as well as Rose's, if he had.

"Were you never tempted, after you wrote those two letters, to contact me again?'' he asked.

She heard the longing in his voice and knew she owed him the truth, no matter what it did to her pride. "I wanted to very badly, but I wouldn't let myself," she said. "I followed your career as best I could, though. Every time you were on some rodeo show on TV or I read your name on the sports page, I wanted to confront you.'' She touched his arm anxiously. "But you have to remember, I had no way

of knowing that you hadn't gotten my letters. I thought
your silence meant you didn't care. My pride wouldn't let
me bother you a third time."

He rubbed at his sideburn with one long finger. "I'm so
sorry."

She reached up to stroke his lean cheek, savoring his
warmth. "So am I."

For a long moment, he searched her face.

"What is it?" she asked, wondering what else they still
needed to sort out. Everything they had already covered
was so overwhelming. The knowledge that he had come
back for her went a long way toward healing her pride,
shredded when she thought he didn't want her or their
child.

Now Donovan astonished her by sinking down on one
knee in the gravel.

"What are you doing?" she demanded as he took both
her hands in his and began pressing kisses to her knuckles.

He raised his head and the love she saw shining from his
eyes almost took her breath away. This wonderful man, so
strong and good and handsome, had chosen her.

"I want you to marry me again," he said. "A real wedding this time. You and Rose and the other children we may
have are my family now and always will be. I love her more
than my own life, but neither she nor anyone else could ever
take your place in my heart." He cleared his throat while
Bobbie's eyes flooded with joyous tears. "You're the other
half of myself I thought I'd never find," he added softly.
"What do you say?"

She urged him back to his feet and then she looked into
his eyes. The love she felt for him almost overwhelmed her.
"We don't have to get married again," she said, more sure
of their feelings for each other than she had ever been sure
of anything. "As far as I'm concerned, we had that real

wedding. My heart made a commitment to you in that chapel. If you want to do it all over again, we can, but I couldn't be more your wife than I already am."

"Sweetheart, I feel exactly the same way." Donovan swept her into his arms and gave her a kiss so tender it curled her toes. "Darlin', I love you," he murmured.

"I love you, too."

"I know that," he said with great satisfaction.

She pulled back and planted her hands on her hips. "Oh?" Lifting her eyebrows, she gave him a sassy stare. "And just how long have you known?"

His grin widened and his eyes gleamed with happiness. "I knew the minute you insisted that I quit the finals just because you were afraid I'd get hurt." He slid an arm around her and bent his head close to hers. "But you can show me how much you love me any time you want," he drawled.

Bobbie looked into his face, glowing with the joy she knew was mirrored on her own. "How about we go back to our room and I'll start showing you right now?" she suggested.

Quicker than a heartbeat, Donovan swept her into the cab of the truck and slid in beside her. Turning the key in the ignition, he told her, "Darlin', I'll have you back there before the buzzer."

Bobbie returned his smile. "And wait till you see your score," she teased. "Just forget about bringing along any more of those red plastic poinsettias."

* * * * *

#1021 MOLLY DARLING—Laurie Paige
That's My Baby!
Rancher Sam Frazier needed a mommy for his little Lass—and a
wife in the bargain. He proposed a marriage of convenience to
Molly Clelland—but he never dreamed he'd long to call the instant
mother his Molly darling....

#1022 THE FALL OF SHANE MACKADE—Nora Roberts
The MacKade Brothers
Footloose and fancy-free, Shane MacKade had a reputation as a ladies'
man to uphold, and he took his job seriously. Who would have thought
a brainy beauty like Dr. Rebecca Knight would cause this irrepressible
bachelor to take the fall...?

#1023 EXPECTING: BABY—Jennifer Mikels
An urgent knock at the door introduced Rick Sloan to his neighbor—
Mara Vincetti, who was about to give birth. Next thing Rick Sloan
knew he was a father figure for the new single mom and her baby!

#1024 A BRIDE FOR LUKE—Trisha Alexander
Three Brides and a Baby
When sister-of-the-bride Clem Bennelli met brother-of-the-groom
Luke Taylor, it was a case of opposites attract. They agreed theirs
would be a passionate, no-strings-attached relationship—but neither
one expected to want much, much more....

#1025 THE FATHER OF HER CHILD—Joan Elliott Pickart
The Baby Bet
Honorary MacAllister family member Ted Sharpe was carefree and
single. But secretly he yearned to be a husband and a father. And
when the very pregnant divorcée Hannah Johnson moved in next
door—he lost his heart, but found his dreams.

#1026 A WILL AND A WEDDING—Judith Yates
Commitment and marriage were two words Amy Riordan never
believed would apply to her. After meeting similarly minded
Paul Hanley, however, she began to think otherwise—and now
the word "wedding" was definitely in her future!

MILLION DOLLAR SWEEPSTAKES

No purchase necessary. To enter, follow the directions published. For eligibility, entries must be received no later than March 31, 1998. No liability is assumed for printing errors, lost, late, nondelivered or misdirected entries. Odds of winning are determined by the number of eligible entries distributed and received.

Sweepstakes open to residents of the U.S. (except Puerto Rico), Canada and Europe who are 18 years of age or older. All applicable laws and regulations apply. Sweepstakes offer void wherever prohibited by law. This sweepstakes is presented by Torstar Corp., its subsidiaries and affiliates, in conjunction with book, merchandise and/or product offerings. For a copy of the Official Rules (WA residents need not affix return postage), send a self-addressed, stamped envelope to: Million Dollar Sweepstakes Rules, P.O. Box 4469, Blair, NE 68009-4469.

SWP-M96

Yo amo novelas con corazón!

Starting this March, Harlequin opens up to a whole new world of readers with two new romance lines in SPANISH!

Harlequin Deseo
- passionate, sensual and exciting stories

Harlequin Bianca
- romances that are fun, fresh and very contemporary

With four titles a month, each line will offer the same wonderfully romantic stories that you've come to love—now available in Spanish.

Look for them at selected retail outlets.

 HARLEQUIN ®

SPANT

Coming in March

from **SILHOUETTE YOURS TRULY™**

It Happened One Week
by JoAnn Ross

Amanda Stockenberg was in the middle of the worst
week of her life, looking like something the cat dragged
in and acting rather unladylike, when she saw *him*.
Her first love. And now she has only seven days
for a second chance at forever....

What Engagement Ring?!
by Martha Schroeder

April Kennan had refused to even *date* attorney
Jake Singleton's brother, let alone marry him, but he
insists she broke their engagement and kept a four-carat
diamond ring! Now Jake's demanding she return a ring
she's never been given—or else!

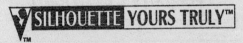

SILHOUETTE YOURS TRULY™

Love—when you least expect it!

YT396

As seen on TV!
Free Gift Offer

With a Free Gift proof-of-purchase from any Silhouette® book,
you can receive a beautiful cubic zirconia pendant.

This gorgeous marquise-shaped stone is a genuine cubic
zirconia—accented by an 18" gold tone necklace.

(Approximate retail value $19.95)

Send for yours today...
compliments of ▼ *Silhouette*®
™

To receive your free gift, a cubic zirconia pendant, send us one original proof-of-purchase, photocopies not accepted, from the back of any Silhouette Romance™, Silhouette Desire®, Silhouette Special Edition®, Silhouette Intimate Moments® or Silhouette Shadows™ title available in February, March or April at your favorite retail outlet, together with the Free Gift Certificate, plus a check or money order for $1.75 U.S./$2.25 CAN. (do not send cash) to cover postage and handling, payable to Silhouette Free Gift Offer. We will send you the specified gift. Allow 6 to 8 weeks for delivery. Offer good until April 30, 1996 or while quantities last. Offer valid in the U.S. and Canada only.

Free Gift Certificate

Name: _____

Address: _____

City: _____ State/Province: _____ Zip/Postal Code: _____

Mail this certificate, one proof-of-purchase and a check or money order for postage and handling to: SILHOUETTE FREE GIFT OFFER 1996. In the U.S.: 3010 Walden Avenue, P.O. Box 9057, Buffalo NY 14269-9057. In Canada: P.O. Box 622, Fort Erie,

---

FREE GIFT OFFER
079-KBZ-R

ONE PROOF-OF-PURCHASE

To collect your fabulous FREE GIFT, a cubic zirconia pendant, you must include this original proof-of-purchase for each gift with the properly completed Free Gift Certificate.

079-KBZ-R

THE BLACKTHORN BROTHERHOOD

Three men bound by a childhood secret are freed through family, friendship...and love

by Diana Whitney

This compelling miniseries from Silhouette Special Edition returns in March with:

THE REFORMER (Special Edition #1019)
Larkin McKay had never thought of himself as husband or father material. Until he met irresistible Letitia Cervantes and her precious son. Could they show Larkin the true meaning of family?

If you missed the first two books—**THE ADVENTURER** (Special Edition #934) and **THE AVENGER** (Special Edition #984)—order your copies today! And be sure to watch for Diana Whitney's next charming miniseries, **PARENTHOOD,** coming late 1996 from Special Edition!

DWBB3

You're About to Become a

Privileged Woman

Reap the rewards of fabulous free gifts and
benefits with proofs-of-purchase from
Silhouette and Harlequin books

Pages & Privileges™

It's our way of thanking you for
buying our books at your
favorite retail stores.

PROOF OF
PURCHASE

SSE-PP118

Offer expires October 31, 1996

Harlequin and Silhouette—
the most privileged readers in the world!

For more information about Harlequin and
Silhouette's PAGES & PRIVILEGES program call the
Pages & Privileges Benefits Desk: 1-503-794-2499

SSE-PP118